MW00639284

Sylvia's Mother

Book Two of The Weather Girls Wedding
Shoppe and Venue

Jennifer Lynn Cary

Tandem Services Press

What Readers Are Saying

The Crockett Chronicles trilogy

"I love historical novels and this one did not disappoint. I was caught up from the first sentence and completely in love with the Crocketts by the end. Can't wait to follow along their next journey. Well done!" –Virginia Denise

"I love this book! The story is soooooo engaging! I can hardly put it down!"—DeNage

Tales of the Hob Nob Annex Café

"This is a well written book that hooks you on the first page. It's a very enjoyable read that makes you forget about all your troubles and step back in time. I loved this book and look forward to what this author writes next." –Ann Ferri

"I loved reading this book! It had me intrigued from the first page, and as the stories began, I could hardly wait to turn the page to see what happened next! Love the mix of true facts mixed with some good, clean, fun fiction! Easy, quick read. I highly recommend this book!" –CatSmit

The Relentless Series

"I lost my heart in this book, caught up in the lives of each character. I remember these times, which made it more real to me. I had tears of joy, tears of sorrow, grief, and smiles in the unexpected. Great story and hard to put down. Keep reading.... You won't regret it."—Novabelle

"I enjoyed another book by Jennifer Cary! As with all her books the story held your attention from the beginning to the end and I look forward to reading all her future books!"—Mary Rima

"I live in Indiana so I know of the places this book talks about. I so absolutely LOVED this story. It's the first one in this series I've read. I'm glad because I feel it should be the first book as it tells of the 2 families & how they connect. It so touched my heart that at times I cried. I couldn't put it down after starting it so anxious to know how things would turn out with all the difficulties Val & Jimmy had. I'm sure the other books in this series are equally as great."—Pat

The Traveling Prayer Shawl

"When her sister's inheritance depends on it, Cami must do the thing she resolved she'd never do, the thing which will break her heart as well as add one more tough task to her already overstuffed calendar. She must fulfill her grandmother's last request - and what's more, there's a deadline that puts in jeopardy her major project at work. As she begins working on the request, she finds even more complications. The inheritance may raise a conflict of interests. How Cami negotiates these and other potential pitfalls made for an interesting and warmhearted story.

Recommended to those who enjoy Christian Women's Fiction and readers who enjoy Debbie Macomber's stories."—Dana McNeely

"I loved this book so much I hated for it to end!"—Cindy

The Weather Girls trilogy

"I just finished all three of the Weather Girls books on my Kindle Fire! I found that once I started, I couldn't stop - and went from one to two to three - in a matter of 4 days! I work so had to leave my evenings to reading - but oh I hated to quit and go to bed! And then I'd run the story through in my mind again!" —Novabelle

"What a fun series! I'm loving spending time in the past with this family and learning more about the girls and their unique personalities." —Erin S

The Forgotten Gratitude Journal

"This incredible book is written in split time. I don't want to give any more away about the story. It's so enjoyable and I couldn't put it down, needing to know what happened to Molly and RJ!"—Annmarie K

"Jennifer Lynn Cary has written a beautiful split time story about love, love lost and love found again! Throw a mystery villain in the mix and you have a romance with suspense and drama! Such a good read for any romance lover!"—Anita Stafford

Cheryl's Going Home

"This book will touch your heart and soul. Cheryl and Aaron's heart-warming story is full of emotions, and you can feel every one of them. This book will make you laugh, cry and feel every emotion in between. I loved it and highly recommend this book and the entire series." —Ann Ferri

"The book is Christian fiction, but it is not heavy handed and fits the characters and the early 1970ties. The book is Cheryl's story, but also her estranged husband, Aaron's story as well. Their two stories, expertly woven together, share the experience of the rebuilding of their relationship from each of their POVs. It's a lovely journey evoking the time and place with musical and celebrity references from the era."—MLRumph

Judy in Disguise

"Wow. I usually don't read strictly romance but this book captured my attention from the back cover and did not disappoint." —Cheri Swalwell

"I love how this author can transport readers back to the 1970's and brings the past to life." —Connie Hill

Copyright © 2022 by Jennifer Lynn Cary

Published by Tandem Services Press

Post Office Box 220

Yucaipa, California

www.TandemServicesInk.com

All rights reserved. No portion of this book may be reproduced in any form without written permission from the publisher or author, except as permitted by U.S. copyright law.

Ebook ISBN 978-1-954986-77-0

Paperback ISBN 978-1-954986-76-3

Cover design by *Alt 19 Creative*

Dedicated to the KHS Classes of

1972 – 1974

Go, Wildcats!

In memory of

Connie Agnew Schneck

who was as kind as she was beautiful.

And in memory of

Shel Silverstien

who gave me fun memories

long before I read his children's books.

And we know that all things work together

for good to them that love God,

to them who are the called

according to His purpose.

Romans 8:28 KJV

Contents

The Cardinal of the Sycamore

Once upon a time, a legend grew from the native people living in Central Indiana.

If a couple really loved each other and they kissed beneath a certain sycamore tree *and* a cardinal landed on the branch above them, they would have a long life together.

In the late nineteenth century, a gas boom hit the sleepy farming town of Kokomo.

A family named Ferguson made their wealth with the event and built an impressive mansion on the grounds of the old sycamore tree. When they did, word of the legend came to them, and they passed it down their generations.

Finally, in 1970 the last member of the family sold Ferguson House to Sunny Day Whitcomb who, along with her sisters Stormy Day Crawford and Windy Day Norman, opened the *Weather Girls Wedding Shoppe and Venue* in the old mansion.

Now when couples come, they have their photos taken beneath the shade of the old sycamore and hope for a cardinal sighting to add spice to their kiss.

Welcome to the stories of the *Weather Girls Wedding Shoppe and Venue* series.

Sylvia's Mother

Book Two of

The Weather Girls Wedding Shoppe and Venue Series

Chapter 1

April 10, 1972, Kokomo, Indiana

"**B**ut, Mom!"

Eileen Avery closed her eyes and counted to five. That was all the time she had. And how did her daughter add so many syllables to that one word? Somehow Sylvia stretched out Mom so far that it gave antidisestablishmentarianism a run for its money. She waved her hand to halt any more nagging. "Sylvia, I said we will discuss this later. You need to get to class, and I have a student coming in early. Here she is. Corrina, I'll be right with you."

The petite freshman nodded but shyly moved farther into the home economics classroom, not making eye contact.

"You always have time for others but never for me. I'm your daughter. Can't you spare a minute?"

How could she say that? But this was not the time. "Sylvia, I promise when we go home after school, we'll talk about anything you want. But right now..." She lowered her voice. "This is important."

Her daughter huffed, but at least she didn't cause a scene or say something inappropriate. Instead, she stomped out of Eileen's classroom. It was like the aftermath of a summer storm, without the physical debris. Tornado Sylvia. Did they name tornados?

Eileen pasted on a reassuring smile and focused on the young teen who'd stood out to her from the moment she arrived as a new student in her class before Easter break. A sweet, quiet girl. Sometimes Eileen just felt that nudge that she could make a difference for someone in her classroom. She swiped her hair from her forehead, sent up a quick prayer for guidance, and hoped she didn't have to explain. "Corrina, thank you for coming by. I have something for you, but please, I hope you will accept it and not feel like I'm overstepping." She reached behind her desk for the brown grocery bag. "I put it in here in case you want to take it home. Or you can use the changing room over there." She pointed to the curtained area where her sewing-class students tried on their creations.

"What is it?" The girl took a few steps closer, still not looking Eileen in the face. Though clean, her dress had seen better days. Just like the other two she rotated in her wardrobe.

"I made this dress a while back for my daughter, but she didn't like the color." That was a big fat lie. Eileen spent Saturday making the outfit specifically for Corrina out of leftover material from another project. Well, her daughter wasn't into coloring Easter eggs anymore, so why not? It'd be time well spent if the girl approved. "It's never been worn and is only taking up room in my closet. You are welcome to it."

A tear threatened to drip down Corrina's cheek. "Mrs. Avery, I don't have money to pay for it."

2

"It's not for sale. I just hate to see it going to waste. However, there are two conditions." The girl stiffened, but Eileen went on. "One, please do not tell anyone I did this. And two, when you don't want it anymore, pass it on to someone who can use it. Can you do that?"

Corrina's smile grew, and now she was ready to look in the bag. "Yes, ma'am." As she pulled out the brown linen dress covered in tiny daisies, her eyes grew too. "Oh, Mrs. Avery, this is beautiful. Are you sure?"

"Yes. Do you want to wear it today or simply take it home?"

"I should find out if it fits first. May I?" The girl showed more animation now than she had the entire week she'd been in school.

So many needs made it into her class, and though Eileen would love to help each one, there was a limit on her resources. But each time she was able to do something for a student like Corrina, she believed she'd found her purpose.

"Of course." Finally, Eileen had done something right for a change. It didn't happen often enough.

While Corrina tried on the dress, Eileen prepped and readied her first hour classroom. In a few minutes, students would wander in. This group would bake cookies, and one team had insisted on peanut butter melt-aways. Thankfully, part of the lesson included cleanup, but Eileen had her Playtex gloves close by. Just in case. Not all cleaned as instructed, and the thought of what a peanut could do to her sent a chill down her spine. Frankly, it terrified her. She should have insisted that the group make something else. But then Sylvia liked to point out that it was "Mom's way or the wrong way." Maybe that attitude carried over to her class. She heard Sylvia's voice in her head. "Ya think?" Her daughter would be the death of her someday.

Corrina came out wearing the short-sleeved, A-line creation. Eileen had guessed right about length—short enough to be cute and stylish, but not so much to be immodest. It looked perfect with the girl's fro and her cocoa-colored eyes and skin.

"I love it, Mrs. Avery. But I don't get why."

Eileen shrugged, trying for her best imitation of nonchalant. "I needed to clean out my closet—this job means I have a lot of recipes, fabric, and sewing materials in my home. But when I pulled this out, I thought of you and, well..." She motioned toward the girl and the dress. "I was right. Perfect. Do you want to wear it today? You can put your clothes in the bag, and I'll hang on to it until after school. Pick it up on your way h ome."

"You don't mind?"

"No, of course not. Go pack up your things, and I'll put it all behind my desk."

Corrina turned to do as instructed.

That gave Eileen a couple more minutes of peace before the first student showed up. She wandered over to the window and glanced at the spring green popping out with the random dandelion.

And that's when she saw them.

Her daughter. And a boy.

Kissing.

It might have been a quick peck, but on the lips? She watched as they went in different directions—Sylvia to the old Main Building and the boy to... Was he heading into her building? The Vocational Building? Most likely for a music or art class. Her heart tightened. He wouldn't be coming here, would he?

No, it was too close to the start of first period. He was headed to his class, and she didn't have any males in this first period group.

Eileen turned away from the view in time for Corrina to leave the changing room, holding the paper bag out to her.

"Thank you, Mrs. Avery. I won't forget this."

Time to pull herself together. "My pleasure, Corrina. I'm glad it has a good home. Better hurry to your class now. I'll see you fifth period."

The girl met her gaze and smiled. If only she could make a break-through with her daughter so easily.

She and Sylvia would have a discussion after school. That was going to happen. No two ways about it. Sylvia needed to understand. Eileen knew the dangers that her daughter didn't.

Sylvia hugged her first hour books to her chest. "She makes me crazy, Luke. I'm up for Stardust Queen and have to have an escort. She's attending as a chaperone, but I need a date."

"You've got me, babe." He looked so cute, all patient and letting her dump her drama onto him. Why he wanted to spend time with her went beyond understanding. But he did. He even gave her his class ring. They were going steady. How did she luck out to have a boyfriend who would tolerate her mother's edicts?

"Yeah. I just can't let my mom find out. If she thinks we're more than school friends, she'll blow her mind and lock me in a dungeon. Or would—if we had one. Better keep my mouth shut before I give her any ideas."

"Why's she so totalitarian? Did you do something?"

Sylvia shook her head, though she'd often wondered that herself. No other kid in school had a parental shadow like she did. "I've no idea. She told me we'll talk after school, so I guess I'll have to wait until then. I promise to tell you what she says. But how I'm supposed to be in front of the whole student body at the dance and be the only one without an escort, I have no idea." Then a thought hit. "She wouldn't try to escort me herself, would she?" Images of her mother linking arms with her and dragging her to the front made her want to sink into the ground, buried alive. It would be less painful.

Luke reached up and wound the curl alongside her cheek around his finger. "Not even your mother is that crazy." The guy was magic with how he could talk her down. "Just stay cool, baby. Get to class, and I'll catch you at lunch." He leaned in and gave her a quick kiss. "Remember. Stay cool."

He sauntered off toward the Vocational Building, shaking his head to move the black tuft of bangs that must have slipped over his brow. No need to see his face. That gesture made her smile. Then she hustled toward Old Main for her first hour chem class.

Would she ever get out from under her mother's thumb? Mick Jagger hummed "Under My Thumb" in her head. That would really set her mother off—Sylvia enjoying the Rolling Stones.

Speaking of setting her mother off, if Mom caught wind that she'd applied to Anderson College along with the Indiana University Kokomo campus for her next year's placement, talk about a scene. But Sylvia had tried to think reasonably. It was a church school, which ought to help, but anything other than what her mother had envisioned wouldn't even be considered.

She had to escape. The thought of living at home another year made her want to scream.

No one knew what it was like. Everyone thought her mother was so kind and thoughtful, the favorite teacher on campus. Always at the events, remembering every student and their ideas. *Oh, Sylvia, your mom is so cool. She's the best teacher at KHS. Wish I had her for every one my classes.*

It was like she respected all the other kids at KHS, but not her own daughter.

Sylvia slipped into class. It was a lecture day—after they received the results of the latest test and reviewed it. She'd aced it. Of course. What else could she do? As a prisoner in her own home, there was nothing to distract from study time. She'd have to be an imbecile not to pass. At this point, valedictorian was a shoo-in. Almost.

Turning Luke's ring on her finger, she enjoyed the feel, the weight of it. He'd asked her to go steady before spring break, but she'd hidden the ring from her mom. It stayed in her locker at school. Luke even understood that. He said she was worth it.

Was she? Why would he choose her when he knew the truth about her mother? He could have any girl at school without the hassle of Mrs. Eileen Avery in his life.

After the lecture, she and her lab partner, Jim Hect, sat together and discussed a plan for their next experiment. They had to show the outline and materials list to Mr. Dolan so they could test it out during tomorrow's class.

With that stamp of approval, they packed up and rapped a few minutes about tomorrow's experiment until the bell rang. Jim never wanted to talk about her mother and tell her how lucky she was to have her. Sylvia liked that. And he was super smart, giving her a run for her money at valedictorian. Still, despite her good grades, he didn't treat her as competition. Just someone who would pull her weight in a team effort situation.

That meant she'd most likely get a great grade, and he wouldn't bug her. Yep.

8

If only all her peers in this senior class of 1972 were like that.

Three more subjects, and she'd see Luke again. Her heart thumped with excitement. This semester they had no classes together, which bummed her to no end. Last year they'd had calculus, and she'd helped him the first couple of weeks—Mr. Etherington had seated them next to each other. It didn't take long for Luke to catch on, and then he used the time to get to know her.

Just remembering that brought a smile to her face.

The bell rang, and she headed for her fourth year Spanish class. No English allowed once you crossed the threshold of the third-floor room. Mrs. Myers was strict about that policy. Funny how Sylvia's Spanish improved when she wanted to keep something from her mother. If only her friends spoke it. Who was she kidding? She'd settle for a group of real friends, forget about the Spanish part.

That class ran fast, but the next one, econ, always made her want to slash her wrists. Oh, she could follow along and do well on the tests, but the subject bored her to tears, though she tried to look somewhat interested so nothing got back to her mother about bad behavior.

"Miss Avery, may I speak with you a moment?"

Miss Avery? Oh-oh. Was she in trouble?

"Yes, Mr. Barsh?" Sylvia approached his desk, watching as he wrote something on a piece of paper.

He leaned closer as if he didn't want the whole class to hear him. "Sylvia, I understand your mother sometimes has her cooking students bake for after school events."

Her mother? This wasn't about her? Her breathing came a little easier. "Yes, she often does that."

"Would you please run this note to her? I've waited until the last minute, but I'm hoping she'll agree."

"Now? You want me to go now?" Popping in on her mom? After their so-called discussion before class? This couldn't be good.

"If you would. Is there a problem?"

Sylvia shook her head. "No, no problem." None that she would explain to him. She took the note, hurrying to the stairs and out a side door for a shortcut to the Vocational Building. Just as she reached for the door handle, something glinted.

Luke's ring.

She popped it off her finger and thrust it into her pocket. Her eagle-eyed mom wouldn't make a scene in the classroom, but she'd have plenty to say once the audience disappeared. Might even take the Stardust Queen nomination away from her.

Nope, better safe than sorry. She patted her pocket for security and headed to her mother's classroom.

"No!" Seth threw himself forward, grabbing at the woman and pulling her down, covering her with his body as something seared into his back. He grew weaker by the second. "Stay down!"

He gasped, the intake pulling him into a sitting position, eyes wide.

It took a few seconds for the vestiges of the dream to fade, allowing him to realize where he was—his mother's living room. Even more ticks of the old mantle clock sounded in steady thuds before his heart rate slowed enough to allow him to exhale. In, out. In, out. His pulse returned to a semblance of normal. After nearly four years, the nightmares still snuck into his dreams.

Especially when he overdid it and irritated the lodged bullet shards. The inoperable lodged bullet shards.

Seth sighed, glad his mother flew to Florida for a month and wasn't here to see this. He'd never explained, and he still didn't want to. There was only one solution. A place of his own.

For Pete's sake, he was a grown man. He didn't need to live with Mom—or his sister for that matter, despite her hinting that it would be the perfect situation for them both.

No, he was definitely going house hunting. And today was better than tomorrow because if he waited, he wouldn't go. He'd tried this before, and the women in his life managed to talk him out of it. If he didn't act on this idea right away, it would sail on without him.

He found the Yellow Pages and searched for real estate agents. Ken Wooley's ad jumped out at him, so he dialed the number. Ten minutes later, he hung up with the promise that Mr. Wooley would call him in an hour to set up a time to look at properties.

There. Settled.

Muncher wandered into the living room, settling his long, narrow snout on Seth's knee, and stared at him with soulful eyes.

"Yeah, buddy. You'll probably like it better once we have a place of our own again too." Mom wasn't all that keen to have hairy reminders of Muncher in her house. He ran his hand through the dog's soft fur. Even if coming back to his hometown had seemed like the best idea, there were still moments when he felt he was letting down those who depended on him—whether or not they knew it. Both clients and coworkers.

Well, he could still be there for the women in his life. They didn't require a fitness standard to keep them safe.

Speaking of fitness... Seth found Muncher's leash. "Let's go for a walk and check out the neighborhood."

It was the same place he'd left when he went away to college. Basically. Oh, a few businesses had morphed into something else, but nothing much. Very few in his mother's neighborhood moved away. Change happened when the homeowners either passed or their children moved them into a home.

Mrs. Thomas still swept her stoop. Like she did every day, right before lunch. He gave a little wave her way, and thought she sort of waved back, he couldn't help but notice the confusion on her face. Oh, well. He wasn't the school kid who roamed the neighborhood on his bike anymore.

Then came the Fosters' home. Seth had spent a lot of time in that backyard playing with the two sons before they all grew up. Wonder where those boys were now? Anywhere local? Did they have sons of their own?

He crossed the street and soon found himself headed for the one place he'd sworn he'd never approach if he returned. The spacious Victorian had baskets of smile-making scarlet geraniums hanging next to every post above the porch railings.

As if anyone could be happy to be there.

Was *she* happy? Was she still there?

No, of course not. Mom had written him at college that she'd married. And he said not to tell him anything more about her.

That house was more fortress than home. It reminded him of some fairy tale where the wicked ol' witch enticed small children inside with goodies and treats only to make the children disappear by eating them. Or maybe he was getting that story mixed in with another.

He crossed the street and turned to the next block. It wouldn't stop the memories, but at least he wasn't punishing himself by staring at the place.

Wonder if the ol' witch had taken notice of him on her sidewalk—not that she owned it, but she thought she did. He shook the thoughts from his brain and scanned the street. Not a time to let down his guard. Peaceful settings could be deceiving.

Fifteen minutes later, he'd lapped back to his mom's place. Mr. Wooley would be calling soon, and he hoped they'd be able to come to an agreement on something fast. He needed his own house, not only for his independence but also because no one needed to walk in on him in one of his moments. If he could get moved out while Mom was gone, it would save a lot of arguing and trying to talk him out of this.

Muncher seemed to sense where his thoughts took him and nudged his leg.

He reached down and scratched the dog's ears. Good boy. As much comfort as this four-legged friend had brought—and the knowledge that any confessions would stay confidential—he still couldn't bring himself to even tell Muncher what dueled with him in his sleep.

He hadn't told anyone. To say it aloud would make it all true. Not voicing it left the possibility of it only being his imagination. Until his back twinged.

The phone rang, and he answered.

"Mr. Matthews? Ken Wooley here. I have a couple of places I could show you. When might be a good time?"

"I'm available now."

There was a pause, and Seth knew the guy was scrambling to figure out if a family could be ready for a showing that fast. "I do have one that is vacant at the moment. How about we start with that? I'll come pick you up. Where are you staying?"

Seth gave him his mother's address and stepped outside to watch for the car.

It didn't take Mr. Wooley long, and it turned out the vacant home sat only a few streets over. "This actually just opened up. No one's done any work on it yet. The owner passed, and the family is eager to sell, so you should get a good deal. However, it is a fixer-upper." He parked in front of a small craftsman with a slab porch.

One look and Seth knew it was for him. Even with the peeling blue paint on the shutters and overgrown weeds. He saw the possibilities. More than that, he could imagine himself working hard to make this house rival its glory days, making him so tired he'd be unable to conjure the nightmares hidden in his subconscious.

"I'll take it."

Mr. Wooley froze. "You haven't been inside or heard the price or seen anything else."

"I don't care. This is the house. Let's check out the inside and then talk business."

"If that's what you want."

Seth nodded as peace settled on his soul. Oh, yeah. That's what he wanted.

Chapter 2

Eileen glanced up from where she helped a sophomore rip out a wonky zipper from the back of her lime green jumper.

Sylvia stood in the doorway. What was she doing here? One more thing to discuss at home. But now she needed her daughter to stay in her own class.

Instead, Sylvia headed her way, a paper extended from her hand. "Mr. Barsh sent me."

Oh.

In that case. Eileen accepted the note and read it. "Tell him my sixth hour class should be able to help him out. And next time I'd..." She chewed her lip to keep from saying something she shouldn't. It was hard to always try to be nice. But this time, she could accommodate him. "Tell him I'll send them to his room once they're all done."

Sylvia nodded before turning to leave.

"And we definitely need to talk when we get home." Eileen almost added "young lady," but figured it would embarrass her daughter in front of the other students. She'd get the message anyway.

Another nod and Sylvia escaped out the door.

Eileen returned her attention to her student and the zipper, only her mind wandered again. How was she going to approach this? What kind of consequence should she impose? There was obviously sneaking around going on behind her back. That had to stop. But how did she keep an eye on her daughter any more than she did? Sylvia was too innocent to understand how this could ruin her life.

Too bad King Solomon hadn't been a single parent. He might have some wise words about that instead of spouting platitudes in proverb form while adding to his harem.

Ouch. Sorry, God.

She glanced at her thumb where she'd just stabbed the seam ripper. A single drop of red oozed. "Here." Eileen thrust the piece back at the student before she dripped blood onto the material. "I'll be back." She grabbed the first aid kit from her bottom desk drawer and fumbled with the Band-Aid. Her mother would mock her for doing something so stupid in front of her class.

If nothing else, it just proved she needed to keep her mind focused on her job. And find a way to keep Sylvia safe so she wouldn't be pulled in too many directions. Her daughter needed that scholarship to help pay for college. A boy would mess up everything. Eileen was proof of that.

Sylvia had to be her main concern. But if she didn't do her job to the best of her ability, she wouldn't have it and then how would she care for her daughter? Such a vicious cycle. If only she could trust Sylvia.

What else had Sylvia not told her?

She had to find out if there were more bits Sylvia wasn't sharing.

Three hours later, she packaged up the cookies for Mr. Barsh, who seemed to think she had nothing else to do but wait on him hand and foot—oops, that wasn't fair. He was a good guy and had apologized for the late request. Still, what nagged at her the most was she hadn't come to any plans on how to proceed with her daughter.

Is this how her mother felt all those years ago? No, Mother was manipulative, judgmental. That's not how she treated Sylvia. Eileen only wanted to protect her daughter, make sure she headed in the right direction, ready for life.

Because life was cruel when you were unprepared.

Sylvia should be arriving any moment so they could go home together once her room was put to rights and prepped for tomorrow. It was important to save their talk until they reached the house. No need of anyone walking in on the discussion. She needed her daughter to understand that.

Of course, Sylvia would be after her right away. She might allow them to get to the car before she started in, but that was about it. Still, Eileen needed as much time as she could get to form the words she had to say. To ask the questions that needed asking.

Would Sylvia be honest with her?

"Ready, Mom?"

Eileen glanced up from her mind-wandering to find her daughter already in the room. When had she entered, and how long had she been standing there?

"In a minute. Just need to set out the recipes at the stations for the first hour tomorrow."

Sylvia took the index cards from her. "I'll do it. You get your things together."

Was she being kind and helpful? Or just anxious to get where they could talk? Why did she have to question her own daughter's motives?

"Ready. Let's go home." Eileen ushered Sylvia toward the door, flipped off the lights, and locked up. No pleasant chit-chat on the way to the teachers' parking lot, and the silence felt cold in the spring warmth.

However, once they had settled into her 1965 Ford Falcon and exited the campus, Sylvia turned in her seat. Just like Eileen knew she would.

"Mom, the Stardust Ball is a little over a month away. I need to have an escort to be a nominee."

Eileen drew in a breath and gave herself the moment. "I said we'd talk at home."

"To be correct, you said when we go home. We're on our way. Doesn't that count?"

She slowed everything in her body to be under her control and lowered her volume like she did with disruptive students. "We're not there yet. You can wait."

Sylvia crossed her arms in a huff and turned to face forward. Though she uttered no more words, the message was clear. This girl was unhappy.

Well, so was her mother. Eileen could have jumped on her the second she arrived after school—or better yet, she could have embarrassed Sylvia in front of her whole class. But she didn't. They would save the discussion for home. Which was not all that far away.

The chilly silence piled up like a mounded snowdrift as they mounted the stairs to the over-the-garage apartment they rented and she unlocked the front door. Two tiny bedrooms, a minuscule living room/kitchen, and a three quarter bath provided for their needs. All Eileen could afford without taking money from her parents.

Then the door closed, and Sylvia began before letting her put her things away. "Mom, you're going to have to allow me to have a date so I can attend the Stardust Ball."

Have to? Eileen bit her tongue and took her briefcase to her bedroom.

That didn't faze Sylvia, who followed her. "We're home, and you promised to talk to me once we got here."

Wordlessly, Eileen pointed toward the living room. Once Sylvia got the idea, she followed the girl there and motioned for her to take a seat on the couch. "Now we will talk. I understand about your nomination for Stardust Queen. That is an honor, and I'm happy for you. However, I am concerned about your behavior of late."

Sylvia blanched. "Like what? My grades are perfect. I never get in trouble. What did I do?"

"I think you know." She waited for her daughter to confess.

Sylvia glanced down, chewed her lip a moment, and then made eye contact. "What are you talking about?"

Sylvia's heart thundered in her chest. What did Mom know? There was no way she was going to confess something, only to learn that it was news to Mom. If she kept her mouth shut, sooner or later, Mom would have to give her a clue.

"Hmm. Maybe something that happened this morning?"

Well, there it was, the clue she needed. Only what did she do this morning that would garner her mother's disapproval?

Then she remembered. Before first period. When she met Luke between the buildings. Had her mother been watching? Oh, talk about a kiss of death.

"I see you do remember. Want to tell me about him?"

Sylvia paused. Did she? Maybe it wasn't a matter of what she wished. Was it ever a matter of her desires? "His name is Luke Rafferty. He is an A student with possible athletic and music scholarships. He's kind and funny and respectful. What else do you want me to tell you?"

"How long have you been sneaking around with him?"

"Mom!" She made it sound so tawdry. "We're not sneaking around. I would like to date him, and he'd like to ask me out. I told him you didn't want me to date until after graduation. So he is waiting. You've never even met him, and I can see in your eyes you're making snap judgments."

"And you're kissing a boy you haven't even dated."

Well played, Mother. "Let's get back to the Stardust Ball. I need an escort, and Luke is truly a good guy, Mom."

Her mother paused, like she always did, giving her the eye. Such a drama queen, drawing out the moment like it gave her power. Sylvia twisted her fingers in her lap. That was an awful thing to think. But anymore, it was getting easier to let those thoughts run free. She was eighteen, for Pete's sake. In the eyes of the law, old enough to get married. Why couldn't she go out with a boy? Dating and jumping into bed were two totally different things. Couldn't her mother see that?

"I would like to meet Luke. That is if you are sure he should escort you to the ball?"

"Yes, I am sure. And I am happy to bring him to your classroom tomorrow to introduce him to you." Saying the words pricked her heart with terror. But if they met on school property, Mom would be on her best behavior. Right? She had that favorite teacher status to maintain.

"I would prefer to wait. Ask if he'd like to come to church. He could meet us there." Mom stared back, daring her to disagree.

But Sylvia would take that dare. "I'm sure that would be great. He's a believer, so I don't see a problem."

"Where does he attend?"

"Redeemer Lutheran." She answered promptly, just to prove she knew the answer.

"I see."

What did that mean? "I'll invite him tomorrow. And if you approve of him, does that mean he can escort me to the Stardust Ball?"

"Let's not get too ahead of ourselves. I'm not sure you ought to go after this stunt." Mom's voice was calm—not chilly, but definitely controlled. She never got overexcited. Instead, she simply spoke slower, lower, calmer the more everyone around got animated. Definitely a great strategy for class discipline but annoying when trying to have a conversation.

Sylvia didn't have that talent. The amount of pressure her teeth were putting on her jaw could attest to that. Her normal reaction would be to explode at this point. However, if she wanted her mother to see her as an adult, or at least ready for adult responsibilities and privileges, she needed to control her words and tone. Still, it ground against everything bubbling inside her personality. "Fine. Then we'll begin with you meeting Luke on Sunday. I am sure he'll accept the invitation. Could we go shopping this weekend and check out dresses? I heard Bethann Connelly mention that there's a better selection in Indianapolis."

Mom sighed. Had she hoped for a tantrum from Sylvia? What a crazy thought. "I don't think we need to go to Indianapolis, but after our hair appointment Saturday, we can walk through the mall. Now get changed and busy with your homework. I'll start dinner and call you when it's time to set the table." She stood and walked away as if everything needing to be said got said.

Sylvia didn't know whether to be relieved or insulted, so she obediently headed for her room to change out of her school clothes. Her hand brushed the pocket of her skirt, noting the lump. Luke's ring. Her heart missed a beat. She'd forgotten to leave it in her locker. In fact, it had stayed in her pocket all afternoon once she'd dropped off the note from Mr. Barsh.

Where to hide it? She scanned the tiny cubicle she claimed as her bedroom. There was no way she could let her mother see it now, not when she agreed to meet Luke and consider allowing him to escort her to the ball.

She pulled out her underwear drawer and tucked the ring into the toe of a cabled knee sock. There. That should do it. She placed the sock ball in the very back corner of the drawer for good measure and blew out a soft whistle. That was close. Sylvia shoved the drawer closed and finished changing into a pair of embroidered jeans and an old baby-doll top before pulling out her books along with her transistor radio and ear phones and taking them all to the small dinette table to work. By the time she had her homework complete—considering she'd gotten most of it done in study hall—it would be time to return her school materials to her room and set the table for dinner.

As she pulled her pencil from the pocket of her binder, Alice Cooper sang "School's Out for the Summer." If only.

Twenty minutes later, she gathered her things together and could only imagine what supper conversation would be like. It wasn't something she looked forward to.

Seth knocked at the door before walking in. His sister didn't stand on ceremony, but his tap on the door frame announced someone was there.

"Hey, what brings you by? Thought you weren't coming until tomorrow." Tammy stood on tiptoe and planted a peck on his cheek. "Of course you are always welcome, big brother."

He wrapped his arm around her in a quick hug. "Glad to know that, Sissy. I have news."

She pulled him into the kitchen and pushed him into a chair. "So give. What's up?"

"I bought a house."

"What?" She collapsed into the seat opposite him. "When? Where? Tell me more."

He leaned back. "It's only a couple blocks from Mom's, which I thought might be a good idea so I'm available if she needs me. It's on Wildridge."

"How did you find it? I didn't realize you were looking again. I thought Mom and I had you talked out of that."

"I called Ken Woolley, and we checked it out. This house is vacant now, and though it needs some work on the outside, the inside isn't too bad. Could use some updating, but for my needs, it's fine. Want to go see it?"

She stared. "You saw it today and already have it?"

He shrugged. "Made a cash offer. The owner was motivated and even said Ken could give me a key because his mother was a friend of Mom's." Seth dangled the key in front of her.

"Let's go!" Tammy grabbed a sweater from the hook near her back door and raced for the driveway, obviously expecting him to follow.

Seth chuckled at her response and headed for his car. At least she was excited now that her opportunity to talk him out of it had passed.

Tammy stood next to the passenger side, so he opened the door for her. "Oh, I'm so used to locking my doors, I just assumed you'd locked it."

That gave him a pause, so he decided to ferret out more information. "I figured we'd be leaving quick so didn't bother. Is there a problem I'm not aware of?"

"Probably not. I just got into the habit after that disruption last fall."

A sliver of ice floated down his back. "What disruption?"

"Oh, they might have made more of it than they should have. Or maybe because they jumped on the problem with the determination to not let it affect our community, things fizzled before getting too bad. Not sure, but I did serve on the parents' committee the high school put together. Almost pulled Luke out to send him to Hayworth High across town, but he fought me tooth and nail. He'd already lost his father. I couldn't take his friends away his senior year. Plus, things finally settled down."

Seth braked at the light. "Start at the beginning. What was going on?" And why was this the first he was hearing of it?

"Last fall there were some incidents, race related. By early November, there were police officers in every hall by every entrance in the school. They even had the kids going to school for half days for a while—about twenty minutes per class or something like that—because the trouble had a habit of erupting during lunches. But the principal, Frank Moore, did some very smart things. He even set up a committee of students to investigate, as well as bringing in that parent group. With everyone working together, the drama ended, and this semester has been more peaceful."

"You and Mom said nothing." Though he tried to keep it an observation, a touch of bitterness crept in. The problem was, he was more upset with himself than his sister.

"You were going through enough with your job and making your decision to accept retirement. We knew it was rough on you, and you didn't need our little predicament to add to that."

He gripped the steering wheel tighter and continued through the intersection with the change to green. It gave him a moment to dial it back. "You two need to stop worrying about me. I'm here to help you. That's the one good thing about retirement. I can be close to my family." Wildridge Drive appeared on his left, and he turned before pulling in front of his new house. It wasn't a home yet, but maybe with some ideas from Sissy and Mom, it would be. And then, with something more permanent, he might get his mind off of what he was missing at his former job. "Don't give me an opinion yet. The outside is rough. Let's go inside and then see if you agree on the possibilities." He climbed out and gave her a hand, though she'd already shoved the door open. With her word of warning in his head, he locked up and guided her to the slab porch before slipping the key in the knob.

Tammy grinned. She was excited for him.

Seth held the door open and let her walk in first—the gentlemanly manners his parents instilled fighting the protective pattern his job had required he cultivate.

But there shouldn't be danger here.

Shouldn't being the operative word.

The stakes here in Kokomo had just gotten bigger.

"Oh, Seth, this is great. It's the perfect size for you, and I can see you living here." Tammy's voice cut through his thoughts. She liked it.

"Think you might want to help me do up the inside? My furniture is in storage, though I don't have a lot. I usually just rented furnished apartments. But I've got some budget, so you can have fun fixing up the inside—"

She squealed, hugging him around the neck and bouncing on her toes. "I'd love to! When can I get busy?"

"I already signed the contract and cut the check. It should be deposited into their account in the next day or two. Maybe you can start by looking through magazines and coming up with a plan? By then it should be official. Nothing should get in the way, but there's a buffer of time just in case."

Tammy released him and dug in her purse for a notebook. "Do you have a tape measure? Never mind, I can walk it out for estimates." She was already stepping heel to toe in front of the living room's picture window.

It brought a smile to him. Tammy had been hit by enough, and even though she still kept a joyful expression most of the time, he knew she hurt from the untimely death of her husband. One more reason his doctor had talked him into taking early retirement—his sister needed him.

Then he lifted up a quick prayer. *Lord, please don't let her make this too girlie.*

Chapter 3

The bit of hamburger sizzled in the skillet while Eileen chopped a small chunk of onion to add to the makings of her spaghetti sauce—a crust of bread between her lips to keep her eyes from watering. She should have made a larger batch for portioning, but there was so little room in the freezer it never seemed to work out.

Just like her life.

Sylvia was upset, and a part of her didn't blame her daughter. However, the girl was naïve at best and woefully innocent of what could happen in this world. There was no choice but to protect her.

But then, wasn't that what Mother tried to do to me?

No. Her mother was controlling and manipulative and completely self-serving. If she'd only listened to Eileen, things would have been different.

Eileen shook the thoughts away and stirred in the onion, the aroma making her stomach growl.

Still one niggle remained, a teasing at the back of her brain until she had to pull it free and examine it. What was she to do to keep Sylvia safe? Was this Rafferty boy really trustworthy?

Even good boys made bad decisions sometimes.

Tomorrow in the teacher's lounge, Eileen would make inquiries about him. With that settled, she finished fixing dinner, adding a small salad to the menu.

Sylvia came in without speaking and set the table. One moment Eileen thought she'd caught her daughter sniffing the air like something smelled good, but still she didn't say anything. Was she simply ungrateful or just too upset to talk?

Their meal at the tiny dinette was comprised of short-phrased questions and one syllable answers.

"Homework's done?"

"Yes."

"How was your day?"

"Fine."

"Anything interesting go on?"

This time, Sylvia stared at her.

"That note you brought from Mr. Barsh was a little unexpected. I don't know what he thinks I do over there all day, but he lucked out that one group was making cookies, or I couldn't have helped him."

Sylvia pushed her dish away. "Why not just tell him no? Why do you have to make yourself the favorite for everyone?"

Eileen's fork clattered onto her Melmac plate. "What do you mean?"

Stay calm, speak slower, softer.

"I mean, you help all these kids in your classes, and they just love you for it. You have time to do all that for them and to always be at every function, or at least all the ones I want to attend, so the staff thinks you are wonderful, always having something extra to donate. You don't have time to teach me to drive or go shopping in Indianapolis. And the worst part of this great honor of being a Stardust Queen nominee? People think they picked me because of you. It's like you invade everything in my life."

Her daughter couldn't have shocked her more if she'd changed into a bug and scurried across the table.

"I'm sorry you feel that way. I promise I had nothing to do with it."

"Oh, I believe that. It's not something you'd ever want me to do. But you'd lose face if you made me decline it without cause. And I haven't given you any. My schoolwork is at the top of the class—I'll either be valedictorian or salutatorian, depending on Jim Hect. Any other eighteen-year-old in that school who's protected to the point you do me would have rebelled by now, and trust me, I feel like it. I keep telling myself you are doing your best, and that I'm to honor my parent like God teaches. But you are making this very difficult."

Eileen breathed slowly. This was not typical Sylvia. "So if you think I wouldn't want you to have a shot at Stardust Queen, why do you think it is my fault that they nominated you?"

Sylvia rolled her eyes, an expression Eileen had seen with other teens at school but not with her daughter. "Because they all love you. I wasn't chosen because of me. I was chosen because of you. I can't even earn an award on my own, no matter how hard I try."

"You had a great part in the musical this year."

"Yeah, because they knew I'd be there, and so would you, so they could get that extra help. I was a two-for-one deal."

Eileen held her breath and counted to ten. "You did a lovely job, and no one else could have done better."

"Yeah, well..." Sylvia scooted back from the table and picked up her plate. "I'm done. I'll grab my shower and read a while before bed. Please excuse me." Moments later, the dish was scraped and set in the sink.

Eileen almost called her back to remind her it was her turn to wash dishes but decided against it. This was not how her Sylvia behaved, and the change threw her for a loop.

She needed to find out what was going on. It was probably that Rafferty boy's fault.

It was as if her mother were in the room whispering in her ear.

No. Eileen didn't want to be that kind of mother. She wanted a close relationship with Sylvia. Heaven knew she'd worked hard enough for it.

But what if this abrupt personality change was instigated by that kid? How could she find out?

The old pipes knocked as the water heated. Soon, the sound of the shower pelting the wall sprinkled a new idea into Eileen's overworked imagination. Maybe there was evidence in Sylvia's room?

Sylvia used to write in a diary. Eileen had seen it a few times but hadn't looked inside, though she'd wanted to. But her daughter never acted this way before Luke Rafferty came on the scene. Did she still keep one? Or perhaps there was a note from Luke in with her homework. She slipped into the hall and grabbed Sylvia's doorknob.

This borders on invasion of privacy.

But how else was she to learn?

It also is something your mother would do.

No, her mother would have tossed her room while Eileen cowered in the corner. This way, she could get the information and not embarrass Sylvia.

Eileen nodded that justification into her brain and entered the room. Usual showers for Sylvia lasted fifteen minutes, but Eileen didn't want to count on anything being usual tonight, so she'd better be quick.

She felt beneath the mattress. Nothing.

Then she carefully combed through all the homework and books neatly stacked on the dresser. Again, nothing.

She raised her eyes and caught her mother's reflection in the mirror right down to the way her lips thinned in disapproval. Even the new gray hairs seemed to point and sneer.

Seriously, she was not her mother!

The shower still ran, so she pulled out the top dresser drawer and felt around for a small book or paper. At the back, her fingers found something solid, hard, bundled up in the toe of a sock. Eileen pulled out the bundle and squeezed it. Yes, there was something there. What could it be?

Quickly undoing the rolled-over end, she pulled the sock with the mystery free and reached her hand in.

When her closed fist reappeared, her heart clenched tight. She knew what the item was before she even looked.

A class ring.

Very much like the one buried in her own undies drawer.

Sylvia had wrapped angora thread around it to make it fit her smaller hand. Eileen slipped it on her finger as memories burst through the ground of her mind where she'd buried them as deep as possible, refusing to be ignored. She held out her hand, admiring and remembering how it felt when he'd first asked her to wear it.

The pipes went silent. Sylvie had turned off the water. Oh, no.

Eileen guiltily pulled at the ring to return it to its hiding place. She was too embarrassed—though not sure if more about behaving as her mother or the brief stroll down memory lane. But either way, she needed to get this ring off.

It wasn't budging.

Now her pulse pounded. Had her finger swelled? *Come off, come off, come off!*

The bathroom door creaked.

She tugged again and the ring flew, landing on the bed. After a scramble to retrieve it, Eileen slipped the ring back into the sock toe and shoved the drawer closed just as Sylvia opened the door.

"What are you doing in here?"

"Just putting something away." It was the truth. But shame chased her to her bedroom as she massaged her finger.

Tuesday, April 11, 1972

"Sure, babe, I'll do that. No sweat."

Sylvia breathed a little easier with Luke's words. After last night's dinner disaster, she wanted to prove to her mother she could behave as an adult. To storm out and skip her turn at dishes wasn't exactly the best method. But if Luke would come to church, then that would be one step because anyone who met him could tell he was one of the good guys.

He put his arm around her and walked with her toward the Main Building. "I just don't get why she's so uptight about you having any freedom."

Sylvia shook her head. "I keep telling myself she's protecting me because she loves me and feels like she's got to do the work of two parents. So I try to give her peace about it. But I'm ready to bust free, and I'm afraid that will hurt her."

"I got an idea. Just now. And I'm not sure if it will work."

She stopped and faced him. "Tell me. I'll try about anything."

He brushed a long loop of blond strands off her shoulder. "I have this uncle. He just moved back. What if I get him to pay attention to your mom? I mean, if she had her own love life to deal with, maybe she'd stay out of ours?"

Sylvia cracked up. "That is the craziest, most insane, and most brilliant thing I've heard in forever. My mother with a love life. Think he'd go for it?"

He turned her to walk toward her class. "Dunno, babe. Plus, I've got track practice after school before I head for work so don't know when I can ask him." He slowed, changing the subject. "Still haven't heard from Anderson College yet. They've got the best music department for what I'm planning to do. But if I can't get the bread to pay for it, I'll have to work full time and save, and those chances at scholarships will dwindle f ast."

Sylvia leaned her head against his shoulder. How could she feel so safe this way when, if her mother caught her, it would be disastrous? But she did. "You'll get it. I need to go talk to Miss Winslow, too, and see what else I have to do to get into Anderson. Mom wants me at IUK, but living at home another year is too much. I mean, it's Indiana University and all, but no matter how good the school, the Kokomo campus would be still living with my mother and her rules."

"Have you talked to her any more about getting your driver's license?"

She shook her head. "No, though I mentioned it when I lost my cool last night."

"What happened?"

"I was still flipped out about the whole conversation we had when we got home—the one where I learned she'd seen us kiss and she told me to invite you to church." She glanced at him.

Luke's face got a little pale, but he kept listening.

"Anyway, I tried to keep my temper under control, but she pushed for rapping about the day. Like everything was A-OK. She finally hit the right button, and I blasted."

"Aww, babe. I'm sorry." At least he didn't say she knew better. Which she did.

"But I have an idea too. Sunday we'll have to go to my grandparents' for dinner. I like to slip away with my grampa. He's pretty cool. It's like he understands a little. He's the one who gave me the radio. Anyway, I was thinking, maybe he'd teach me to drive."

"That's a great idea. And now I need to get myself to my class." He scanned the area before leaning in to brush a soft peck against her lips. So sweet, so fast. And she appreciated that he checked. "I'll catch you later."

Sylvia watched him head toward the Vocational Building. Was being with Luke all a dream? Would she wake up clutching her troll to her chest only to find it was still day one of her freshman class with four more years of living with her mother to go? She cringed.

After slipping into first hour chem, she gathered the materials she and Jim Hect had listed they'd need. He joined her seconds later, and together they set up the equipment and got ready for their experiment.

Mr. Dolan gave them the go-ahead, and the two of them got busy. Jim wasn't one for a lot of conversation while they worked, and whatever he did say had to do with the experiment. Which meant it was usually pretty quiet in their portion of the room.

She could overhear other students who used this time to catch up on gossip and talk about their crushes and the latest episode of the *Partridge Family*. Not that Sylvia watched that much TV. Since her mother didn't own a television, it made it difficult to get into any particular show. But apparently not everyone was into David Cassidy.

"Roxie Latham should've been a Stardust nominee. I can't believe they overlooked her."

"You realize why they did."

"Yeah, but it's not right. I think we need to start a petition to get her added. Or, if not added, have you-know-who taken off and replaced by Roxie."

Sylvia's stomach clenched. She could guess who you-know-who was.

"They'd never do that. Not with her mom a teacher and all. Plus, her mom's such a goodie-two-shoes helping with everything, they wouldn't want to make her upset."

The beaker slipped from Sylvia's hand and suddenly she felt the spotlight of a million eyes staring at her.

"You okay, Syl?"

She raised her gaze to Jim's.

"Miss Avery, is there a problem?" Mr. Dolan's voice cut through.

"Excuse me, please." She tore off her goggles and raced out the door for the restroom, giggles chasing her to the hall.

It was worse than she thought.

Tuesday night dinner at his sister's was turning into the highlight of Seth's life. Sure, he appreciated having time with his mom, but she seemed too worried about him all the time. He hated all that probing. *Are you sure you're okay? Did you talk to Doctor Schwartz and get your medical files sent to him?* Which made him doubly glad she'd extended her visit with her friends down in Palm Beach.

Tammy was also concerned—he could see it in her eyes—but she was less likely to interrogate him. Besides, he had penetrating questions he could ask her as well, and he knew she wouldn't like that. So time at her house around the dinner table was more enjoyable, if not a little chaotic.

It usually consisted of Tammy and his niece, Kimmie, and him. On rare occasions, Luke put in an appearance, but with his after-school activities and job at the radio station, he normally wandered in much later and grazed through the leftovers while completing his homework. It'd be nice if he'd listen for once and let Seth just take care of them all.

But he and Luke had been through this before. As the man of the house, Luke said he needed to step up. He knew he couldn't contribute to the financial stability the way his father had, but he wasn't about to let his mother pay for his college education when she needed that money to manage their day-to-day expenses.

Not that she needed to with big brother Seth there. But Luke not only was as stubborn as his mother, he was as responsible. And Seth had to respect him on that count.

He pulled into the driveway and checked his watch. Tammy gave him what-for when he showed up too early. But fifteen minutes prior was his on-time. There was no telling what could happen that would mess up a schedule, and one had to be prepared. At least that's what he'd told her the last time he'd wandered in before expected. Seth didn't mind that she put him to work as penance. Besides, the sibling banter was something he'd missed in his years away.

Still, he sat in the car until 5:45. More than fifteen minutes, and she'd be fit to be tied.

Even with the wait, though, she gave him a squint when he entered the back door. "Grab an apron. You know the drill."

He did, picking a frilly one to give her a laugh. It worked.

Delicious aromas filled the kitchen, his mouth watering in anticipation.

"You're on potato duty. Drain'em, then smash them with this." She handed him a gizmo that had a wooden handle on one end and a disk with holes on the other. He was no genius but figured out he needed to press the disk into the hot, soft spuds. "Once you've got them pretty squished, put these in and mix'em up." She pointed to a partial stick of Chiffon margarine and a bit of milk in a Pyrex measuring cup.

"Not sure if I can make them look pretty all squished but mashing I can do."

"Ha. Ha. Funny man."

Seth put his focus on smashing the little white cubes. He'd seen his mother make mashed potatoes his whole life. How hard could it be?

"Say cheese."

A flash of light nearly blinded him. "What in the world?" He blinked until his vision returned.

"Mom's going to want proof." Sissy set her Instamatic on the counter—the detonated peanut bulb a blistered blue—before she grabbed her loom-woven pot holders and opened the oven door. A savory scent of beef and tomato blasted the room. Her meatloaf—that might as well be art—was brought from the hot cavern and placed on trivets sitting on the counter top.

"Yeah, well, next time give a guy some warning."

"Oh, no. You show up at my house whenever you choose despite the time you are invited. If you get the unvarnished me, there's no mercy for you, buster." She followed up with a wink, and it made for more fun while they got dinner to the dining room.

Somewhere in the middle, Kimmie wandered in to set the table. "Is this what I have to look forward to with my brother?"

Seth and Tammy shared a glance before they both cracked up.

"You just answered my question. Oh, joy." She shook her head as she pulled the utensils from the drawer and shut it with her hip. The motion made Seth see her for a moment not as the little girl who used to ride on his knee but as a young woman.

He stopped chuckling as a wave of protective mode washed over him, reminding him she was now a high school sophomore.

"I think we've got everything. Luke's going to be late again, so we might as well get started. Kimmie, how about you say the blessing tonight?" Tammy sat on the chair Seth held for her and nodded to her daughter.

"Thanks, God, for this food and for Mom and Uncle Seth even when they get silly. Thanks for Luke and bring him home safe from work. In Jesus's name, Amen."

Seth couldn't help but study his niece a moment. He and Tammy had discussed how the death of the kids' father had affected Luke, but not so much Kimmie. Was she starting to feel concern for her brother being away from home? One more reason he needed to step in and help them.

Plus, though Tammy was willing to talk about the kids regarding Carl's death, she wasn't so forthcoming about herself. In time, maybe. However, Seth just wanted to help. He wasn't schooled in dealing with a widow's emotional problems. A completely different animal than the big-brother-little-sister trials he was used to growing up.

Just as Tammy pushed away from the table to go after coffee, the back door creaked open, and Luke wandered in.

"You made it in time to sit with us." Tammy raised on tiptoes and kissed the boy's cheek. "Leave your books in the kitchen, and I'll get you dipped up."

"Hey, Uncle Seth. I'm glad you're here. Think we can talk before you leave?"

"Sure thing." That was a new development.

The kid inhaled his food like he hadn't eaten in a month but made a point of thanking his mom for the meal. "Those potatoes were extra creamy tonight. Really good."

Tammy tossed him a wink. "Thank your Uncle Seth. He made those. And you should have seen him at it—wearing my pink, flowered apron no less."

"And I made them pretty, just like your mom ordered."

Luke snorted milk out his nose.

"Gross!" Kimmie jumped up from the table and threw her napkin at him.

"Yep, that photo is going to be golden." Tammy giggled.

After dinner, Tammy put Kimmie to washing dishes while she set the kitchen to rights, giving Seth and Luke time to speak in private.

"Uncle Seth, I've got this girlfriend whose mom is like some prison warden."

All at once, a vision from his high school days floated through Seth's head like a big gray cloud raining pity for his nephew. "I can imagine."

"Doubt it. This is really out there. I can't figure out why she's so strict, but she found out about me and wants to meet me this Sunday at her church. Sylvie and I thought up something, and I'm hoping..."

"I'm not helping you elope, kid."

"No, nothing like that." A tinge of red crept up Luke's neck to his cheeks. "We thought, or rather I figured out a plan, sort of..."

"Spit it out."

"Would you ask her mother out on a date?"

Seth stared at his nephew. "What did you say?"

"Listen, we just want her out of our business, at least some. We're both eighteen and would like to spend some time together besides between classes at school. If her mother had her own love life—"

"Whoa. Wait a minute. I see where you're going, and I don't need a matchmaker. And just so you know, I won't lead a woman on like that. I've never even met her."

"We get that. We'd just like you to meet her and *if* you hit it off, and if you could spend some time with her, could be she'd loosen up a little with Sylvia and me."

Seth sighed. Maybe if someone had offered to help him back in the day. But no. That ol' witch had been married and no one in their right mind would've wanted to ask her out. "Tell you what. How about I go to church with you on Sunday? I'll do that much. Maybe after I meet her, I can give you some ideas."

There was no way she could be as awful as Mrs. Lawson.

Chapter 4

Saturday, April 15, 1972

"So then I told them..."

Eileen kept her eyes closed and tried to focus on the sensations running through her hair as her head rested against the shampoo sink. The scalp massage helped release tensions that had built all week, though the gossip flowing from nearby clients kept her from fully relaxing. She didn't want to hear about their troubles. She had enough of her own. And she definitely didn't need the buzzing in her ears like some intrepid swarm of mosquitoes. Thankfully, the beauty technician working on her today understood and didn't attempt to engage her in conversation.

Every once in a while on her bi-weekly trips, she'd be greeted by one of her former students working at Catalina Beauty College, and then they'd chat while the student put her hair in rollers or after she came out from under the dryer. But today the girl helping her was a stranger, so Eileen retreated into her mind.

The water turned off. "All set." The girl raised the chair. "Let's go back to my station. You just want a trim and set, right?"

"Right." Eileen followed her to the styling chair and returned to the thoughts that had chased her since Monday night.

Sylvia had definitely been hiding something. But was that all? There was no place for anything else to go on, and Eileen knew where her daughter was every minute of the day—she'd made sure of that. If Sylvia skipped a class, Eileen would be the first to know. So what else was happening?

How had she developed this crush on a boy anyway?

At least her inquiries into Luke Rafferty's background had turned up good reports. A well-liked student and respectful young man who'd just lost his father about a year ago. She had a moment of sympathy for him and his family. Still, what boy would remain interested in a girl who wasn't allowed to date? Was he pressuring her daughter? Did he have one of those charismatic personalities that just made people like him so no one saw the wolf he really was? A mental picture of Sylvia in a red hooded cape and a wolf strolling arm in arm jolted her.

The whole situation made Eileen's stomach roil.

Sylvia sat in the chair two stations down, getting her blonde snarls combed out and the split ends removed from her waist length hair. They'd end up using the biggest rollers Eileen had ever seen to give the straight-do some body but keep it long and silky, though the little curls that dangled in front of her ears were on tiny sponge curlers.

Her daughter was downright beautiful. No wonder that boy was interested.

As long as he didn't entice Sylvia to rebel against her upbringing.

"Mrs. Avery, do you teach at the high school?"

The question startled Eileen out of her revelry. "Yes, yes, I do. I teach home economics. Why do you ask?"

"I thought I recognized you. My sister had you for home ec. Rochelle Gann."

"I remember Rochelle. Outstanding student. How is she doing?" She smiled, recalling the intelligent brunette who'd showed so much potential.

The tech continued to comb and section Eileen's hair. "Well, she's doing okay for now. She dropped out of college and got married. They have a baby due any day."

Something cold settled in Eileen's chest. "She dropped out? But she was a straight-A student, and I thought she wanted to become a teacher."

"She did. But plans change. They're happy, and she'll enjoy hearing we met."

"Yes. Please give her my best." Oh, that poor girl.

The beauty tech student didn't say more, and Eileen was grateful, though it hit her as the girl turned on the hair dryer's timer that she hadn't caught Rochelle's sister's name. She'd make a point of asking once her hair was dry.

Or had the girl already given it to her, and she'd been so wrapped up in her thoughts that she'd forgotten? Was it simply pinned to the front of her smock?

Hopefully she'd get a glance at a name tag and not face the embarrassment of getting caught.

In the meantime, her ruminating continued. Tomorrow she'd officially meet Luke. If he turned out to be as nice as all the reports claimed, should she allow him to call Sylvia? She could listen in on conversations that way. Maybe she could let him stop by the house.

But for what? She didn't even own a TV for them to watch together. Maybe they could do homework and that way Eileen could keep an eye on them. Plus, that would give her a glimpse of his studiousness. Would their tiny apartment embarrass Sylvia? Maybe she wouldn't want him to see where they lived.

Eileen was getting ahead of herself.

Tomorrow. Take it one day at a time. She drew in a slow breath, willing her heart to slow as well.

Sylvia was definitely looking forward to Sunday and church. Eileen could tell by the way she talked to her hair-dresser-in-training about making sure her style was just perfect.

It reminded Eileen of how she'd tried so hard to look her best for that special someone so long ago. Yes, if things had been different, if he'd been trustworthy and true, she wouldn't be pinching every penny and nervous about paying for Sylvia's Stardust Ball gown.

The girl was sure to be disappointed to learn she'd have to wear something handmade. But it would be the most professional-looking homemade gown ever worn to a fancy prom. She'd see to that. As long as her budget held out.

Her stylist, Sandy—Eileen got a glance at her name tag—lifted the dryer and led the way back to her cubicle and chair to finish the style. A bit of teasing and spray and Eileen's regular hairdo was ready.

At the cash register, Eileen flipped back and forth in her mind up to the last second about what to do. If she didn't tip, word might get out that she was stingy and not the person she presented to the world. If she did tip, was it enough to not make her look cheap? And would it cut into what she'd saved back to get the material for Sylvia's dress?

Finally, with a prayer for her money to stretch enough, she slipped a dollar bill into Sandy's hand.

Well, that was awkward. Sylvia watched as her mother tipped her stylist but not the girl who'd worked on her.

Sylvia dug into her purse and came up with a few quarters she'd earned helping her grandfather. It wasn't as if she ever got a chance to spend money on herself anyway.

Mom held the door for her and leaned in once they were outside. "That money I gave my girl was for both."

"But you didn't tell her that. How would she know?"

Mom stopped and gave her a puzzled look.

It wasn't that going to the beauty college was unusual. They went every other Saturday. And Mom usually slipped a tip to the girls. But she also made a point of saying it was for both, and she didn't this time. Guess she didn't realize that.

"So, can we go look at dresses now?"

"Yes, but just look." Mom turned to the car parallel parked a few feet down from the shop.

"But what if we find something? We could put it on layaway. Then it wouldn't be such a sizeable chunk all at once." Sylvia had overheard a couple girls talking about doing just that with their dresses during her English lit class.

"We'll see."

Sylvia kept her tongue wedged between her teeth, locking the words she was thinking inside. Mom always said that instead of saying no. Why couldn't she just say what she meant? After all, Sylvia had been interpreting her mother's hidden messages since she was a toddler and was skilled in avoidance language. But if she spoke out now, it would sound petty and childish.

No, Mom needed to see her as an adult with abilities, capable of managing her own life choices.

So she clammed up and climbed into the passenger seat. Like always.

Now that she was eighteen, she could go on her own and get her driver's license. Though she wouldn't be on her mother's insurance, so what was the point when she had nothing to drive? But it would give her a grown-up feeling to have that official form of identity.

Maybe Grampa would help with this. They'd need time alone to talk, which wouldn't be too hard. Maybe he could give her lessons on Sunday afternoons, if they could slip away. But getting a chance to go to the BMV to take her test would be a challenge. That would require planning. However, the learning part came first, and if he wasn't willing, she'd need a whole different idea.

Mom took Sycamore Street east to the highway and then south to the Markland Mall, finding a parking space on the north side.

Sylvia couldn't help it. As she opened her car door, hope rose that somehow Mom's *we'll see* would really mean she'd consider layaway, despite her brain trying to keep her sane and mature.

They headed into Sears to the prom section. The influence of the movie *Romeo and Juliet* still showed in the styles, with so many being empire waisted. Everything from capped sleeves to those with flowing chiffon hung on hangers, waiting to be picked.

Mom took over and chose three gowns in Sylvia's size.

"What about this one?" The dramatic navy velvet bodice contrasted against the cream taffeta and lace skirt.

"It's pretty, but not your style. It's too bold for your coloring."

And something she liked, so of course, it wouldn't be considered.

All of Mom's selections fell into pastel hues with pink being dominant. "These colors are more complementary to your skin tone, Sylvie. Trust me."

Sylvia didn't. But she took the hangered dresses anyway and headed to the changing rooms without stomping—an enormous feat considering what was going through her head.

However, there was nothing Sylvia could do to hide her disappointment in how she looked in the gowns—like a little girl playing dress-up.

"I don't think these work, Mom." She made a slow spin in front of the three-way mirror while her mother rubbed her chin.

"I think you're right."

"Can we go on to the Kokomo Mall and try Ward's or Penney's?"

Mom sighed and finally nodded.

Sylvia had gotten a concession, and it stunned her since she'd expected the cryptic no. She shimmied out of the last dress and returned it neatly to the hanger before donning her clothes and hurrying out.

Mom took the gowns and handed them to the sales clerk with a thank you before they left to go south to the next shopping mall.

Sylvia tried on four dresses at Penney's before they crossed to the other anchor store, Montgomery Ward. It was there Sylvia finally saw it. The gown. It had all that she loved and fit what her mother had been trying to find. Yes, it was pink, but not a little girl pink. More of a peachy-rose velvet with embroidery on the bodice and a soft, pale, shell-pink skirt made of three layers—taffeta, lace, and chiffon. The top layer shimmered. Sylvia was in love.

Until she looked at the price tag. *Oh, please don't let it fit, so I won't have to hear Mom say no to this dress.*

She took it to the try-on room, her hands shaking as she slipped out of her slacks and button-down top. As the material dropped over her head, waves of pleasure washed down her.

And it fit. Perfectly.

Sylvia didn't know whether to laugh or cry.

She stepped from behind the curtain, her focus on the carpet. No need of Mom seeing the desire in her eyes.

But the gasp made her look up. Her mother's face glowed, and she knew they agreed. It didn't happen often, but when it did, Sylvia knew.

"I love it, Mom."

"It's beautiful on you, Sylvie. Go stand in front of the mirror, and let's check it out from all angles."

She did and was so taken by how it looked, she nearly missed how her mother studied each part of the dress.

Oh, no. Mom wasn't going to buy it. She was going to make her own version.

Sylvia would wear a handmade dress to the Stardust Ball. If only she could just die right here on the spot.

Sunday, April 16, 1972

Seth completed the half-Windsor knot on his tie and ran his comb through his hair one more time. As much as he remained firm about not leading on the mother of his nephew's affections, it still felt like an inroad in his relationship with Luke. It was the first time the kid had actually asked for help with anything. Maybe if he started here, then he could advise and finally help the way he was prepared to. Heaven knew he had the means and the time, and more importantly, the need to do something for his family.

The face that stared back didn't look all that hopeful. Was he digging himself a hole—and Luke too, for that matter—because he didn't gather enough information?

The familiar scenario and subsequent gut-clench had extracted an idea that had morphed into a promise to attend the girlfriend's church this morning to help the kid look trustworthy. Responsible. Anyone who knew Luke realized he was those things, but a stranger with an innocent daughter might have doubts.

Tammy would have been a better choice to attend with the kid, proof he possessed a loving mother. But Kimmy had something special going on, and Sissy needed to be with her. For a moment, Luke had tried to get the whole family to go with him, but when that failed, he was determined his old uncle make a respectable appearance.

"Hope this meets with your approval, kid, because it's the best I've got." Seth tossed a wink at his reflection, slipped his wallet into his hip pocket, and donned his suit jacket. Time to head for his car.

Minutes later, he pulled into his sister's driveway.

Luke waited on the porch. Hopping off the edge and bypassing the steps, the kid raced to the passenger side and climbed in.

"You're not excited or anything, are you?"

Luke glanced over, and instead of joy beaming in his eyes, Seth spotted fear. "Um, just a little nervous."

"Hey, nothing to worry about. You are a good guy, the type any mother would like her daughter to meet. Hard-working, intelligent, and you get your good looks from me, so you should be in like Flint." Seth offered a grin and caught the twitch at the corners of Luke's mouth. "See, nothing to fear. Now, where is this church?"

While his nephew navigated, Seth drove as instructed. The church, Wabash Congregational, wasn't far. He'd noticed it while cruising through the area but hadn't caught on that this was the place.

"Sylvia says her mom realizes she needs an escort to the Stardust Ball, so this is the test to see if I'm allowed to take her. She said her mom might only let me meet them there so I can walk her to the stage but not be on a real date."

"It sounds like Sylvia's mother keeps a tight rein. Are you sure she's worth it?" Seth glanced toward Luke while driving through the parking lot, searching for a spot.

"She's worth it. Uncle Seth, she's the most beautiful girl I've ever met, and she pays attention to me. I was struggling in Calculus last fall. It was hard to even think after what happened to Dad. And she helped me.

Didn't figure I was stupid or anything. Very patient and all. I think she could have any guy she wanted if her mother wasn't so strict."

"Has she ever mentioned why her mom's like that?" There had to be a reason.

"She thinks her mom's afraid, though she's not sure what of. Said her grandmother was tough on her mom, still is from what I understand, telling her how to raise Sylvia and what to allow her to do and what not to do. It's really messed up, but you'd never hear it from Mrs. Avery's students. The girls who take her class all think she's the best teacher on campus. They haven't a clue how she is with her own daughter."

Seth found a vacant parking space at the edge of the lot farthest from the church entrance. But walking never hurt, or at least shouldn't. Sometimes the fragment twinged, making mobility painful, but since there wasn't any other choice, he pushed through, and usually with some stretches, he was able to keep going. It was the sitting at the desk all day that did him in. When he no longer could be a field agent due to not meeting the physical standards, the desk or medical retirement became his only options. He tried the desk—heaven knew he tried—but it only made him weaker.

So here he was, retired before his fortieth birthday, and getting set up on a blind date. That is, if his nephew had anything to say about it. The things one did for love.

He shut off the ignition and turned to face Luke. "I'm here for you. Just want you to be sure this is what you want."

"It is. I'm sure." Luke looked like he was breathing normally. Finally. Then his eyes widened. "They're here. I see her." He pointed to a girl.

Who made Seth stop breathing.

How could it be? She was the spitting image of Leenie. Lithe and blonde and sweet.

And a teenager.

No way.

But then someone came from the other side of the car. And he knew.

"Luke. We need to talk."

"What? Why? I gotta get out there."

"Wait." Seth grabbed his nephew's arm. "Just a minute. There's something I should tell you."

"Hurry then. They're waiting."

How did he say this? How did he tell Luke that he already knew Sylvia's mother? That she was the one he fell in love with his senior year of high school. That Sylvia's grandmother drove them apart and that his Mrs. Avery was the real reason he'd stayed single all these years. "Um, I —"

"Tell me after church, Uncle Seth. I really need to get out there." Luke popped open his door and was gone before Seth could pull his thoughts into cohesion.

Eileen Lawson. Avery. He had to remember she had a married name. But a lot of things now made sense. Of course Eileen would raise her daughter the only way she knew how.

The problem was, what would she say when she saw him show up with Luke?

Asking his uncle to come along might be the worst mistake his nephew made. And Seth was powerless to protect him from whatever was about to happen.

60

Chapter 5

"He's here!"

"Sylvia, we don't race out. Show some self-control." Eileen realized she was talking to the closed passenger door before she'd uttered her last syllable, and that her daughter hadn't heard any of the advice. Oh, well. She couldn't blame Sylvia for being a little excited.

However, it was more anxiousness than anticipation that ran through Eileen. This was a new path on the journey to her daughter growing up. One she'd accepted was coming but still wasn't ready for.

So it was time to face the future.

Eileen climbed from her car, tucking her keys into her handbag after locking the doors.

The boy standing with Sylvia was closer now than when she watched from her classroom window. She saw him much clearer.

And gasped.

Black wavy hair. Tall, thin build—well over six feet already. And that crooked grin that had lit her world twenty years ago. Had Seth married, settling here in town, and she never knew? No, the boy's last name was Rafferty.

God, this isn't funny. You can't make my Sylvie go through what I did. We have to protect her.

Eileen willed her heart to a normal beat, inhaled and exhaled, then raised her chin a notch and strode over to where her daughter held hands with Seth Matthews's doppelgänger. That was going to have to stop.

"Hello, Luke. I'm Mrs. Avery. Nice to finally meet you." She offered a handshake just as someone approached.

Withdrawing her trembling hand, she covered her mouth and stepped back, stumbling.

Then she was caught by a familiar yet long-forgotten sensation that kept her upright.

Her breath whooshed out with his name. "Seth."

"Leenie."

It was him. It really, truly, was him. Just as she began to allow instinct control and pull him into an embrace, the pain of his silent rejection all those years ago flooded back. She pushed away and darted a glance toward Sylvia and her guest.

Both teens stared back with wide eyes.

No, she would not behave like some ingenue in an epic love story movie. She had pride. With determination, Eileen pulled herself together, patted her hair, and then offered to shake Seth's hand as if they were meeting for the first time. Or as if they were old high school acquaintances making polite reintroductions. "Hello, Seth. It's been a long time."

Not that her pulse was all that cooperative.

He cocked his head slightly, giving that unnerving gaze that used to send shivers all over her. "It certainly has been, Leenie."

"Leenie?" Sylvia and Luke echoed each other.

Seth coughed into his fist. "That was what I used to call Mrs. Avery back when we were in high school. Together."

The way he tacked on together caused Eileen's face to heat. Almost as much as hearing his pet name for her. No one else had ever called her Leenie.

"So, you already met my uncle. I was about to introduce you. He's just moved back to town."

Eileen turned her gaze back to his. "You have?"

"Yes. In fact, I bought a house not far from here."

Suddenly, her brain filled with blinking caution lights and sirens. So not good. *Stay poised.* "How nice for you." What else could she say?

They all stared at her. Did they expect more of a response? Then, one by one, their gazes seemed to go anywhere but at her, which was even worse.

Seth nudged her elbow. "Perhaps we should go inside?"

That's what she needed. A point in the right direction. "Yes, let's go in and find our seats."

He continued to guide her, gently touching the sleeve of her good blue suit. Even though she couldn't feel it through the fabric, the heat of his fingers penetrated to her arm, sending shock waves all throughout her system. How was she even supposed to think with him so close? And why, after all this time, could he show up and do this to her? It was not fair. She and God were going to have a stern discussion once she had an alone moment.

The kids walked in front, and Luke held the door for everyone. She didn't want to like him, but so far he had proved to have manners. And now that she knew *who* he was related to, she really didn't want anything to do with him. Or his uncle, for that matter.

Sylvia led them past the usher, who doled out bulletins, and toward the pew where they regularly sat, stepping aside for Eileen to go in first.

Oh, no. That wasn't happening. She motioned for her daughter to go ahead.

Sylvia shook her head, then nodded for her mother to enter.

Eileen straightened and gave her daughter the look.

Her daughter stubbornly shook her head.

Just as she opened her mouth, Luke put his hand on Sylvie's shoulder, guiding her into the pew and following.

No, no, no. Wrong plan. With pursed lips, she scooted in, only to be seated between Luke and Seth.

Ooh. A whole lot of awkward going on.

Seth grabbed a hymnal from the rack in front of them and handed it to her before selecting one for himself. "Nice little church. I don't remember it being here when we were in high school."

"It was a smaller congregation back then and met on the other side of downtown." She paused, a question burning through her desire to be proper. "Why are you here?" And why wasn't he as upset as she felt?

"What do you mean? Here in town or here at your church?"

She wanted to slap that innocent, self-assured expression right off his still too-handsome face. The one that had matured to show a few crinkle lines near his eyes and streaks of silver at his temples.

Snap out of it!

"Let's say at church, for now. We can discuss your return to town later." Because she wanted to learn about that too.

"So there'll be a later?" He twisted at a ring he wore on his right pinkie. Maybe he was a little nervous. Good.

"I'm assuming since we're in the same area that we might meet again. But we don't have to. Back to my question. Why are you here?"

"My nephew, who is a wonderful young man, by the way, was nervous to meet you and asked if I'd tag along so you could see he comes from a nice family." He smiled.

If that had been Luke's intention, he didn't choose as wisely as he thought.

The wounds might be a couple decades old, but the sharp pain that caused them felt as fresh as the day it happened.

"Did you know?" Luke's whisper tickled Sylvia's ear.

She shook her head and then glanced toward her mother. It was the first time she'd ever seen her so rattled. There was something bigger here than what anyone was sharing.

Her mother had a secret.

Talk about wild.

Mom in high school. That was hard to imagine. Sylvia had sort of figured her mother started off an adult, though of course common sense and sophomore biology class said otherwise. She tried to picture a six-teen-year-old Eileen Lawson and somehow couldn't make it happen. At least not until she glanced at the woman on the other side of Luke, whose face was slowly gaining extra color in her cheeks. It only piqued Sylvia's curiosity. There had to be more.

How well had she known Luke's uncle?

Maybe that was why her grandmother was the way she was. Had she discovered a relationship with Luke's Uncle Seth? Images bloomed in her mind. Oh, that would have been a scene.

Could this be why her mother was so strict? Had Mr. Matthews done something awful to her mother?

She sneaked another look. Mom sat so proper, her hands folded in her lap and her face almost as flushed as when she had to dig the car out of the snow last winter. What could be going through her mind right now?

Then she had an awful thought. *What if Mr. Matthews is my father?*

No, that couldn't be. Her last name was Avery, and her father died when she was a baby. Too many people knew that. Besides, she'd seen a photo of when her parents eloped. Her father was blond, like her and M om.

But what if?

Sylvia shook her head, knocking away that ridiculous notion.

Luke glanced at her, a furrow building between his eyes.

She smiled and hoped that was enough of an answer.

However, her imagination came out to play so loudly that focus on Pastor Mussing's sermon was outshouted. Normally, Mom would ask her questions while in the car after the service. The purpose was mostly to make sure Sylvia paid attention, but she actually enjoyed the ritual, finding ways to keep her mind off going to her grandmother's and ideas where she could debate with her mother in an intellectually equal way. Mom usually seemed to appreciate the thought Sylvia put into her answers and questions. However, she wouldn't be able to put enough thought into anything today since the only question she could come up with was "What did he say?"

But then, a peripheral glance at her mother left little doubt—the drive to Sunday dinner would be different. Maybe Mom was too shaken to interrogate her.

At the door, as Pastor Mussing shook hands with everyone, Sylvia introduced Luke and his uncle, who received an invitation to come visit again.

And then they were back in the parking lot.

Luke had a funny look on his face, like he was trying to decide how much affection he could get by with. He settled for squeezing her hand,

and even that little gesture caught Mom's eagle eye. Oh, well. They'd made it through, no one was injured or maimed, and with the fact Mom knew Luke's family—or at least his uncle—she should give her permission to let them go to the Stardust Ball together. *Please, God!*

"It was nice to see you, Leenie. I hope that it won't take two decades before it happens again." Luke's uncle held out his hand to Mom.

Time crawled before her mother finally accepted the handshake.

Mom's face was frozen into that proper expression she'd borrowed from some royal princess's magazine photo. "You too."

That was it? That was all Mom had to say? Something really bad must have happened. And she couldn't wait to talk with Grampa about it. Or should she?

The ride to Sunday dinner was silent. Something about her mother's demeanor kept Sylvia from asking all the questions she was dying to have answered. She'd never seen Mom like this before, and to be honest, it was a little scary.

But once they parked in front of Grandmother's house, Mom shut off the car and turned to face her. "Do not say a word to Grandmother about Luke or Seth. Do you understand me?"

The fierceness—or was it terror—on her mother's face demanded compliance. "Yes, ma'am."

Mom swallowed and squeezed her eyes tight. "I can't explain, at least not now. But I'm trusting you with a lot to obey me on this, Sylvia."

"I said I would, Mom." Then she paused, really searching her mother's face. "Are you okay?"

Her mother took a moment before replying. "No. I was not ready for that. But if you will do as I say, I'll be able to get through this meal, and we can go home, which is all I want to do right now. Promise me, please."

Now Sylvia was worried. It was worse than she imagined. "I promise."

Mom patted her hand. "Good." She sighed, then added, "Thank you."

"You can count on me, Mom. But we better get in there before she comes storming out to learn what's taking us so long."

"You're right. Let's go."

Once inside, they headed immediately to the dining room since Grandmother made it clear they'd taken too long to arrive and she'd had to do everything herself, so they'd better not let the food get cold.

The meal was more awful than normal. No conversation except to ask for something to be passed. Grampa kept his head down, focusing on his plate. Grandmother stared at Mom while she slowly raised her fork to her mouth bite after bite, and Mom simply nibbled and pushed her food around on her plate.

"Sylvia, would you please cut slices of cake for everyone and bring them in?"

Though it sounded like a request, it was a command, and Sylvia obeyed without pause. Grandmother scared the snot out of her.

In the kitchen, Sylvia found the cake server and plated four desserts. There was never an opportunity to say no. The best one could hope for was to not be noticed leaving food on one's plate. She loaded up the four slices of chocolate cake and backed into the swinging door.

As it opened behind her, Grandmother's voice carried. "I saw him walking the neighborhood last Monday, so I'm aware he's back. You will stay away from him. Am I understood?"

A plate slipped from Sylvia's fingers, crashing into a mess on the carpet.

"Stupid, clumsy—"

"It was an accident, Mother." That was the boldest thing Sylvia had ever heard her mother say.

Grampa, however, left his seat and came to her aid. "Set the others on the table while I clean this up, Sylvie." He even winked at her, wiping away Grandmother's outburst.

She did, giving everyone but herself a dish. Her stomach wouldn't like the rich dessert anyway, not the way it was roiling with all the tension.

There was no getting around it. Luke's Uncle Seth and her mother had a history, and Grandmother was not pleased.

"Stop sign!"

Seth slammed on the brakes, nearly knocking his nephew into the windshield. His heart thudded to a halt as well. What had he almost done? Seat belts. He had to make everyone wear seat belts. His pulse jackhammered.

"What's with you, Uncle Seth? You've been freaky ever since we left the parking lot."

The pounding in Seth's chest subsided. "I just got caught unaware. Not good in my business—my former business. Proves I made the right decision to retire." And that he needed to brush up on his skills. He was better than this.

"Want to talk about it?"

Seth shook his head. "Not really. But I understand what you're going through more than you can imagine." So much more than he could begin to imagine.

"Oh, I can imagine pretty good. It's obvious you and Mrs. Avery have a past. Who'd have guessed?"

"Your mother, for one. Wish she'd have given me a heads up." Seth still couldn't believe Sissy didn't warn him about what he was about to walk into. She knew. She had to remember.

"I've never mentioned Sylvia's name to anyone before you. We didn't even say it when I was inviting Mom and Kimmie to church. Though I think if Kimmie hadn't made such a big deal and I hadn't gone to bed when I did, Mom probably would've been probing for answers. But I know how she gets, so I avoided her." Luke shrugged, as if that could explain everything.

71

Seth pulled into the driveway at Tammy's house. "Well, it's about time we got some of this in the open." Maybe. To dig into old wounds would be painful though.

They climbed out, and Seth slammed his door a little more forcefully than intended, causing Luke to scrutinize him. "Just go. I'm coming."

"Yes, sir." The kid took off at a run for the house, undoubtedly to fill his mother in on the strange morning.

Seth leaned against the car and pounded his fist on the roof over his doorframe. That was all it took. The fragment chose that moment to send a twinge down his leg, making his knee buckle. He grabbed the driver's side door handle to catch himself and took a couple deep breaths. *You're right, God. I need to slow down and think clearly. No charging ahead. Got it.*

The twinge subsided, and he walked through the back doorway to see his sister's eyes wide and staring. "Oh my goodness, Seth. I had no idea." The pity in her gaze said more than her words. Luke had definitely brought her up to speed.

"I know. Plus, I told you and Mom that I didn't want to hear any more about her, so there wouldn't have been any clues to help. It was just... Let's say Shakespeare could've made a great comedy out of it."

She hugged him. "That's fair. He'd already had the tragedy to work with from before."

"So does anyone want to clue me in? This is affecting my love life. Me, right here." Luke plopped into a kitchen chair and stared at them.

Sissy pulled away. "You want to fill him in, or should I?"

"I'll do it." That way Seth could control how much got shared and the light shown on the players. He sat alongside Luke and gathered his thoughts that took him on a not-so-lovely trip down memory lane. "Leenie, Mrs. Avery, was a junior when I was a senior in high school. I remember it took me two weeks to get up the gumption to just speak with her, let alone ask her out. But, as you can guess, her mother was controlling. We tried to abide by her rules, my stopping by and staying on the porch while we chatted and Mrs. Lawson listening in or sitting with us. At school, we could talk without being overheard and, well, we fell in love. She even wore my class ring. I was headed for college while she started her senior year of school and...things happened." That would have to be enough because he wasn't going to go into the rest. Not this soon after seeing Leenie for the first time in almost twenty years.

"What about you, Mom? Why didn't you say anything about you and Mrs. Avery from when you were in high school?"

Tammy shrugged. "Since Seth didn't want to hear about her and I wasn't fond of her for what she'd done, I chose not to keep track of her. You never took a home ec class, and Kimmie hadn't picked that for her elective yet, so there was no need to bring it up. Besides, if your sister ever did have Mrs. Avery for a teacher, she wouldn't have figured out the relationship, and that would be for the best, I'm sure."

Luke sighed. "So now what do I do?"

Seth shared a glance with Sissy. "You wait. Didn't you say they had Sunday dinner with Sylvia's grandparents?"

"Yeah."

"Well, I'd bet money that Leenie will avoid all conversation concerning me with her mother. It could get ugly, and Leenie will shy away from anything that will bring about her mother's wrath."

"Oh?"

"Trust me, the subject of you won't come up before they reach home. Unless they live with Mrs. Lawson?" That was something he hadn't considered.

"No, they live over on Maple. Sylvia says it's a converted apartment over an old, large garage. I know where it is, but she doesn't want me to go there. Says she hates that place." Luke ran his fingers through the hair at his temples, making it stick out. He had to be stressed because Seth had never seen him with a strand out of place, even if he did wear it longer these days.

"Let's give them some time, and then maybe you and I can go for a walk."

"Seriously, Uncle Seth? Wouldn't that just destroy any chance I have?"

Seth glanced at Sissy, who averted her eyes and started wiping her kitchen counter. "Right now it doesn't look too good for you because of me. I think if we have more time, and maybe if I try to make some peace with the woman, you'll get to take Sylvia to the Stardust Ball."

"But that's not everything."

Tammy turned back to them. "What else is there?"

"Sylvia has my class ring. We're going steady. I've been looking into the cost of things at Anderson, and I think if we don't wait for college graduation but get married before we start, we could save money living in married housing and pooling our resources."

It was more serious than Seth realized. "You don't marry to save money, Luke."

Tammy pulled up a chair at that point. "Seth's right. You marry for love. It's the only thing that will hold you together through the storms."

"But I do love her. And I want to marry her. I'm just saying, if we do it right after graduation instead of waiting four years, it will save us while we get our degrees."

Seth twisted his ring before he braved the inevitable question. It was key and would determine his next move. "What does Sylvia say?"

Chapter 6

E ileen clenched her eyes closed and forced herself to maintain control—slow breathing, dropping her voice. If it worked in her classroom, maybe it would work with her mother. Only it never did. Wasn't that the definition of insanity? Doing the same thing over and over, hoping for a different result?

Well, she didn't have the courage to simply yell at Mother, that was for sure.

"I have no expectation of ever seeing Mr. Matthews, though the fact that he has moved back to Kokomo means there's always the chance of running into each other at the grocery." She hoped that had the right amount of respect and common sense.

"If you do, you are to turn and go the other way. I will not have you getting into a discussion with him." Mother paused. "And how did you know he had moved back to town?"

Eileen's breath froze in her chest. How did she answer that? "You said you'd seen him walking the neighborhood. Maybe he is only visiting."

Mother stared hard, her eyes narrowing. But she didn't question the response. "Just see that you stay clear of him."

"Yes, ma'am." Eileen crossed her fingers that lay in her lap, neatly hidden beneath the edge of the tablecloth.

"Sylvia, you may cut yourself another slice of cake but make it small. No need to waste it." Mother needed to prove she was magnanimous.

"No thank you, Grandmother. I feel bad about your plate. I am so sorry." Sylvia knew the right words to say.

"It's perfectly fine. I think I can find a replacement for the dish on my next trip to Indianapolis, so there's no need to forgo your dessert." Mother nodded toward the kitchen door. "I insist."

Force-feeding sugary treats to her granddaughter. If that wasn't love... Eileen pulled her thoughts away from the sarcasm and searched her brain for an exit strategy. She had to get out of this asylum and back to her home where she had some control.

Sylvia slowly scraped her chair back and left the table for her piece of cake. That she didn't want. Besides the fact that Mother was not the best cook, if Sylvia's stomach was flipping anything like Eileen's, eating dessert was just one more form of torture.

Once she returned, Sylvia glanced at her watch. "Um, Mom, I have homework I need to get done."

Good girl. "Then I think we ought to help get the table cleared and dishes done so we can head for home." Mother would not let them out of the house without doing that first. Eileen stood and picked up her plates and utensils.

"Why are you so in a hurry to leave?"

Father glanced up then. "Ethel, they have lives outside of here. It was good to have you both to dinner today." He rose, following suit.

"Carson, they are here every week, and every week they behave as if they only dropped by to fulfill some duty. I want my family to stay and spend some real time." Something telegraphed between Eileen's parents.

"Well, then, Sylvie, how about you and I take care of the dishes while your mom and grandmother go into the living room to chat?"

Sylvia glanced her way, so Eileen nodded. At least her daughter wouldn't have to follow her into the lion's den.

Waiting for her mother to stand first, Eileen followed obediently to the living room, whose decor hadn't changed since before she was born. Heavy draperies, massive furniture, flocked wallpaper. She could tell where every pattern began and ended, how many repeats between the chair rail and the ceiling, the exact number of drapery hooks which hung from each ornate rod. Whenever she'd been forced to sit in this room and silently attend to a lecture, she'd developed a skill of making it look like she paid attention while her brain calculated the number and shape of things in the room. She'd be able to identify anything from here if it showed up elsewhere.

"... and don't think for a moment you have me fooled young lady. You think you know better than me, but I tell you, if you allow your daughter to attend that awful dance they insist on having, you will lose her. She'll pick up those radical thoughts like one of those hippies, and the next thing she'll be smoking marijuana and doing who-knows-what with boys. Eileen, are you listening to me?"

"Yes, Mother."

"And while we are talking, you still attend that Wabash Congregational church. I told you we were leaving when the music got too contemporary with all those choruses. Now you and Sylvia will start coming with us. That way, you won't be so late for Sunday dinner."

Change churches? Eileen thought she'd won that battle. Ah, but no. Her mother never gave up. "Mother, Sylvia is doing well under Pastor Mussing's teaching. I do not want to pull her away and maybe cause a problem with her faith. She's a good girl, and I want to make sure she continues to receive the support she needs."

"You and I are her support."

"Yes, but Pastor Mussing is a safe male role model in her life. She trusts what he says."

Mother nearly rose from her seat. "You don't leave her alone with that man, do you?"

"Of course not. The only males she encounters where I am not present are at school and there are lots of people. She's never alone. I keep very close tabs on her." Except for Father, who was alone with Sylvia in the kitchen, but no need to remind Mother of that.

"Humph. Your problem started at school, too, where I couldn't be with you." Mother's eyes narrowed. "That's another reason she is not to attend the dance. She'd need an escort. Just tell her to turn down the nomination for her own good and let some other girl get pregnant out of wedlock."

"Mother!" Eileen had been married. Even if her mother didn't approve. And just because her mother was right about Doug Avery didn't mean she was right about all men. Was she?

Sylvia slipped on the Playtex gloves and opened the faucet to fill the sink. A generous squirt of Palmolive built mounds of foam while she slipped the dirty plates into the water. "Grampa, we have to have the most uncomfortable Sunday dinners of anyone on the planet. I don't get it. Why does she have to behave that way?"

"Which she are you talking about?" He nudged her shoulder while she rinsed a fork.

"Grandmother. And why can I call you Grampa, but she has to be Grandmother?"

He sighed. "I couldn't tell you, Sylvie. When I got back from the war, she'd changed a bit. She'd had to care for your mom by herself while I was overseas, so when I got home, I was told not to interfere. Plus, she might have been a little afraid of me after having spent time in that POW camp, coming home when she thought I was dead. So I abided by her wishes."

"But you still stayed."

"Yeah. I stayed." He dried a handful of utensils and put them in the drawer.

"Why?"

"What else was I to do? I made a promise when I married Ethel. A solemn vow. There's no changing that." Grampa's shrug was the saddest thing Sylvia had ever seen.

She let go of the plate she'd started, allowing it to sink back onto the stack, and wrapped her drippy hands around her grandfather before jumping back, realizing what she'd done. "Oh, I'm sorry."

"Nothing to worry about, Sylvie. It's just water." Grampa flashed a sweet smile.

"Won't she get all bent?"

"That's life. Let's not talk about her right now. We've got time to ourselves. What's going on with you, Squirt?"

She plunged her hands back into the soapy foam and found that plate again. It was the perfect opportunity, so she breathed in a prayer and took the leap. "Well, it's still up in the air, I guess, about me going to the Stardust Ball. I really want to go, and I'm hoping Mom will let me. But what I really want, more than anything, is to learn to drive. I'm old enough to get my own license, but without training on how to drive or having anything to drive, it makes the whole legal thing sort of useless."

"I see. Do you have a solution?"

She paused scrubbing and turned to him. "Would you teach me to drive, Grampa? Please?"

"I'm not sure when I could do that." He looked down at the patterned china bowl in his hands. "I'd have to come by to pick you up, and your mother would figure out what was going on. And then you-know-who-else would learn of it."

"Yeah." Defeat felt like a deflated balloon.

"But it shouldn't take too many practice sessions..."

Sylvia glanced over at him.

"And maybe I could ask if you could go with me when I need to run errands on Saturday or Sunday afternoon after dinner."

Springs invaded Sylvia's feet as she bounced on her toes in anticipation. "Oh, Grampa, I'd hug you again, but you are wet enough."

He chuckled. "But we need to keep this between the two of us, all right?"

"Deal. So when do we start?"

"I'll think on it. Might have to wait for summer, just to be safe."

Keeping her drippy hands over the sink, she stood on tiptoe and brushed a kiss against his cheek. "Thank you for being the sanity in my life, Grampa."

"We'd better get this finished, Sylvie." But he grinned and winked at her. He was her safe place. She could tell him anything.

Well, almost anything. Besides the fact Mom had sworn her to secrecy about Luke and his uncle this morning, Sylvia had the feeling Grampa wouldn't want to hear about her having feelings for a boy. He might be ready to teach her to drive, but she doubted he was ready to hear she was becoming a woman with adult-sized emotions.

She nodded, and they finished the dishes in silence.

Once the kitchen looked perfect, or as perfect as they could get on her grandmother's perfection scale, she hugged her grandfather one more time. "I ought to get in there and rescue Mom."

"You're probably right. It's not hard to believe that some creatures eat their young. I've seen Ethel in action for too many years. Let's go."

When they made it to the living room, Mom popped up from her chair. "Oh, good, you're ready to leave."

"Just remember what I said, Eileen."

"I will, Mother. Thank you for dinner."

Grandmother sort of smiled.

"Yes, thanks, Grandmother." She couldn't add on that it was delicious. It wasn't. How her mother could be such an amazing cook and her grandmother so awful, she had no idea. But that was the truth of it.

"We're glad you two were here. We will see you next week. Plan to attend church with us."

Sylvia froze, glancing from Mom to Grandmother. "Um, I'm supposed to be part of the youth choir next Sunday." If they were singing next Sunday, that is.

"That's right. I'd forgotten. I'm sorry, Mother. It will have to be another time. Sylvia has an obligation."

Grandmother's lips puckered as if she'd bitten into a lemon. "Very well. I guess one more week won't hurt."

Grampa stepped forward. "Goodbye, then. Drive safely."

It wasn't even a mile to their house, Sylvia wanted to point out. But instead, she flashed him a smile. She knew what he was doing and loved him even more for it. "Bye." She opened the door for Mom, who scurried past, and then followed her mother to the car.

Once they were inside, though, her mother looked like she'd just toured a haunted house, so pale and jittery. It even took her two tries to insert the key into the ignition. With shaky hands, Mom pulled away from the curb. "Let's get home."

Sunday dinners were always horrible, but today Mom seemed beaten worse than normal. In fact, Sylvia had never seen her so...unnerved.

"You okay, Mom?"

"Yes. No. I don't know. I just need to be in my own home where she can't touch me."

Sylvia wanted to say "I get that," but instead remained silent. Mom might not understand. And, the truth was, Sylvia was just beginning to. Mom might do a lot of things like Grandmother, but her motives were always kinder, more loving. Because when all was said and done, Sylvia did not doubt her mother's love, just her parenting skills.

However, there was no love involved with her grandmother. As least as far as she could see.

And right now, that broke her heart for her mother.

Seth glanced at the avocado wall clock hanging in his sister's living room. Yeah, he needed to inform Sissy that was not his style before she got him one for his new place. But for now, it was pushing three, and Sunday dinner was over, and everything cleaned up. He figured Eileen had enough time to get home from her parents' house as well. "Ready?"

Luke glanced up from the game on the TV. "Now?"

"They should be back, and the walk will do us good."

"Yeah, but…" The fear in Luke's eyes was understandable. He didn't want to do anything stupid now that his future with Sylvia was in the balance.

"Just c'mon. It'll be fine." Seth hoped he spoke the truth. But he was driven more by his desire to see Eileen again than making it all good for Luke. Selfish? You bet. But if this worked out for him, it would also work for his nephew. Really, what could go wrong? His brain fired up multiple options. He shoved them all away.

They walked in silence for a block or two. Luke had his hands shoved in his pockets as he stared at the ground.

"Snap out of it, Luke. You were the perfect gentleman today. And I'm the one dragging you along. You've done nothing for Mrs. Avery to count against you."

"Easy for you to say, Uncle Seth. Her reasoning isn't always what I'd call logical, and if her behavior today means anything, my being linked with you might be a deal-breaker."

Seth chuckled. The kid was right, though logic wasn't what drew him toward Leenie's house.

"We turn here." Luke pointed out the direction, and they continued until they stood on the sidewalk in front of a large two-story garage.

"This is where they live?" Something told him that Leenie had found a bit of independence even if she hadn't cut the cord all the way. Her mother would never approve of these living arrangements. They were too small, too modest. So this must be Leenie's try for freedom. He imagined it took everything she had to do it.

"Hey, there they are."

Seth glanced over in time to see Leenie's car pull into the driveway.

She hopped out quickly, racing over even before Sylvia could, though the girl was close on her heels. "What are you doing here?"

"We were out for a walk and thought we'd say hi. It was good seeing you today, Leenie."

Confusion flashed through her eyes, followed by fear that raised her perfectly sculpted brows. "You'd better come inside before someone sees you out here." She turned and marched up the steps. Looking over her shoulder at the three of them on the sidewalk, she motioned. "C'mon."

Seth followed while Luke and Sylvia held hands and joined the parade to the second-floor entrance.

Leenie stood, holding the door open. "Hurry before someone calls my mother." Once everyone was inside, she closed the door and leaned against it like she'd just run a mile. "Now, again. Tell me why you are here, and don't you dare give me any drivel." Her stare was a bullet ready to assassinate anything that didn't ring true.

He rubbed his hand over his mouth. How he answered was more important than the actual answer. "Um, I wanted to see you. It's been a long time, and you surprised me this morning. Guess I needed to make sure you weren't some apparition."

She softened before his eyes, her glance becoming shy. "Oh. I understand that." After looking over at her daughter, Leenie straightened her spine. "Well, you're here. Go ahead and have a seat. Would you like something to drink? I can make coffee, and we've got some cookies—"

"Mom, why don't you sit with our guests while I plug in the percolator? I'll bring those chocolate chip cookies over too." Sylvia even gave her mother a tiny push toward the sofa.

"I'm perfectly capable of being a hostess, Sylvia."

"Of course you are, Mom, but so am I, and you have a guest. Go sit while I take care of this."

Leenie glanced between her daughter and his nephew before sighing. "Fine." Luke would be helping with the refreshments, that was a given, but at least she resigned to sit while waiting to be served.

The living room and kitchen were actually one open room, so it was no problem to keep an eye on the two teens. Despite being small, it was nicely decorated. Was that how to describe it? It wasn't cluttered with a lot of knickknacks, and the furnishings were comfortable with clean lines.

"I can't believe you're here." She glanced at him and then back at her hands, folding and unfolding them in her lap. Her voice dropped to a whisper. "I never thought I'd see you again."

"I understand. How are you, Leenie? Really."

"At the moment? Unsettled. I've got my mother telling me she saw you out walking. She warned me to have nothing to do with you and insisted I not allow my daughter to attend the Stardust Ball because she'd need an escort. I'm getting pulled apart worse than when we were in high school, and all I want is what's best for Sylvia."

Seth flashed her a smile he hoped showed he was harmless in all this. "It sounds tough. But Sylvia is a lovely girl. Looks like you've done a great job with her, from the little I've seen. Luke says she's kind and that she's a good kid."

That got a smile from Leenie in return. "Thank you. She is a good girl and at the top of her class."

"Where's she going to college? Have you decided?"

She shook her head. "She needs to go. She's too bright to stop her education now. But I worry for her, so I'm planning to have her stay home and attend IUK. I just don't want her making my mistakes."

"Your mistakes?"

Leenie raised her left hand and wiggled her fingers. The diamond ring glittered.

"Ah, I see. But I thought you were a widow."

"Even widows have bad marriages."

Seth slipped his arm over the back of the couch and settled his ankle on his other knee. "Want to tell me about it?" His back disapproved the position, so he returned his foot to the floor.

"Not really. At least not when Sylvia is so close."

"They're not paying attention. Look. They're in their own world." He nodded toward where the kids were quietly laughing while Sylvia got out cups and dessert plates.

"Doug was a whirlwind. I met him in my English lit class at Anderson. He followed me like a puppy, wouldn't take no for an answer. Said we had to go out. After two weeks of dating, he assured me we needed to get married. So he gave me this ring, and we eloped. Next thing I know, I'm pregnant and he's in a terrible accident. Mother brought me home, but she was growing more controlling, so I finished my teaching degree at IUK and found this place. It puts a buffer between me and my mother, though it took all I had to do that much. We still are required to have dinner on Sunday, and she's moved from making strong suggestions to out and out demanding I do things her way."

He used his free hand to capture hers, and she didn't fight him. "Like what?"

"She is insisting that Sylvia and I attend her church and that my daughter can't be part of the Stardust Ball. Seth, she said some awful things today, and all I wanted was to run back here and..."

"And what?"

"Run away? Change my name? That woman has pushed me to the brink, but I don't think I'm brave enough to do what I need to." Her grip on his hand grew tighter.

"I'm here if you ever want to talk."

She glanced at him, then all at once pulled her hand away, scooting farther from him. "Um, but for how long?"

"What?"

"For how long will you be here? How can I be sure I can trust you?"

"This is me, Leenie. You can trust me. You always could."

She shook her head. "The last time I counted on you, you deserted me."

Chapter 7

Eileen felt more than saw Seth pull away, like peeling back a layer of her heart.

"You think I deserted you?"

She should've kept her mouth shut. But Seth had always dragged things out of her that no one else had. "I mean, you took off for college, and I thought we were good for most of that first year, but when I was planning to join you there, no more letters." A vise twisted in her chest as she remembered. "You didn't call when you came home to visit. And when I finally got to Anderson, you'd switched schools. I even checked with enrollment, and they said you hadn't registered for that semester. You just up and disappeared." She swiped at the tear that had disobeyed and broken through.

Now he turned and stared as if she spoke a foreign language. "What do you mean? I got your letter. The one where you said you'd changed your mind and weren't coming to Anderson and that we shouldn't see each other anymore."

He had to be kidding, right? "What letter? I never sent you a letter like that. Do you still have it?"

Seth sighed and raked his fingers through his hair. "I... Why would I keep such a thing? I just did as you asked. But, Leenie, you're the one who broke up with me."

Eileen heard the misery in his voice, but her own shouted louder. "That's not true." It wasn't. She'd never have done that, not when she was so in love with Seth that she was defying her mother with plans to marry him.

"Then I've no idea what happened, Leenie. All I know is I got that letter and out of respect for you, I did as it said. I'm sorry."

Eileen closed her eyes, drawing in a breath through her nose. She held it, counted to four, let it out. Then it made sense. "Mother."

"Your mother? She'd go to that extreme?"

"Between the two of you, I'm more likely to believe you over her. I've seen her in action over the years, so there's no doubt she's behind our breakup. I'm sorry, too." She patted his hand before glancing up into the kindest eyes she'd ever seen.

He cupped her cheek, gently gliding his fingers over her temple.

She closed her eyes while she rested against his palm, pulling her back to when she was seventeen and the same touch made her universe right.

"Leenie."

His breath was close, so close that it whispered what he was about to do. A forgotten desire so strong welled from the depths of her soul.

"Um, should Sylvia and I go for a walk, Uncle Seth?"

Eileen's eyes popped open, and she jumped to the far end of the couch, the magic erased. "No need for that. No. We're good. Good."

Sylvia eyed her while holding a tray of cookies and small plates.

"Just set them down, and we'll help ourselves." Eileen brushed invisible musses from her hair, dodging eye contact with everyone, especially her daughter.

"I bet you will."

"Sylvia!" Eileen's face caught fire from embarrassment, and her daughter's grin didn't help. "Go on." She motioned to the tray that now sat on the coffee table before glancing at Seth.

His neck was red, but he also sported a smirk as he reached. "May I get you a cookie, Leenie? Want to share a plate?"

"Oh, Mom never eats a whole cookie. She just goes for the crumbs. Fewer calories that way." Sylvia giggled.

"Well, that's true. I get a taste, and it's enough." She leaned over and pressed her fingertip onto some scattered crumbs before licking them off. Only it really wasn't enough. But it was all she would allow herself.

"That's the silliest thing I've ever seen. They aren't that big. Just have one, Leenie. It won't hurt you. Trust me." Seth offered her a plate with a lone chocolate chip circle of deliciousness.

Trust him? She used to trust him with everything. Could she again?

"It's just a cookie."

Eileen nodded and accepted the plate.

Sylvia and Luke dropped to the floor, crisscross style like only the young can do.

"So, Mom, I realize you wanted time to think, but since Luke is here, would you please tell us what you've decided about the Stardust Ball?"

As if triggered, Mother's caustic comments echoed. *She is not to attend. Let someone else go and get pregnant out of wedlock.*

A long-lost voice of reason—or was it rebellion—shoved and stomped on her mother's pronouncement. "Yes. Yes, you can go. Luke, you may pick us both up, since I will be chaperoning the dance." *So there, Mother.*

Sylvia and Luke's smiles faded, and Eileen thought she heard a soft groan.

"Wait, do you need chaperones? I'm happy to do that. Then the four of us can go together."

Eileen spun to Seth. "To... together? Like a date?"

"Sure, why not? The kids can be our chaperones." He winked at Luke.

Sylvia giggled, and this time Luke's groan was more audible.

Eileen glanced between the teenagers and the man on her couch—she had a man sitting on her couch! How did that happen? And it was Seth. She stood. "I..." Her mother's persimmon-puckered stare dared her to agree. "Sure. Why not?" And then something rusty and unused for a long time burst out of her.

A giggle.

She picked up her cookie, glanced at the others, and then plopped back on the sofa and bit into the sweet concoction. It was as if she heard the chains dropping with each morsel.

"Well, then, we'd probably better get going. I'll call you later, Leenie, to make the arrangements." He stood and tapped Luke on the shoulder. "C'mon, you'll see her tomorrow."

Luke stood as if he simply rose to his feet. How did young people do that? Had Eileen ever been that flexible? The boy brushed his hand over Sylvia's shoulder as if sprinkling youth dust on her and she popped to her feet as he had. "Tomorrow before first period. Our spot."

Sylvia nodded.

They had a spot?

Was Mother really right this time?

Clink. She'd just shed those chains. She wouldn't let them make her a prisoner again. *Mother, you are wrong.* Eileen shook away the restraint before it snapped closed.

After rising, she walked with her guests to the door. "I'm glad you stopped by, Seth." But she couldn't help but glance outside to see if any neighbors might be paying attention.

"Me too, Leenie." He brushed a kiss at her temple. Causing her knees to want to buckle.

"Goodbye."

She and Sylvia watched them go down the steps to the sidewalk before she closed the door.

As it latched, Sylvia suddenly squealed and pulled her into a bear hug. "Thank you, Mom! Oh, thank you, thank you."

"You must never say anything about this to your grandmother. And Sylvia, I am trusting you."

"Mom, you're going with us. I'm double dating with my mother. How in the world could I possibly get into trouble?"

Eileen shook her head. "It's not that. I think you and Luke probably heard enough, though we tried to be quiet. If my mother would stoop so low as to forge my name to a letter to get rid of Seth, then there is no telling what she'll do once she learns we are seeing each other again." She paused. Was that what was happening? Aside from being an extra chaperone, he hadn't asked her out. No, she was not going to let her heart run amok and get broken to pieces again. "So, in case he ever does ask me out, your grandmother must never learn of it. Understand?"

Sylvia kissed her cheek. "I understand. You two make a cute couple. I hope he asks you out." She turned to clean up the refreshments, taking the tray to the kitchen sink.

Eileen moved the curtain of her front window to gaze out on the sidewalk where Seth had been. Being with him, talking with him, was almost like picking up where they'd left off nearly two decades ago. Only a lot had happened in those nineteen years. Was it too much to get over?

Water ran in the kitchen as Sylvia washed the dishes.

Eileen let the curtain fall back as her daughter's words repeated in her brain. *I hope he asks you out.*

Me, too, Sylvie. Me, too.

Monday, April 17, 1972

"How weird is it?" Sylvia shook her head as she swung hands with Luke on her way to her first hour class. "I can't believe they had a thing way back then."

"Uh huh. Uncle Seth kept asking me questions about your mom. Stuff I couldn't answer." He shrugged. "It was like he needed to fill in all the blanks on a test."

"Mom just got quiet. She pulled out her old Sargasso yearbook and tried showing me all sorts of things. She'd wanted to be a cheerleader, but Grandmother never let her try out. After yesterday and watching them together at dinner, it felt like the first time I'd really seen what my mom went through. I mean, she's pretty strict with me, but it's nothing like how Grandmother treated her."

Luke paused. "Think she'll let you wear my ring in public now?"

The fear of Mom finding out came rushing like a winter dip in Wildcat Creek. "I don't think she's there yet. Remember, she's only letting you take me because I need an escort, and she insisted on going with us."

"Yeah, and then Uncle Seth jumping in like that. I don't see us making a habit of double dating with them, do you?"

Sylvia giggled. "I think they're cute together. Besides, wasn't it your plan that he keep my mom busy? Maybe we can slip off if he does."

Luke's slow grin tickled the edges of her heart, making her brave. Wrapping her arms around his neck, she kissed him in front of God and KHS and anyone who chose to glance out a window. Including her mother.

But he didn't respond as she expected.

"Oh!" She jumped back.

"Hey, I'm down with it." Then he sobered. "But just in case we have witnesses." He winked and slid his fingers down her arm to capture her hand for a squeeze.

She squeezed back. "I'd better get in there. Supposed to get our chem tests back today."

"You did great, babe. I'm sure you did. Go on. I'll catch you later. Maybe your mom will let me call you this evening."

Sylvia chewed her lip. "Maybe. Love you."

"Yeah, me, too."

She slipped into her seat just as the last bell rang. Mr. Dolan was passing out the tests and laid hers face down on her desk. Despite having studied like crazy, the fear of missing a question or not getting full credit on an essay section formed a ball of lead in her stomach. With shaking hands, Sylvia lifted the stapled edge of the packet and turned it over.

A+

She'd even gotten all the bonus points offered.

"Hey, how'd you do?" Jim Hect was glancing her way.

The smile refused to be contained. She held her test results for him to see.

"Nice. Me, too." He held his up for her.

It was coming down to the wire. If either of them slipped in a class on anything, it would mean second place at graduation. Salutatorian. Mom wouldn't like it. And Grandmother would be on the phone demanding a reevaluation.

Nothing like embarrassment.

Mr. Dolan reviewed the test with them. Apparently, Sylvia and Jim were the only ones in all of his classes to rate perfect scores. One more thing that pointed to the race between the two of them.

"Yeah, everything is just so peachy when you're the favorite teacher's daughter."

Sylvia whipped around to spot Lyla Godes and Karen Nucum staring at her, nasty smirks twisting their lips. Hot tears rose and tried to escape, but she turned to face the front and blinked them away. She would not let them see her cry. Hadn't she jumped through enough hoops in her life? Didn't she work her backside off to earn her grades?

How dare they? How dare they try to label her as someone who had the world handed to her? Did they even have a clue?

And what made them feel they had to be so mean? Did it give them a charge, make them feel superior? Why did anyone need to bully or pressure others to fit into their conformity?

Sylvia declared enough. She'd taken their crap, those malicious gossipy comments whispered just loud enough to reach her ears. But no more.

She stood and glared in their direction. "Do you have something you want to say to me?"

Lyla and Karen's eyes grew wide, and she knew they hadn't expected this reaction.

Sylvia tipped her head, put her hands at her waist, and tapped her foot. "Well?"

"Miss Avery. Is there a problem?" Mr. Dolan stepped next to her.

She stared at the girls who now cowered, much to her delight. "I don't think so, but thank you, Mr. Dolan." She took her seat and glanced at Jim, the aftermath now making hot blood rush to her cheeks.

Jim flashed a smile and then winked.

Funny, she'd never noticed, but he was sort of cute.

Not as cute as Luke, but when he smiled, he definitely had potential.

The period ended, and Sylvia gathered up to go to her next class. A few more hours and she'd meet Luke for lunch. They'd eat their home-packed brownbag meal together on the back steps of the Main Building. With the weather turning nicer by the day and everyone else heading for town to Fenn's or Scotty's or Coney Island, it gave them privacy, and she looked forward to that.

The big question was if she would tell him about Lyla and Karen. It wasn't as if there was anything he could do. And it would only upset him.

"Hey, Sylvia. Want to go to Puckett's and grab a deli sandwich for lunch? I'm parked in the senior lot." Those were more non-class related words to come out of Jim's mouth than Sylvia had ever heard.

She needed a minute to wrap her mind around the fact that Jim Hect had invited her to lunch. In his car. A glance at him staring at his shoes, hands in his pockets, and the toe of his Keds twisting as if it were working a hole in the flooring, and she saw him in a whole new light. The guy was sh y.

And she had to say no.

First off, she had a boyfriend. Second, her mother would never allow her to leave campus, especially with a boy, though she might approve of Jim over Luke.

It didn't matter, though. If Luke weren't in the picture, she might do it, just to let that streak of rebellion have some fun. But she had promised herself to Luke. He was her steady, and more importantly, she was in love with him.

"I'm sorry, Jim. I can't. I'm meeting my boyfriend." She flashed her hand to show off Luke's class ring.

He sort of nodded while he dug his toe deeper. "I should have figured that. Never took the time to... How did I miss that ring?" Jim shook his head. "Proves I need to get my head out of my textbooks, I guess."

He continued walking with her as she headed toward her next class—to the corner staircase and up two flights.

She held her books to her chest, not needing to visit her locker yet. "It's okay. I don't show it off, and my mother is very strict, so I can only wear it where she won't see."

"So she doesn't know you're going steady?"

Sylvia shook her head. "No. She just barely knows we like each other. We finally got permission for him to escort me to the Stardust Ball, but she insists she's going with us."

Jim stopped, his eyes staring. "Seriously?" It might be only one word, but Sylvia heard "Whew, dodged that bullet."

"It's okay. You don't have to say anything. We both feel the same way. That's why Luke talked to his uncle about paying some attention to my mom. Maybe that way she'll be more interested in what's going on in her love life than mine."

Jim chuckled. "That's a great idea. Hope it works for you. Hey, this is my next class. See ya tomorrow in chem."

"Yeah, see ya." Sylvia smiled and kept moving. Until she heard a giggle behind her. She glanced over her shoulder to spot Lyla and Karen, heads together, thoroughly pleased about something.

And right behind them stood Luke. Only he wasn't pleased. In fact, if anything, with his heightened color and that black curl drooping on his forehead, his face looked stormy.

Thursday, April 20, 1972

Most of the shutters had been removed from his new home, but not this one. Uh oh. That screw was more stubborn than anticipated, but Seth rose to the occasion and grunted as he gave one hard twist. The heavy wooden piece dropped onto his foot.

Causing him to lose his balance on the step stool. Arms flailing, he landed with a thud and lay there in the newly sprouting grass, assessing the damage.

As bad as his foot felt, his lower back screamed louder from the sudden fall.

"You okay?" Sissy raced from the front door and she knelt at his side. "Do I need to call someone? Stay still, don't get up."

"I'm all right." He brushed grass from his pant knee and started to rise. Then thought better of it as shock raced up his spine. "Maybe I'll give it a moment."

"Have you been in to see the doctor since you got here?"

Seth shook his head, his teeth gritted. "Calling is on my to-do list once the phone company arrives. Today. Don't worry. It's only a spasm. Give me a second, and I'll be fine." He wiggled his toes inside his work boots just to make sure he was telling the truth and breathed normally when they moved. "Want to give me a hand up?" Hopefully his grin would chase away the worry lines on his sister's face.

"I think you need to rest there a bit longer. Then go in the house until you can hire someone to do the outside renovations for you." She stretched her legs out, not going anywhere but keeping him company. He didn't know whether to hug her for sticking with him or be frustrated that she wouldn't allow him the privacy of pulling himself together.

"You might be right, at least about taking a break. I could use one. And maybe about hiring someone, though I'd want them to work with me, not for me. This is my project." Would she accept that as a compromise?

"Hm. Well, it is almost lunch time. Okay." Tammy hopped up. "I'll fix us something, provided you stocked your refrigerator."

Seth groaned. "Not yet." He cautiously moved to grab his wallet from his hip pocket and yanked out some bills. "Want to go grocery shopping for me?" The addition of a smile and wink should do the trick.

And it worked. She reached for the money. "Fine. But I'll pick up burgers at Scotty's for lunch on the way back from Marsh's. Still need a hand up?"

He shook his head. He hadn't really wanted her help in the first place, just hoped it would make her stop hovering. After she left, he would employ his uncoordinated maneuvers and get to a standing position.

Tammy ran back for her purse and was on her way in a couple of minutes. As soon as her car drove out of sight, Seth stretched out and rolled to his side where he drew his knees up and shoved himself onto all fours. From there it was a matter of using the old shutter as a cane and pushing himself upright. His back wasn't too happy, but as least it wasn't screaming at him anymore.

Inside, he limped through the rooms to see what all Sissy had accomplished while he'd been working on the exterior.

A lot.

The living room was set up with mostly new furniture that fit his personality as if he'd owned it for some time. Strong and heavy. His sister knew him. His bedroom had a spread with coordinating drapes in masculine earth tones.

Yeah, this would end up being a comfortable place where he'd find a bit of peace.

A knock at the door startled him.

"Phone company."

Seth let in the forty-something technician and led him to where he wanted his phones hooked up—one in the living room, one in the kitchen, and one in his bedroom.

The guy seemed a bit surprised to have to install so many. But Seth knew that racing from one room to the next to answer the blamed thing wasn't a good thing with his back. Besides, he could afford it.

Fifteen minutes later, the phone guy had all the lines installed and had added an extra-long cord to the one in the living room so he might take the set any place where there were seats. "You're all hooked up."

"Can I make calls now?"

"Yup. Sign here." He held out a clipboard and pulled a pen from behind his ear.

Seth scribbled his name, and the guy was gone, leaving the means of communication with people he'd been wanting to call ever since he had that talk with Sissy. He grabbed the living room phone and settled in his easy chair his sister had tried to throw out—some things were sacred—and dialed the long distance number.

"Chet Barker here."

"Chet, it's Seth. How's it going?"

There was a chuckle. "You really can't leave this place, can you?"

"Guess not. Actually, I was wondering if you'd check on something for me. Hoping you had information on some rioting that happened in Kokomo, Indiana, back in the fall." He wanted to explain that he'd been in the hospital and Tammy had tried to shield him— he was sure she was downplaying it—but he decided less details with his request was better. Besides, if he was going to sort this out and proactively protect his family, he needed to investigate.

"I don't have that info off the top of my head, but I can look into it for you. You said it was last fall?"

"Yeah. Things seem pretty peaceful now, but I want to know what happened."

"Sure, I get it." The sound of shuffling papers came through, a sure sign Chet wanted it known a lot was happening, and he was busy.

"So, what's going on there?"

Chet sighed. "You're no longer cleared for that. However, I'll just say that nothing has been reported that concerns your area."

Okay, so that helped, but it didn't take away Seth's desire to stay abreast of important events. The evening news and Kokomo Tribune would never replace the data coming through the FBI field office. Well, he'd made his request, and his friend had a job to do. Seth should let him do it. Then another thought struck him.

"Do me one more favor?"

"Aw, c'mon, man. I can get into trouble with this."

"No, nothing like that. I just wanted to see if you can locate when and where a guy named Douglas Avery died and what happened. He'd attended Anderson College in Anderson, Indiana, got married maybe around 1953 and died soon after."

"Does he have a sheet?"

"Not that I know of. I'm sort of friends with the family and hoped to learn more."

More paper rattling and sighing came through the line. "Sure. I guess I can do that. Give me your number. Can't say how long it will take to get the information, especially since I'm up to my eyebrows on a hot case right now—and no, I can't tell you what it is."

"Got it." Even though he hated the fact. Seth read off his new phone number from the strip across the phone base and ended the call.

Once the receiver was in the cradle, he sat with the set on his lap, wondering if he'd done the right thing. It was none of his business who Leenie had married. And even if her mother was the real reason they broke up, they weren't together anymore. She could marry anyone she wanted.

That didn't mean he had to like it. Besides, she'd said it wasn't a good marriage. What had the guy done? This whole thing aroused his investigative curiosity. What kind of man swooped in on an innocent girl who, according to what she shared, had been heartbroken? If she'd felt anything like he did when he got that letter, she was more like devastated.

He'd never been able to move on after. Even the few casual first dates he tried only left him missing Leenie all the more. After a while, he stopped trying and decided he'd remain a bachelor. There was no need to marry, and with his injury, and the possibility of paralysis in his future, why do that to a woman?

But now Leenie was back in his life. Could they move forward? He had no idea. There was way too much water under the bridge to make that assumption. And maybe she wouldn't want to be saddled with a guy who might end up in a wheelchair—or worse—for the rest of his life, just because he zigged when he should have zagged.

Still, she was here. She was talking to him. And old feelings were rushing back like an overflowing dam.

Okay, so he was being nosey, maybe even pushy, digging into her life where he had no business. But hadn't the key to his success with the FBI hinged on having enough background information to understand what the next moves should be?

And she never had to know.

It would just be so he had full understanding. Besides, this was the only way he knew to fill in the holes from the last nineteen years and be prepared to do what was necessary to keep her safe. If riots broke out here once, they could again. It only took a tiny spark to start a blaze.

So, though he might not be able to offer her a future, he'd darn well offer her protection along with the rest of his family.

And he would start by finding out exactly what happened back then.

Chapter 8

Friday, April 21, 1972

E ileen pressed her index finger into the crumbs left from her fourth hour group. She'd taught them to adapt cookie recipes into bar cookies. A handy skill, but she'd have been happier if they'd moved faster in class so she didn't get stuck finishing their clean up.

There was always holding them over and writing late passes.

She sighed, realizing her brain spoke the truth but...

She wanted to be liked.

Eileen licked her finger and wiped the counter clean. It was her own fault, and she knew it. They'd been given plenty of warning about the time left in their kitchen before the bell rang. Next time she'd stand firm. Not give in. Be the disciplinarian she should be.

But sometimes, after maintaining all that control to keep Sylvia safe, she had no more discipline left in her. At least they had gotten the dishes washed. It was just a matter of wiping down the workspace. She rinsed the dishcloth in the sink and hung it to dry as the next group of students arrived. This bunch headed for the sewing machines to continue work on their projects.

"Mrs. Avery, what do you think? Should I add some machine embroidery here?" Corrina held up a white polyester knit and pointed to the small Nehru collar and slash neckline.

Eileen imagined the addition of the color brilliance against the stark white on the girl's dark skin and knew it would be the perfect touch. "I like that idea. Think you're ready to try machine embroidery?" The new sewing machines had cams, so it was an added skill to teach.

Corrina set the dress aside. "Yeah, but I don't have the colors. I'll have to see about getting them this weekend."

"I'm sure I have some. Let's check the supply cabinet." Sure enough, there were several jewel tones of rayon thread available, and she handed them to the girl who showed such promise and effort.

"Thank you." Corrina took the spools and returned to her Singer to wind up some bobbins.

That allowed Eileen to check on her other students who, for the most part, were busy pinning, measuring, or trying on if they weren't at their machines. Good. Her prep period came after next hour and then one more class before dismissal.

It had been a long week with too many thoughts about Seth and barely enough time to get Sylvia's gown finished—the girl had been beside herself trying to play it cool but still nagged. Eileen shook her head. They'd gone after school on Monday to pick up matching shoes and new gloves. And Eileen still had a compact purse in white sequins that she'd convinced Sylvia to use, plus the weather was nice enough that she shouldn't need a wrap.

Corrina's embroidery question had reminded Eileen she still had a bit more to do, and tonight was the last chance. She really should get Sylvia to try it on, but more than that, she wanted to see her daughter's face light up when she saw the finished piece. Would she like it? Or would she still wish for a store-bought dress?

Only time would tell.

If she weren't trying to keep it such a secret, she'd have brought it with her to work on during her prep period. Still, she had enough work to do that her prep was never long enough anyway. Might as well use it as intended.

The last two classes ran swiftly, especially her last hour advanced class. She would have to come up with some challenging plans for that group, since they seemed to have imagination to spare. The creativity they'd shown in the kitchen was beyond anything any other advanced class had demonstrated. And they were respectful, most of the time cleaning when she told them to. The last student was walking out the door when Sylvia showed up.

"Ready, Mom?"

"All set."

Sylvia had been more communicative this week than she'd been in a long while. Whether it was due to her being allowed to attend the Stardust Ball or something else, she couldn't say. But why question the gift?

Her daughter even helped get dinner together since the ball was the next night and most teachers hadn't assigned homework. It was fun working around each other, and the banter made Eileen relax. For the first time in forever, she and her daughter just enjoyed life at the same time.

"Go ahead, Mom. I've got the dishes. You do something you want to do."

The kindness made Eileen's eyes blur with moisture. "If you're sure. I have something to work on in my room. Just holler if you need me."

With a gentle shove toward her bedroom, Eileen decided to take advantage of the moment and put the finishing touches on Sylvia's gown.

It wasn't exactly like the one her daughter fell in love with in the store, but it was as close as she could make it. And she hoped the hours of embroidering tiny flowers over the pink velvet bodice would be worth it.

Eileen pulled the dress from her closet and shook it out, brushing her hand down the lacy, chiffon-covered skirt. She'd skimped on groceries to have enough money for the material. In the evenings, she closed her bedroom door. To muffle the machine noise, she'd shoved a towel under the threshold and gave up valuable sleep. But the dress would be finished on time. She imagined her Sylvie dancing in it, her flowing long hair hanging down with baby's breath tucked in with a barrette in back.

Her little girl was just way too beautiful.

God had blessed her with this precious life when she thought her world was ending. And now she couldn't fathom the world without her Sylvia.

"Hey, Mom."

SYLVIA'S MOTHER

Her bedroom door opened.

Eileen tried to shove the dress behind her.

"What's that? Is it my gown? Oh, can I see it? Please?" Sylvie was already trying to peek around to where the dress was sort of hidden.

"I wanted to have it completed first."

Sylvia froze. "It's not done? Will it be done on time?"

Eileen pulled the dress to her lap and smoothed out the skirt. "It'll be finished on time. Nearly there now. Just a bit of hand work. Here." She held it out to Sylvia and studied her face.

"Oh!" Instead of taking the gown, Sylvia's hands flew to her mouth.

"You don't like it."

"No, oh, no, Mom. I love it. It looks identical. I don't think I've ever seen you make something so..."

"What?"

"So amazing. May I try it on, please?"

"Go ahead."

Sylvia took the dress and stepped into her own bedroom, returning a few minutes later. "I can't get the zipper. Would you, Mom?"

Eileen drew the slider up the elements, while Sylvie held her hair out of the way. "The hook at the top is one of those last-minute things. Want to see?" She stepped aside so Sylvia had a clear view in the mirrored closet doors. Better than seeing that the dress fit to perfection was the look in Sylvia's eyes. It matched the one she had when they'd gone shopping and found the original gown.

That was what Eileen needed.

115

"Go get your shoes on so I can make sure the hem is right, and I'll dig out my sequined bag for you."

Sylvia rushed to obey, coming back to change shoes while sitting on Eileen's bed.

"Are you sure you like it?" It might be silly, but Eileen needed the reassurance.

"Like it? Mom, I love it. This is custom *haute couture*." She bounced up and wrapped Eileen in a bear hug. "Far better than I imagined. And I'm sorry for having any doubts. You were right. This is perfect." Sylvie pulled away and returned to looking at herself in the mirror, swishing the skirt to and fro.

She liked it. Sylvia more than liked it. She loved it and even apologized for her doubts.

Did that mean she was proud of her mother? That would be something, Sylvia being proud of her. Far more than she would have expected or even hoped for.

If there was a way to freeze this moment in time and save it, Eileen would do it. Because Sylvia's apology revealed the girl was growing up, becoming an adult. And no matter how much Eileen tried to protect her, keep her safe and close, the time to let her fly was approaching like a train at full speed.

And that terrified her.

Saturday, April 22, 1972

Sylvia squeezed her eyes closed while the beautician-in-training sprayed half a can of Aqua Net over her finished hairdo. Mom had skipped getting her hair done in order to run by the florist. Somehow it felt weird to be here alone with no chaperone to ensure she stayed out of trouble. Maybe Mom was beginning to trust her.

Or maybe she didn't think she had a choice.

Either way, the freedom felt great, even if it was only for a quick moment.

When she finally opened her eyes and took in a breath of chemical-tinged air, she noticed Connie Agnew two chairs over on her right and Maria Volikas coming in the door. Both girls were up for Stardust queen, and they had far better chances of winning. But they both seemed genuinely kind girls, though somehow through the four years at KHS, they'd never been in situations where they might become friends with her.

No problem. She made a point of waving and saying hello on her way to the front.

They returned the gesture but didn't start a conversation. Oh, well.

Sylvia couldn't help but wonder what their gowns would look like. As pretty as the one Mom sewed for her, bet theirs weren't homemade.

Mom walked in at that moment, paid the bill, and they left together. "Hungry?

"Yeah, maybe we ought to eat now rather than later." First, Mom decided to forgo a hair appointment and now was offering to eat early? Things were feeling a bit weird, that's for sure.

"Don't look at me like that. You'll feel better eating first and then getting ready." Mom winked.

"I was wondering why you didn't have your own hair appointment." Sylvia had felt hesitant to ask but curiosity won out.

Mom shook her head. "I just had it done last weekend. It's better if I stick to my schedule." With that, they climbed in the car and the conversation lagged.

At dinner, Sylvia picked at her plate of Salisbury steak and mashed potatoes, noting that Mom wasn't eating all that much either. Anticipation churned her stomach. This was so momentous—not necessarily being nominated, though that was pretty huge. No, it was that Mom was allowing her to go out with a boy, even if she was riding shotgun over the whole thing. This was Sylvia's first date, and she'd waited a lifetime for it. The expectations mounted with each second.

Afterward, Sylvia grabbed her shower, careful to keep her hair protected, while Mom cleaned the kitchen. Then Mom showered while Sylvia did her makeup. She'd had to wait until she was sixteen before being allowed to wear any and even now what she put on was minimal—no eyeliner or foundation. Just a touch of blush and lip gloss and mascara. Still, it made her feel pretty.

Mom peeked in. "Would you like a little help with your face? I think this eyeshadow might look nice." She held out a soft blue.

"Yes, please!"

Sylvia tried hard not to sneak a peek in the mirror while her mother added the color to her lids. But when finished, she felt like a true woman, a grown up. And once her dress was on and her hair back the way it had been styled, she stood before her mother's mirror, not sure she recognized the person staring back.

"Sylvie, you look stunning."

"I think I do." Then she heard her words and covered her mouth. "I didn't mean that the way it sounded. I just can't believe what I'm seeing is me."

"Oh, it is, darling girl. It is." Mom squeezed her shoulder. "Now I have to get me ready. Be careful not to muss yourself."

"I will." Sylvia went to the living room to pace. Sitting would only add wrinkles. Luke should arrive in less than half an hour and the ball started in an hour. Most couples ate dinner afterward. Restaurants in the area remained open late on Stardust Ball night. Wonder where Luke planned to take her? Did they have to sit with Mom and Seth, or could they have their own table?

Ten steps to cross the room, ten to go back and repeat. Sylvia's new shoes pinched, and she hadn't even had a chance to dance in them.

Mom came out after a while. "Honey, relax. They'll be here soon."

But after thirty more minutes and no sign of their dates, even Mom had furrow lines popping up between her carefully tweezed brows. "Where are they?"

"I don't know, Sylvie. But I'm sure there's a good reason."

Just then, the phone rang. Sylvia beat her mother to it. "Hello?"

"Sylvia, this is Seth. I just spoke with Luke. Their track meet ran long, so he's jumped in the shower. We should be there in twenty minutes."

Her heart beat again. "Thanks for calling. We'll be ready." Nothing like making an entrance, but everything was okay, and they'd be at the Oriental Dreams-themed gym eventually.

She relayed the information to Mom, and the guys arrived as promised. Luke brought her a lovely wristlet of pink rosebuds and baby's breath that matched what her mother had twined in her hair. As she was pinning a pink carnation boutonniere to Luke's lapel, she noticed the pretty yellow rose corsage Seth had for her mother. "Ready to go?" He glanced at Mom and winked.

However, Luke answered first. "So ready, Uncle Seth."

They all chuckled and filed down the steps to Seth's car.

Sylvia thought for a moment her mother would make the guys sit up front while she and Mom sat in the back, but no. Mom took the front passenger seat and allowed her and Luke the semi-privacy of the rear seat where they could hold hands. Tonight was turning magical, and they hadn't even arrived yet.

Once at the gym, Sylvia barely noticed the work the Boys' Legion had put in as several members of the track and field team started on Luke.

Apparently pole vaulting was scheduled last at their out-of-town event, and as Luke was doing well enough to be in the running for an award, he had to stay to the end, which made everyone late for their dates.

"Dude, people were already arriving when our bus pulled into the parking lot, and we still had to go home to get ready. I'm just glad my girl was willing to understand."

Luke squeezed her hand. "Me, too." Then he turned to her. "Want to dance?"

She was too excited to speak, so she simply nodded.

He led her to the dance floor while Dale Updegraf crooned a cover of Harry Nilsen's "Without You."

She was in his arms, dancing with him in public, in front of her mother, and no one was getting upset. It was the best night of Sylvia's life. It stayed in the slow dance mode for "Precious and Few" and "Walking in the Rain With the One I Love," before the beat picked up a bit with "Brandy, You're a Fine Girl."

It only got better as the time passed. She even caught her mother giggling over something Seth whispered in her ear.

About fifteen minutes before she was to be ready to head for the stage, more of the track team found Luke, still giving him what-for, only it was more playful this time as they all stood around the punch table. One of the guys asked him to come see something, and he turned to her, the question of permission clear in his eyes.

"Sure, go ahead. I need to go to the ladies' room anyway. I'll meet you here, okay?"

He kissed her cheek. "You're the best. I'll be right back."

As Luke headed left with the guys, Sylvia turned right for the restrooms. It was a better idea to go now than to feel like she needed to up on that stage.

Once in the stall, she thought she heard others who had the same idea, but coming out to wash her hands, it was only Lyla and Karen.

Lyla stepped forward. "So, you're really going through with it?"

"You're talking to me? I thought you just talked about me behind my back."

"Ha, she thinks she's clever. But why'd you insist on showing up tonight? Why didn't you just drop out so Roxie had a chance? Still, you won't be queen. We'll guarantee that."

Before Sylvia figured out what she meant, something icy cold and wet dripped down her head, over her face, through her hair. She wiped her eyes and cheeks with her hands while turning toward the mirror, spotting what looked like a pink rat drowned with red something—it had to be the punch.

Not only was her hair and makeup a mess, her dress was ruined.

She glanced back in time to see Lyla and Karen beating a quick exit while another girl entered.

"What happened?" The girl grabbed fistfuls of paper towels from the dispenser and dabbed at Sylvia's dress. "You work on your hair and face. Maybe we can get you presentable. Sorta."

Sylvia's mind loosened and questions flooded. Why had Lyla and Karen done that? What was she going to do about going on stage? How did she get out of there with no one noticing? "Why are you helping me?"

The girl's dark face showed a friendly smile of bright white teeth. "Your mom has been good to my sister. I figured you could use the help." She shrugged and stepped back, giving a scan of what Sylvia was eyeing in the mirror. "What are you going to do?"

"I don't know." She bit her lip to keep from bursting into tears in front of the girl.

"Me, I'd hold my head high and march right up there. You didn't do this. Let those girls feel embarrassed. Especially if you win."

"You knew I was nominated?"

"Sure. I even voted for you. Figure the popular girls will get plenty of votes." She smiled her friendly smile again.

Sylvia turned to the mirror. If she ran and hid, Lyla and Karen won. She straightened her spine and took a breath. They were not going to win. She'd been nominated, and by gum, she would be on that stage.

"Yep, I thought you were the type to stand up for yourself. I think this is the best we're going to get, except maybe I can fix your hair a little." The girl picked up a section of hair only to drop it back in place. There was no fixing it.

"What's your name?"

"Carma."

"Well, Carma, thank you for helping me and for the pep talk. You're right. They're not going to keep me down."

With that, Sylvia stepped out of the ladies' restroom.

"Relax. Everything's going to be fine." Seth hoped he spoke the truth as he gave Leenie's hand a gentle squeeze. She looked amazing, and he couldn't help but wonder what it would've been like for them to chaperone their own daughter's dance. Or maybe they'd have had a son.

If only Leenie's mother had kept her nose out of their business.

That thought raced him back to the present. Tension rode his shoulders as he took on his protector persona. If something were to happen, tonight would be the perfect setting. As he continued to keep a sharp lookout, he remembered Tammy gave him the same advice while he'd paced her living room waiting for Luke to get back from the track meet. *Relax, brother dear. Everything's going to be fine.*

"Do you see them?" Leenie's height, or lack of it, made it difficult to keep track of Sylvia and Luke though she tried. Her standing on tiptoe in her high heels made her wobble enough that she let him keep hold of her. The thought made him smile.

"Yes, they were at the refreshment table when some fellows spoke with Luke. He said something to Sylvia, and she nodded before heading to the ladies' room where she still is. Luke followed the guys but is now by the punch bowl." Maybe she'd be impressed with his powers of observation.

"Luke didn't stay with her or escort her?"

Seth sighed. "Leenie. She's a big girl and can go to the ladies' room on her own. Honestly, I've kept an eye on the door. Two girls went in after her and then exited as a third girl entered. She should be out any time."

As if on cue, the restroom door opened, and someone came out. It took a second glance to realize it was Sylvia. And Leenie was going to have a fit. He coughed before he spoke. "Ah, there she is."

The girl looked like she'd bathed in red water. Her hair hung limp, tinged pink. Her dress was splotched with red over the soft pink tones, and her face appeared as if most of her makeup had been removed.

But she stood outside the ladies' room entrance with her back straight and chin up as the third girl to go into the restroom came out. Seth's line of vision followed her back to a small group of black students.

Luke must have spotted Sylvia then, as he shoved through the throng to get to her side. They had a huddled communication before he mirrored Sylvia's stance—ramrod spine, firm jaw.

Whatever happened, they were going through it together.

The music stopped, and a boy about Luke's age grabbed the mic. "One, two, three, we on here? Yeah? Okay, just wanted to say welcome to the 1972 Stardust Ball hosted by the Boys Legion. It's that time, and I won't make you wait too long. How about we get our Stardust Queen nominees up here? I'll start with the freshman class. Give it up for Robin Levy."

The couples clapped, and it hit Seth all at once. He realized what Sylvia and Luke were going to do.

"Do you still see Sylvia? Did Luke find her?"

"Yes, he found her." Oh, Leenie was going to go nuts, and there was no way to prepare her.

The sophomore candidate was announced followed by the two junior candidates and polite applause.

"Maria Volikas." A pretty dark-haired girl was escorted to the stage.

"Connie Agnew." This time, a perky blonde with a bright smile was led to the front.

"Sylvia Avery." He felt Leenie holding her breath and then her death grip suddenly attempted to crush the bones in his hand as it nearly brought him to his knees.

The gasps of the crowd replaced the sudden silence as the clapping died out.

"What... What happened to her?" Leenie released her hold and he had to grab fast to keep her from stopping her daughter on the way to the front. She tried to shake him off. "Let go of me. I have to get to her."

"No, Leenie. Don't. She needs to do this." He pulled her into his arms. "Sylvia knows what she's doing."

"Her evening is ruined."

As Sylvia and Luke reached the stage, the other nominees left their escorts and surrounded Sylvia, a show of solidarity.

The announcer stood, shaking his head. "Um, folks, I'm not sure what happened."

Sylvia stepped forward. "It's okay, just a little mishap. Please keep going."

The girls on the stage grouped together, all holding hands and staring at the announcer who held an envelope aloft.

He tore it open and pulled out a folded paper. "Okay. Here's the news you've been waiting for. The Stardust Queen of Kokomo High School for 1972 is...Connie Agnew."

Cheers rose from the gym floor.

Connie looked as shocked as anyone with her eyes big and her mouth shaped like the perfect O, though Sylvia raised the girl's hand and grinned while the announcer kid put a crown on Connie's head.

Moments later, Luke escorted Sylvia down from the stage and over to her mother.

"What happened, Sylvie? Who did this to you?"

Sylvia shook her head. "It was an accident. Can we go now? I'm feeling sort of sticky."

"Sure." Seth leaned over to Leenie. "You won't get in trouble for leaving your chaperone job early will you?"

"No, but I ought to let someone know. Excuse me, I'll be right back." Leenie headed over to another adult a few feet away for a quick explanation.

Which gave Seth a moment. "Sylvia, are you sure you want to cover up for whoever did this? It's going to get out. Your mother will definitely be pushing, and you'll probably get called into the office on Monday." If she'd confide in him, he'd help her.

"No. I'm not going to dwell on this. Let's just get out of here."

Luke glanced over her head. "Uncle Seth, how about after Sylvia changes, we take them out like we'd planned?"

"That's up to Leenie and Sylvia." Seth tried to gauge what Sylvia might say.

"I'm all for it. But it might take a bit for me to get this gunk out of my hair. You don't have anything too fancy planned, do you?"

"Too fancy for what?" Leenie joined them.

"Mom, the guys are going to drive us home so I can get cleaned up and then take us out to dinner."

"Oh, I don't think that's such a good idea."

"Why? I'm the one who got messed up, and I'm willing to save our evening. Can't you go along with it?"

Leenie froze. "I just don't think it's right."

Seth turned her to face him. "Leenie, let's not spoil the night any more than it has been. C'mon. You were willing before this all happened. What do you say?"

She huffed. "I'm going to regret this, but fine. Let's go."

He tried to hold her hand again, but she pulled away. It was the only outward sign besides her silence that she was angry at him—well, that and the fact that she insisted on riding in the back seat with Sylvia.

Once they arrived at Leenie's place, he and Luke dropped them off, agreeing to return in thirty minutes.

SYLVIA'S MOTHER

Sylvia assured them that would be enough time. And it gave Seth and Luke a chance to change out of their fancy duds into something more comfortable.

Thirty minutes later, the girls were ready as promised. Sylvia had washed her hair but wound it into a bun on top of her head.

Seth had made reservations at the Casa Grande restaurant, and they were a bit early, but the hostess said it was no problem and led them to their table. He'd looked forward to this meal all day, imagining the T-Bone steak with his name on it and enjoying it in the company of the one woman who still made his pulse skip beats.

Only Leenie still wasn't talkative.

Finally, after they'd placed their orders, he leaned closer to her. "Would you step out to the lobby with me a moment?"

She peered at him. "Fine." After scooting her chair back, she allowed him to lead her out of the dining room. "What do you want?"

"Tell me why you are so angry with me."

"You don't think I should be?"

"I'd at least like to know what you think I've done."

Leenie huffed again, glanced over her shoulder toward the dining room, then zeroed in on him. "First, you gave me no warning when you saw something was wrong. I'd have helped her get out of there before anyone saw her."

"She didn't want that."

"You don't understand. It's not a matter of what Sylvia wants. She's still my child, and I make the decisions. And speaking of that, undermining me about going out, siding with her like that, I won't stand for it. I am responsible for my daughter and will protect her with everything I have. Going home and resting after such an ordeal would have been better and maybe then she'd have told me what happened."

He shook his head. "That's what's eating you, that she won't say who did it. Well, I have a good idea, and if I learn anything, I'll tell you." Seth paused, accepting that she did have a point. "I realize I'm no expert on parenting. And even if I... Never mind. Your daughter. I get that. But in the meantime, for Sylvia and Luke's sake, can we call a truce?" He held out his hand.

It took her a moment, but finally she shook it. "Truce. Let's get back in there."

But as they reentered the dining room, it seemed all eyes were on the young couple in the corner.

Luke was on one knee, slipping a ring onto Sylvia's finger.

Chapter 9

Eileen shook from the tip of her roots to her big toe nail bed. *How? Why?* She sputtered, trying to get the words out. "Get up. Get up, get up, get up and move away. Now. What were you thinking?" She pulled Sylvia by her arm. "C'mon, we're leaving."

Sylvia shook free. "Mom, no. You are not going to ruin this moment."

"Moment? You mean the biggest mistake of your life? I can't let this happen. We'll call a cab. C'mon."

"Mrs. Avery—"

"Leenie—"

She spun on the men who looked so alike. "I trusted you. A truce, you said. Look where that got us. How can you stand there and think this is okay?"

Seth leaned in, his voice low. "You're causing a scene."

Eileen took that second to scan the room. The gaze of everyone in the dining room focused on their little corner table and the catastrophe surrounding it. She dropped her voice. "Then let's go, Sylvia."

"No." How did her daughter remain so calm yet stubborn?

"Leenie, sit down and let the attention fade." Seth reached for her shoulder, but she shrugged him away.

Still, he made sense, even if she didn't like it. So she sat, making sure to be between Luke and her daughter, and gritted her teeth. "Fine. I'm seated." She turned to Sylvia. "What in the world are you thinking? You haven't even finished your first date with this boy. How can you believe you are prepared for marriage? You cannot let him chase you into something before you are ready."

"Who says I'm not ready? Mom, Luke and I love each other. We might not have been able to date like normal people, but we've spent every moment possible together. We've shared our thoughts and dreams. I can't imagine loving anyone else, and I'm honored he has asked me to be his wife."

Any response she might have made shriveled, dying on Eileen's tongue. Her daughter was heading toward that same awful choice that had cost Eileen so much. The very thing she'd tried to protect Sylvia from was having its way. Tears welled as fear cut off air to her lungs.

"Mrs. Avery, we mean no disrespect. But Sylvia is right. We've spent all the time we could find to be together, learning about each other, and I love your daughter more than I can say. I realize I'm just a high school kid this minute, but we aren't rushing too fast, and we've thought this through." Luke laced his fingers together and leaned her way. "I've been working while going to school and have gained both an athletic and a music scholarship to Anderson College. Plus, Sylvia has been accepted the re—"

"What? You applied after we decided you'd stay at home and attend IUK?"

"You decided, Mom. Not me. I don't want to stay at home. I've lived in a straight-jacket too long."

Straight-jacket? That's what she thought of the loving care Eileen had cocooned her with?

"You see, Mrs. Avery, if we get married this summer, there are bonuses to assist our college funds. We'll be able to share expenses, help each other with homework, plus we'd both qualify for the work-study program and for married housing. The original plan was to marry after getting our degrees, but this way we can save some money and still do what we'd planned."

Eileen stared at the innocent, earnest faces. It wasn't that Luke was the villain. He was clueless.

But Seth should know better. And yet he sat silent, letting these children make life-altering decisions. "You have nothing to say?"

He cleared his throat. "It's not my call."

Before she jumped on his cop-out, he continued. "And for the record, I think there are other possibilities, sure. But they are eighteen and getting ready for adult life. They need to make their own decisions and, if necessary, deal with their mistakes. Maybe it's not a mistake. Maybe this is exactly what they need to do. But they have the right to decide, and I'm not the person to try to stop them."

Eileen fell against her chair back, all retorts whooshing out of her like a runny mix in a decorating bag. "I can't believe you said that." Until that moment, she'd still hoped he would be her ally.

"Leenie, they aren't us. They aren't you and your husband, either. Some marriages work no matter what gets thrown at them, and others don't no matter how hard the couple tries. We can't decide this for them. They have to figure it out for themselves."

"No. No, they don't. I forbid this wedding and all talk of marriage." Something told Eileen she needed to breathe, drop her voice, and regain control, but all she could do was blindly grasp.

"Mom, you can't do that. Luke and I will figure it out, just like Seth said. You can be happy for us and support us, or not. But this is our plan." Sylvia reached across the table toward Luke who clasped her hand in his.

The waitress chose that moment to deliver their meals, and the table grew silent.

After she left, Seth's gaze connected to hers. "Want me to ask the blessing?"

Blessing? Eileen stared back, but he apparently didn't heed her voiceless response.

The kids bowed their heads.

Shame and anger mingled, but Eileen finally closed her eyes.

"Father, we ask Your blessing on this food, this time together, and all decisions made here. It's been quite an evening, but we look to You and ask for Your wisdom to do things Your way. In Jesus's Name, Amen."

The kids echoed amen while Eileen squeezed back tears.

Maybe she needed to quit fighting and instead pray more fervently. Let God do the heavy lifting on this one. He had to realize how hard she'd tried to do what was right for Sylvia. Considering He'd entrusted this beautiful girl into her care, He knew what all she'd be facing.

"Excuse me, please." Eileen stood, spotting the doubt in all their eyes. "I'll be back. I just need to use the powder room."

She held it together until she'd made it to the makeshift sanctuary. How had her world fallen apart so fast?

You let Sylvia attend the ball. I told you this would happen.

Mother's voice reverberated in her mind. "No, you're wrong. She is not pregnant and..."

She will be if you don't put a stop to this. Do you want her to go through what you did?

Eileen shook her head as her sobs overpowered her.

The door opened, so she rushed into a stall and pushed the lock in place.

"Mom, it's me."

Sylvia came after her?

"Mom, I've tried to follow your rules, honor you by being obedient even when I hated it. I've wanted to go out with Luke for so long, but I didn't. But now you've got to start letting go, at least a little. I can't live in your prison for the rest of my life."

Prison? Eileen opened the stall door. "What prison? I've only tried to keep you safe."

"I know that's what you intended. I do. But you have to see, especially after what your mother put you through, how it feels."

Was she really so much like Mother?

"Mom, I know you love me. I do. And you made your decisions out of love, not trying to control the world like Grandmother. Your motives aren't the same, but your methods are. And before it kills me and all my dreams, I need to start doing things on my own."

"Like getting married at eighteen?"

Sylvia sighed. "We really had planned to wait. But the cost and wanting to be together has changed our timetable, just not our plans." She stepped closer. "Mom, I love him so much. I wish you'd be happy for u s."

"I love you, too, sweetie, more than I can say, and I only want you safe. Maybe we can negotiate this. I'll loosen up some, and you wait some."

An angry cloud settled in Sylvia's eyes. "I didn't come in here to compromise. I am going to marry Luke this summer. You can help me plan or you can get out of my way. But if we're to have a relationship, I think you know what you need to do." She turned and left the restroom. Leaving Eileen more alone than nineteen years ago when her husband walked out on her, leaving her to raise their child on her own.

Sunday, April 23, 1972

The car pulled between the white lines of the parking space. Sylvia didn't wait for her mother to turn off the engine but hopped out as soon as the car stopped. Since last night, confined places with Mom were torturous. That included their apartment. Once her mom had figured out that Sylvia wasn't about to change her mind, she turned on the deep freeze. The atmosphere had remained icy throughout their quick breakfast and ride to church.

She scanned the lot, spotted Luke standing by his uncle's car, and headed in his direction. There was no reason to hide their affections now, so she kissed him, relishing his embrace in this public area.

"Sylvia!" Mom raced up. "You've been taught better."

Sylvia slipped her hand into Luke's, their fingers lacing, and leaned against his shoulder. "I'm done hiding."

"You still can show some decorum in public. We're at church, for goodness sakes."

Seth stepped forward then. "Good morning, ladies. Hope you slept well."

If Mom's glare had been a laser beam, the man would've been split in two pieces and imploded into a gooey mess on the blacktop.

Luke gave her hand a gentle tug. "Let's go find our seats." He led the way, still holding on to her, leaving the two older ones behind to deal with each other.

Once inside the sanctuary, Luke kept Mom from sitting next to her. She didn't even have to tell him that she'd dreaded that part. Mom would've been whispering throughout the sermon. "Did you get that part? Are you listening?" Hard to pay attention when her mother was trying to make you pay attention. Besides that, the space would do them both good, even if it was only on either side of Luke.

Apparently, her mom's anger at Seth had calmed enough that she was speaking to him, though the tension on both their faces revealed their conversation was anything but cordial. Would she ever just accept that Sylvia was old enough to make decisions about her own life?

The pastor must have been listening in on their conversation because his sermon was from the Song of Solomon and about not awakening love until it was ready. Mom would be using that as a weapon later.

After church, Seth suggested they all go to lunch and talk, but Mom reminded them of the standing dinner appointment at Grandmother's house. For a brief moment, Sylvia had forgotten about that awful trial.

"Maybe tell her we're not feeling well?"

Mom glared. "You want to lie to your Grandmother? It's going to be hard enough because she'll demand I tell her if I kept you home last night. And if you won't return your ring to Luke, you'd better at least take it off before she spots it and you-know-what breaks loose."

"She's really that bad?" Luke glanced at each of them in turn.

"Yes." It was the one thing Sylvia, Mom, and Seth agreed on, and Luke winced as they all answered together.

"Okay then." He stared at the ground and swung their clasped hands between them.

Mom stared at their hands until they hung limp. But Sylvia wasn't about to let go.

"Speaking of the ring, does your mother know about this, Luke?"

"Um..." He glanced at Sylvia and shrugged.

"There's my answer—"

"Seriously, Leenie, don't you think there's a way to skip today? I really think if we try to listen to each other, maybe we can find some peace in all this." God bless Luke's Uncle Seth for bringing the conversation back on track.

Mom shook her head. "There is no peace. This is going to blow up and I will be taking the brunt of it. However... I'm not eager to face that firing squad, so I guess I can call her. But I also don't think going out to eat is the best answer either. Too many strangers eavesdropping."

"We can go to my house. The only one to listen in would be my dog. And as long as I've had him, he hasn't spoken a word in English." Seth shrugged, the corner of his mouth twitching.

"Yeah, it's not far, and there's plenty of room." Luke's gaze focused on Mom, who would be the naysayer if anyone would.

"Fine, we'll follow you there. I can call my mother once we arrive. Do you have food?"

Seth's slow grin, so much like Luke's, spread across his face. "I've got enough raw ingredients to fix a banquet. I'm sure I can whip up something."

Mom nodded and turned for her car, her words echoing over her shoulder. "Let's go, Sylvia."

"I'll see you in a few." Sylvia stood on her tiptoes to get a kiss from Luke.

"Love you, babe."

"C'mon, lover boy, before this all backfires." Seth jingled his keys, and Luke stepped away.

Once in the car, Sylvia leaned against the seatback and closed her eyes. Her mom was taking an awful chance with Grandmother. Eventually, this would all come out. Sylvia would be in Anderson, but Mom would be left in Kokomo to face the Dragon Lady of Indiana. It melted her resolve a tiny bit. But she'd never give up Luke just to appease Mom or Grandmother's control issues. Even Mom should realize that after what had happened with Seth.

Besides, she had a lot of questions to ask Mom about that, especially since Luke had filled her in from what his mother had shared. Mom knew what it was like to be in love, in a loving relationship, even if she was only seventeen. She'd even learned that Grandmother had caused their breakup. So why was she so against Sylvia being in love?

Yeah, all sorts of questions, but it was safer to remain quiet on the drive.

A part of her worried that Mom had acquiesced too easily and was really going to just take them home, or worse, to Grandmother's. But she was true to her word and followed Seth's car to a cute little house with a white slab porch. It was obvious that the place was in the middle of a fix-up with the shutters, blue and chipped, leaning against the side of the house. But it was the type of place Sylvia had always hoped to live in someday. Less cramped than the over-the-garage apartment, and homey looking.

Mom parked at the curb, and they climbed out.

Seth motioned from his driveway. "C'mon in." He unlocked his front door and held it open for them.

Luke, however, met Sylvia on her way and linked hands with her again. Somehow when they were apart, it felt like she was incomplete, but once the magnetism of their love had them in the same place, their hands joined, and she was whole.

By the time she and her mom were inside, having been welcomed by a sweet, furry four-legged greeter, Seth was already going through his kitchen cabinets. "How about hot dogs and beans?" The dog barked. "Sorry, boy, I mean tube steaks. I can even fire up the grill."

"Let me get my call made, and I'll come check things out." Mom's hand, like her voice, shook.

"If you want privacy, Leenie, you can use the phone in my bedroom."

Mom's face blanched and then became rose red. "Um, your bed-room?"

"It's safe. Just go down the hall. Second door on the left. You won't be interrupted."

Sylvia couldn't help the sympathy that welled up. "It's gonna be okay, Mom." She reached out and squeezed her mother's hand.

There was a glimmer of gratitude in Mom's eyes, though she still resembled a prisoner walking toward the gallows. Without a word, she headed down the hallway.

Luke flipped through the albums next to the stereo. "Should we put on some music—"

"No." Sylvia stopped him before he picked a record. "If Grandmother were to hear anything, she'd realize we aren't at home. It's best to wait. For Mom's sake."

He nodded and, with a look at the dog, let the guy out back. Just in case.

Seth joined them in the living room, and while Sylvia and Luke took the plaid couch, he sat in the brown Naugahyde easy chair to wait in silence.

Moments later, Mom stepped into the room, her face pale. "She knows."

"Knows what?" Even though Luke asked, Sylvia feared she knew the answer.

"Apparently someone from the *Tribune* was at the dance last night and snapped a photo of Sylvia with a caption about who would do such a thing, and of course, Mother reads the *Trib* every day. She said she was going to go to our church this morning to speak to us but felt, for decorum's sake, she'd wait until we got to dinner. But since we weren't coming, she had no qualms about informing me what a horrible parent I am." Mom melted onto a hassock, her shoulders shaking with her sobs.

Sylvia slipped to her side, settling on the floor beside her. "Mom, you are a wonderful, caring, loving parent. Last night didn't happen because of you doing something bad. It was because some girls didn't get their way."

"Girls?" Seth cocked his head.

Oops, she'd said too much. "I'm not going to tell you more. Just remember it's not your fault, Mom. And even if we disagree, I still love you." She wrapped her mom in a hug and let her cry. Maybe now she'd get past the fear and start to be reasonable.

Maybe.

The woman crawled in the wrong direction. Seth dove on top of her as something hot seared through his side. "Get down!" He held on as she squirmed to get free. "Stay still!" More gunfire. It hit something metal. Where did it ricochet?

A scream filled the air. A woman.

Seth jerked awake.

It was only the dream.

Had he cried out?

That's when he saw her. Leenie. Standing in the kitchen doorway, a dish towel and pan in her hands, watching with eyes big enough to take in the entire world.

"Are you all right?"

He nodded, too shaken to trust his voice. A civilian had seen him in this nightmare state.

Worst of all, it was Leenie.

His lungs roiled like waves beneath his shirt, and an ocean of sweat made his clothing stick.

She set the pan and cloth on the credenza and stepped closer. "Are you sure?" Reaching out, she lightly brushed his hair from his forehead. "Does this happen often?"

Seth heaved out air and nodded again. "Often enough."

"Have you talked with anyone about it?"

This time, he shook his head. "No. Not family or anyone outside the bureau. I don't want anyone to know. Please, don't say anything."

Leenie knelt by the chair. "Seth, it's okay to get help. Even if you don't tell your family, you can talk to a professional."

"A shrink?" He smirked. "Nah. Tried that. A requirement after my... After it all happened. Not doing that again."

"Why? Are you too good for that?"

"No. It just doesn't work. Unless you've been there, you'll never understand. Those doctors have no comprehension, and I don't need their feely fluff." It was the same thing he'd said to the psychologist, though he'd started to wonder about that recently. Was he wrong? Should he talk to someone before the nightmares overtook him? Maybe contact his supervisor and see if someone had a recommendation? He wasn't the only agent to have been through something like this. Could be there was a doc in the area who knew his stuff? Maybe.

She wormed her fingers under his and held his hand. "Everyone needs a little help now and then. Do you want to tell me about it?"

No. But she'd seen him and hadn't run away. Besides, if they had any chance together—and he prayed they did—he needed to share at least the highlights that got him to this place. He cleared his throat and stared straight ahead, not daring to watch her face as he poured out his guts.

"No one has the whole story." Seth took a couple breaths, needing a moment to go back to before his career tumbled down the mountain. "I was part of the group sent into Dallas the day we got word that Dr. King had been assassinated. Rioting was expected, and the FBI wanted to quell things, find the agitators, and keep things as calm as possible. Add support to the local enforcement.

"There was this lady—"

He couldn't get more out. Instead he saw the woman, remembered what he'd learned about her after. Somehow she'd got caught in the mess. He figured she hadn't heard the news because of her job. And there was an eight-year-old son at home.

He tried again. "A sniper targeted people in the crowds. I should have spotted him, should have realized..." No. It wasn't all going to be said, though it was playing out clearly in his head. They were all so focused on the rioting that he missed the signs until shots blasted past him. A man in front of the woman went down. Seth jumped on her to keep her from being next. *Get down. Get down.* A bullet slammed in his side, splintering off bone. A second bullet ricocheted off a lamppost, went through him to her. She bled out beneath him.

Seth hadn't spoken the words since his debriefing in the hospital four years ago. He still couldn't.

Meeting Eileen's gaze returned him to the present. "You should know this, Leenie. I had to take medical retirement. There are still bone fragments near my spinal column. It's inoperable, and the chances of me ending up in a wheelchair, paralyzed from the waist down, are pretty good. I try to follow doctors' orders normally, but I will not stop living." Speaking this aloud to her, though, was like a reminder to himself, and a shift in his priorities smacked him between the eyes. He looked away, fearing the pity that was to come.

Her touch on his hand forced him to meet her gaze. "What things can't you do?"

Bless her. She hadn't gone to sympathy with her words, but simply gathered more information. He could deal with that. "Anything that puts extra stress on my lower back. I need to be careful on how much I lift, how I step, those types of things."

She scrunched up her mouth as if thinking hard. "When was the last time you spoke with a doctor about this? Maybe there's new technology."

He shook his head. "I'm not going to get my hopes up. I'd rather be grateful for what I have, for the time I have. Besides, my family definitely doesn't need to have me laid up in a hospital where I can't protect them."

"From what?"

Seth stared. "How can you ask? Haven't you had to deal with your own riots at KHS?"

"That was last semester. Things have gotten worked out."

"Have they? What about Sylvia? Who dumped the punch on her?"

Leenie stood. "You know as well as I that she isn't talking about it."

"Could be she's afraid." Though he knew the moment he said the words, that wasn't the case.

"No, that's not it."

He reached for her hand, and she didn't pull away, so he took a chance. "Could she be protecting someone? Maybe you?"

She yanked her hand back. "Me? I have no problems with students. There's never been an incident in any of my classes, and I treat everyone with fairness and kindness. I can't imagine a reason for her to feel the need to protect me."

"Maybe she's aware of something you aren't. Could be the girls said something to her?"

Leenie stared at him as if he'd lost his mind. It was time to change the subject.

"Where are the kids?"

She brushed off her skirt. "Out back. I was watching from the kitchen window. They're just sitting and talking." She paused, and he could see her thoughts before she voiced them. "I'd better get back in there so I can keep an eye on them."

There'd be no talking her out of it. "Yeah, you might as well."

She turned to go but stopped at the doorway. "I'm sorry, Seth. No one should go through that." Then she grabbed her towel and the pan and hustled back into the kitchen.

She was right about that last part. He'd never wish this on his worst enemy, and he couldn't tolerate pity from her.

Instead, he needed to keep in mind the chances of him ending up in that wheelchair. It would be too easy to open his heart to being with Leenie again, hoping for a future together. But what kind of man would put the woman he loved in that type of situation? *Yeah, would you marry me and, by the way, when I end up unable to get around on my own, will you hoist me into my wheelchair, and help me bathe, and change my diapers?*

Even now that he'd been up front with her and she had a peek at what lay ahead, there was no way he would tie her to that sort of promise.

Still, if the riots erupted again—and there was always that possibility no matter how calm it had been for the last few months—Leenie was smack in the thick of where they were most likely to hit. He needed to protect her. And Sylvia, and Sissy, and Mom. He was still useful enough to do that and would continue until God knocked his legs out from under him.

He just prayed it wouldn't be anytime soon.

Chapter 10

Monday, April 24, 1972

"Eileen, do you have a moment?"

Eileen glanced up from her desk to see Imogene Winslow, the dean of girls, coming into her classroom, and stood. "Of course, Miss Winslow."

"You've been here for how many years and still won't call me Imogene?" Eileen's boss, or one of them, shook her head.

"I was a student here before I became a teacher. I mean no disrespect."

"And I don't feel any. In fact, it makes me feel old. But that's not why I'm here. Can we sit for a moment?"

"Sure." Eileen indicated chairs by the sewing machines and took one after Miss Winslow sat. "How can I help you?"

"Well, there are two things. First, we'll be having the annual mother/daughter tea on Saturday, May 13th. Can I count on your students to again provide the cookies? The Girls' League will manage the rest of the refreshments and decorations, as usual, but your classes make such outstanding treats." She smiled, and Eileen wasn't sure what to do with the praise. It was so rare coming from someone in authority.

Oh, her observations and yearly reviews were good, maybe even great, since they all gave her above standard ratings. But to hear someone Eileen looked up to and respected say that, and after the fiasco of the weekend with her mother's cutting remarks, it took everything in her power to not break into sobs.

"Thank you, Miss... I mean Imogene. You have no idea what that means to me." She cleared her throat and changed the direction of the conversation. "I can have them ready for you by the end of day Friday, May 12th. How many dozen do you think you'll need?"

"Let's go with fifty dozen. There will be other things as well. And I have a stipend for you to cover the extra cost, like before. No need to blow up your budget at the end of the year, right?"

Eileen accepted the offered check. "Right, and thank you. Any particular type of cookie?"

"You've never sent over a bad one. Just make it a variety." Miss Winslow paused. "And that brings me to the second reason I'm here. I'm so sorry about what happened to Sylvia last Saturday. It was inexcusable, and I intend to get to the bottom of it."

"Thank you. I appreciate that." Maybe Miss Winslow would have better luck with getting her daughter to talk.

"I called Sylvia to my office this morning. She really is a lovely girl, inside and out, and she is determined not to reveal who poured the punch over her."

Eileen slumped as her latest hope disappeared like a new batch of brownies. "I'd hoped that when you said you were on it, that she'd confide in you. Sylvia won't tell me either."

"Is she planning some type of retaliation?"

"No... Actually, the idea never occurred to me. But she isn't that sort of person." She wasn't. Was she? Eileen shook her head at the thought.

"Then perhaps she's afraid. Maybe they threatened her?"

That notion had continued to flit through Eileen's mind after her conversation with Seth, though Sylvia didn't appear to be afraid. If anything, she seemed to have grown up and become more secure in who she was. "The only thing she's let slip was that it was more than one girl. And she was not happy that we caught that."

"We?"

"Her boyfriend and his uncle were there when she said it. We're all trying to get her to confide in us about what happened, but she's clammed up, and I can't get through to her anymore." She folded over the check in her hands to avoid seeing the pity in Miss Winslow's eyes.

"I wouldn't worry too much about it. Sylvia is a senior and getting ready to step out into adult life. Sometimes she's going to feel overwhelmed or frightened, and sometimes she'll try to feel out things on her own. It's normal. I don't think you have anything to worry about with her. However, I do want to catch the culprits and make sure nothing like this happens again. So if you learn anything, please let me know. It's not enough for someone to say they saw people coming from the restroom. I need a firsthand account. Sylvia can give that. However, we will be talking to anyone who was in the area in case they witnessed something." Miss Winslow stood, and Eileen rose too.

That's it? She wasn't going to say who might be witnesses? And what if no one saw anything? What then?

No, she couldn't push. Miss Winslow was her boss. "Thank you. Again. And I'll have those cookies boxed and delivered before I leave that Friday."

"I trust you will. Now I've got to get back to my office." Miss Winslow smiled and headed out the door.

There wasn't much time left in Eileen's prep period, but she made notations in her planner when the cookies were needed.

The classroom door opened. Eileen glanced up to see two girls from her next class filtering in, Corrina one of them.

"Hey, Mrs. Avery." She came closer and dropped her voice. "How is your daughter? Is she okay?"

The question startled her at first. She hadn't spotted Corrina at the dance. Not a lot of freshmen went. Did she attend the Stardust Ball? Did she see something? Though Eileen hadn't noticed the girl there, it was over almost before it started for Sylvie and her. And then, of course, the newspaper ran that photo and article so everyone in Kokomo pretty much knew. "She's fine. Thank you for asking."

"My sister said it was awful."

"Your sister?"

"Yeah, only she won't say much else. Like there's more, but..." Corrina shrugged. "As long as your daughter is okay." She turned and settled in at her sewing machine.

Could Corrina's sister know something? She'd have to go to the records room and see if she could learn the sister's name and then maybe ask her about it.

But how did she do that? The only time left today was after school and Sylvia would be by. If she thought Eileen was going behind her back, she'd have a fit.

Tomorrow. Tomorrow on her prep period. It would be easy enough to tell the secretary that she needed information about one of her students. And that would be true. It just wasn't all the story.

Sylvia faced Luke, her fingers feathering through his sideburns to the jet black waves dipping over his ears, rising on her tiptoes.

"Wait a sec, Sylvie." His face picked up color to where even his lobes looked slightly sunburned. He glanced around.

She pulled away. "You don't want to kiss me?"

"It's not that, but we're more open in this hallway, and Miss Winslow and Mr. Stucker get a little crazy about lip-locking in the school."

"Oh." She turned from him and to her locker. "I'm just tired of having to hide anymore."

He pulled her into a quick hug. "I get that. Me too. But not in the hall, 'kay?"

She shut the door and spun the dial. "'kay. But don't ask me to like it." And just to show him she wasn't all that upset, she tossed him a wink. With her books pulled to her chest, she changed the subject. "Mom's been putting the pressure on ever since we got home yesterday. She wants me to say who poured the punch."

"I don't get why you won't. Don't you want them to get what's coming?"

Sylvia shook her head. "If I do that, I'm no better than they are. I need to feel like I can move on, and honestly, a part of me is trying to do what I think Jesus would do. Turning them in isn't going to change things. In fact, it would only make them madder. But this way they didn't stop me. They lost out. Maybe they won't try anything like that again since it didn't work."

Luke's sigh was proof he wasn't sold on her explanation. But the shrug said he wouldn't push. "I'm not sure I agree, but I get what you're saying. Okay. So, what do you plan to do?"

"Nothing. Just keep living my life, being who I am, working toward being who I want to be."

He stopped her, turning her to face him. "And who would that be?"

Sylvia wiggled the fingers of her left hand in front of him. "Mrs. Sylvia Rafferty." The giggle slipped out as his grin spread.

"Right on. I can dig it." He gave her a quick hug before they continued to her class.

"I was thinking."

"Uh, oh." He shook his head, but his grin peeked out.

She smacked his arm. "I think you're going to like this idea. There's these ladies at church who have a wedding business. The Weather Girls Wedding Shoppe and Venue. I don't know them really well, but I've heard about them from others in the youth group. What if I call them and see what they can do for us?"

Luke slowed. "Ah, sure. Why not."

"You don't want me to?"

"I didn't say that."

She watched his eyes. They always gave him away. "You didn't sound all that excited. Do you want to get married this summer?"

Those beautiful blue eyes softened their gaze, and his lips curved into a smile. "I want to marry you as soon as we can make it happen. If you say talk to the Weather Girls, then that's what we'll do."

Relief flooded through her like the perfect temperature of bath water. Calming her nerves, pouring a balm over her frayed emotions. "Good. I don't want any more confrontations or arguments. Mom is also trying to get me to give back the ring."

"No."

"That's what I told her. We're engaged. I'm not changing my mind." She slipped her fingers with his and gave a squeeze. "I'll call them when I get home. Mom won't like it, but that's too bad. Maybe she'll get the idea that we're serious."

"I think she's figured that out already." He chuckled and stopped in front of her class door. "You'd better get in there before you're counted late."

"Same goes for you. Just glad your econ class isn't too far away. Love you."

He glanced about, then brushed a kiss against her cheek. "Love you too, babe. See ya."

Twenty minutes later, Sylvia left with a pass to go to the library. It suddenly occurred to her that Mom could easily hide the phone books and then she wouldn't have access to the Weather Girls' phone number. But if she asked to be excused to look up something for her class, she could also peruse the phone books housed in the school library. At least she hoped it would have the directories.

It did. And after writing down the pertinent information, she made sure to look up something she could show as proof to her teacher. Now she only had to wait it out until the end of the day and then try to make a phone call without her mother losing her mind.

After school, Sylvia headed for Mom's classroom and helped with the final cleanup. Mom was ready to go in a few minutes, leaving Sylvia hoping to get home before the Weather Girls closed for the day. She had no idea what their hours of operation were, so it needed to be the first thing she did once she was home.

They'd done little talking since breakfast when Mom pressured her once again to speak with Miss Winslow. Trying to explain went nowhere. So silence was the only other way to keep from arguing. Apparently, Mom got that, too.

They climbed the staircase to the apartment, where Mom unlocked it and let them in. "Go change your clothes and start your homework while I get dinner going." It was the same directive every school evening when they arrived home.

She didn't even acknowledge the order but went to her room and closed the door to put on something more comfortable. That's when she thought about the telephone in her mother's room. She could just sneak in there and make the call. Mom wouldn't even notice.

But that's not how she wanted to be.

If she was going to make adult decisions, she needed to do it in the open, not behaving as a child trying to get by with something. Mom was sure to notice if she used the phone in the living room. And would probably think Sylvia was trying to be in-your-face with the whole thing. But that wasn't the aim.

It wasn't a matter of flaunting or hiding. It was simply about being who she was, working toward who she wanted to be. Mrs. Luke Rafferty. Sylvia Rafferty.

She brought her books to the table and set them down before pulling out the paper with the phone number. Drawing the telephone toward her, she began to dial—Mom never splurged for a princess phone with push buttons.

"Who are you calling, Sylvie?"

Sylvia held up her hand as a voice answered, "Weather Girls' Wedding Shoppe and Venue, Stormy speaking. How may I help you?"

She glanced toward her mom, took a breath, and jumped in. "Hi. I was wondering about what services you offer. Do you have a brochure?"

"Yes, we do. I could mail it to you. Or if you'd rather, we could make an appointment, and you could come in and see for yourself. The appointment is free, just a chance to go over everything and get all your questions answered. Would that be something that might interest you?"

Mom left the stove to stand close.

Sylvia cleared her throat. "I think that would be great. I'm a student, so it would have to be on the weekend or evening."

"Either is fine. I have an opening for Thursday this week at seven. Would that be okay?"

"That's fine. My name is Sylvia Avery."

"Let me get your phone number."

"452-7022."

Mom now stood over her shoulder, trying to hear the other end of the conversation.

"Sylvia, I look forward to meeting you. Do you know where we are located?"

She glanced at her mom, giving her a signal to back off some, but it didn't work. "Yes. Thank you. See you then. Goodbye."

"Who was that?" Mom didn't even wait for her to hang up.

"That was a private phone call. And one more thing I do not want to discuss. I'm going to start my homework now."

Sylvia sat at the table, opened her chemistry textbook, and turned on her transistor radio after putting on the earphones. A part of her, the part that was still somewhat childish, wanted to grin at her mother's discomfiture. It wasn't nice. And definitely not on her to-do list for becoming who she wanted to be. But as she stared down at the reading homework, she still smiled.

The telephone's shrill tone pierced the peace of an afternoon of shutter painting for Seth. He'd set up in his backyard and had cleaned all the former chipped colors—looked to be at least three—and now the first ready shutter rested on sawhorses awaiting his brush strokes. Except the blamed phone had to cut into his project right then.

It better be important and not take much time.

Thankfully, he hadn't dipped the brush into the white paint, so he dropped it on the tarp, loosely set the lid on the can, and made it to the kitchen to answer by the fifth ring. "Matthews here."

"You sound out of breath. Not getting enough exercise?" Chet.

Despite the poke, if his contact at the bureau was calling, he had something to share. Best to not get riled. "Had to race from outside. I've still got it, don't you worry about that."

A chuckle drifted through the line. "Don't doubt it. Anyway, I picked up some news on one of your requests. That Doug Avery guy. Are you sure you want this? I mean, it's not big news really, but you do have your facts wrong."

"What do you mean?" What had been inaccurate? He'd given everything exactly as Leenie had shared, and she had the firsthand knowledge.

"The guy's not dead. He's married and living in Galveston."

"Texas?"

"No, Indiana."

"There's no *Gal*veston in Indiana. Here it's Gal*ves*ton." Having grown up in the Hoosier state, that was something Seth knew for sure.

"Oh, well. However you say it, he's in your backyard, so to speak. Looks like he has a family, three kids. Two boys and a girl. His wife is named Alma."

Seth grabbed a kitchen chair and plopped. Did Leenie know? Had she lied or been lied to? Did the guy even know Leenie? And if he did, was he aware he had another daughter?

"You're awful quiet there, guy."

"Just absorbing. Do you have his address?"

"Sure. But hey, you're not going to cause any trouble are you? I'm already out on a limb getting this data for you."

"No trouble. I promise. Just need to get to the bottom of this. I'm concerned that some people I care about don't have all the facts they should." Or had they been hiding and manufacturing their own?

Chet read off the street address, and Seth wrote it down on the pad he kept on his counter.

"Thanks, man. I owe you one."

"Probably owe me a few, but I'm not out to collect. Just be careful with your information, and don't get me in trouble."

"Deal." Seth thanked the guy, and they hung up.

Then for a good ten minutes he just stared at the numbers and street name he'd recorded. What kind of guy let his wife and daughter think he was dead? Had there been a divorce? Had there ever been a marriage to begin with? He'd never expected so many questions.

But the shutters still waited for him, so he circled the name and address one more time and set the pad on the counter under where the phone hung and headed out back.

The joy of getting something more accomplished on his house had faded, overshadowed by the news about Doug and his family and the inevitable questions concerning Leenie and what she knew about the whole thing. He'd come up with all sorts of possibilities when another question would materialize. They were taking over his brain.

Until he stepped wrong and kicked the whole can of paint over.

White goo poured across his boots and the paint tarp. The can had been three quarters full.

What a mess.

At least it brought him back to the present. Seth removed the shutters and sawhorses from the tarp. Grabbing the paint can lid, he scooped as much of the unaffected liquid back into the can as he could. Then, giving up on saving more, he rolled up the rest of the mess and took it to his garbage can in the alley.

Seth had changed into older work boots to do this job, which was a blessing, but now they were done for. He unlaced and removed his left boot. His black sock was now the color of the shutter. Wonderful. With a groan, he mentally added socks to his shopping list. Then he peeled them off and padded barefoot into the house to his bedroom for other shoes so he could add his paint-infused Tony Lamas to the trash in the alley. Seth had only figured to splatter a little on them at the most. That he could deal with. And yeah, he'd owned them for a good ten years, so they'd seen other bits of abuse, but to have to throw them out now that they were perfectly broken in really hurt.

Painting day was officially over.

That left no excuse. He could drive north to Galveston. It wouldn't take over ten, maybe fifteen minutes tops, to get there. A little longer to find the address, but it wasn't like Galveston was all that big.

Seth scrubbed at the sink, changed his clothes, and returned his ring to his pinkie. After all these years, he felt naked without his father's legacy on his finger, yet wearing it while painting wasn't a great idea either.

The time to get presentable gave him a chance to think through what he planned. If he did this, what would he say? Would he say anything? Did he want this Doug Avery character to be aware he was being watched? Or did he just jump in and start interrogating? Would the man even answer the most basic question when this stranger popped up on his step?

He could pull out his FBI ID—even though it was clearly stamped "RETIRED." If he flashed it fast enough, Avery might not catch on.

Or it might get back to the bureau that he'd misused his credentials.

Okay, so he might not know what he was going to do when he arrived, but he'd better get a move on or the whole point was moot for the day.

Seth backed his car out of his drive and headed for Davis Road. Soon he was in Galveston, cruising for the man's place. Howard Street finally appeared, and he headed west until the numbers matched, and he parked across the street.

Kids were out in force, probably getting home from school. It was about that time. Two boys, looking to be about ten and twelve, held the hands of a little girl, around six years old. She didn't seem all that happy to be guided toward the house, but the older one leaned over and whispered in her ear, and she stopped struggling. They mounted the front porch steps of the gray bungalow with the green shutters and walked in with one of them calling, "Mom, we're home." The words floated back on the breeze through his open car window.

It wasn't the first time Seth had worked surveillance. But it was the first time he'd done it for his own agenda. How long should he stay? How long before Avery came home? Would he come home? Maybe he was in the habit of starting families and then leaving them for another.

No, something told Seth that wasn't the case.

About the time he'd convinced himself that this was a fool's errand, a white '67 Ford Fairlane with red interior pulled into the driveway. More important, a blond man climbed out. Seth noted he stood approximately five foot nine inches and most likely weighed about 185. His powers of observation were still good. The guy wasn't remarkable looking at all. Very average. But Seth knew this was Doug Avery.

And he needed to talk to him.

Seth left his car and crossed the street to meet the man on his porch steps. "Douglas Avery?"

The man scanned Seth, though he flashed a friendly enough smile. "Yes, can I help you?"

Now Seth needed to come up with something to say. He couldn't just blurt things out, and if he came on too strong, the guy could just go in his house and even possibly call the police. "Um, does the name Eileen Lawson mean anything to you?"

The friendly smile disappeared. "Why do you ask?"

Truth. That's what he needed to share. "My nephew is engaged to marry a girl, Sylvia Avery, who's been told by her mother, Eileen Avery, that her father is dead."

A sadness clouded the man's eyes. "Oh. You haven't mentioned me to her mother, have you?"

"No, I just learned of you today. But why wouldn't you want me to tell her?"

Avery motioned to the porch chairs, so Seth obliged and sat waiting to hear the answer to his question.

"Eileen and I were young. She was the prettiest thing I'd ever seen, and I was sure I was in love. We should've waited, but we were college kids with a first taste of freedom, especially Eileen. After I proposed, eloping was her idea, and I was a little surprised she didn't want the whole wedding deal, but she said her mother would sabotage things, so it was better to ask forgiveness than permission." He chuckled and shook his head.

"Then what happened?"

"Her mother. We thought everything was hunky-dory. But then Old Lady Lawson cornered me at my after-school job. Told me she'd put me through Purdue and pay me a monthly fee for ten years if I'd sign a letter saying it wasn't working out and I was leaving Eileen. You've got to understand, I was young, over-my-head broke, and starting to rethink the rush of getting married. She said she'd work it all out, and eventually I got a document saying we were officially divorced. All I had to do was agree to never get in touch with Eileen again."

"What about Sylvia?"

"Who's Sylvia? You mean your nephew's girlfriend?"

"I mean your daughter."

"My daughter is in the house right now, getting ready to have dinner. Eileen and I didn't have any kids. I wasn't there long enough."

"Are you sure?"

The guy's eyes suddenly widened, and Seth could tell there was doubt.

Chapter 11

Thursday April 27, 1972

This was getting so out of hand. Eileen sat on the edge of her bed and slipped off her school shoes. A part of her was frantic enough to want to ask for help from her mother. But then she'd pay for it. For the rest of her life. *You don't have what it takes to be a mother. You never should have allowed Sylvia to go to that dance.*

It wasn't just the dance, or the fact Sylvia wouldn't confide who had poured the punch over her. There was the new attitude she'd developed. It wasn't so much disrespectful. In fact, she probably was more helpful and thoughtful than she'd ever been. But she also was keeping things to herself. Like that phone call she made the other evening. The old Sylvia would have told her everything. No, the old Sylvia would have asked permission to use the phone.

This new Sylvia had confidence. Which was good. Right? But it also felt like she was separating herself, that they weren't as tied to each other.

Eileen had put her whole life into Sylvia and her upbringing. Didn't that count for something? Why now, when she was just starting to bloom into adulthood, would she want to try things without her mother's guidance? It wasn't as if Eileen was as cold-feeling as her mother had been. She made a point of showing Sylvia how much she was loved and had imagined they would remain best friends for the rest of their lives.

In fact, Sylvia was the only good that came out of her marriage to Doug.

Thinking back, Eileen could see all the signs now. The daily arguments, how different they were. Still, she would have honored her vows. Even as disagreeable as he got when he was tired from working after going to school all day, he was still easier to live with than her mother.

But for him to go off and leave her like that with only a letter. The wound still hurt.

The salt her mother rubbed into it as she supposedly rescued her only increased the scars. Sylvia had been too young to remember but getting out of there and into this tiny apartment had been the best decision Eileen ever made.

She hung up her work dress and slipped into a pair of double-knit slacks and a button-down shirt. There was dinner to get going, even if her daughter still avoided all conversation with her.

The phone rang, and she picked up immediately.

"Mrs. Avery, it's Luke. May I please speak with Sylvia?"

This was the last straw. She couldn't keep them apart at school, and church was open to anyone who chose to attend. But she didn't have to allow him contact in her home. "No. She's not available at this time." Please don't let Sylvia pick up the other extension.

"Mrs. Avery, please. It's important. I really need to speak with her. I'll only keep her a minute or two. Not long enough to interrupt her homework or dinner."

He was polite and courteous. But so had been Doug. It didn't matter that Sylvia believed they were engaged. This wedding would not happen, and she'd do what she had to in order to keep them apart. "I'm sorry, Sylvia isn't available."

"Does she know?"

"Know what?"

The line grew silent a moment. "I don't want to bring up hard things, Mrs. Avery, but—"

"But what? What are you talking about, Luke?"

"Your husband, Sylvia's father, is alive."

Eileen dropped to her bed. "No he isn't. He died in 1953. And I would appreciate it if you didn't bring up such lies ever again." The shaking in her hand traveled up her arm and lodged in her throat.

"Mrs. Avery, I'm sorry. But it's true. He lives in Galveston."

"I don't believe it. I won't believe it. I thought you were a nice young man, Luke, but I was wrong. To say such things, that is plain cruel." He had to be lying.

"I'm sorry, Mrs. Avery. Tell Sylvia to call me as soon as she can."

"So you can fill her with these same lies? No. And you are to stay away from her at school. If I have to leave my classes in order to walk her to hers, I will do so. Stay away from my daughter." She heaved for breath as she got out the last words.

"I'm sor—"

Slamming down the receiver, she fell back on her bed, her eyes squeezed shut.

What if he was right? What if Doug were still alive? What if he learned about Syl— The bedroom door banged open.

"What was that all about?" Sylvia glared at her from the doorway.

"What was what?"

"Don't play innocent with me, Mom. I was listening. I should've spoken up, but I wanted to hear how far you'd go only to discover I have a father who is alive and a few minutes' drive from here?"

Icy fingers of fear clutched Eileen's heart, keeping her from thinking. What should she say? What could she say?

"He's lying, Sylvie."

"Luke is not a liar. Why would he? He has nothing to gain. He's only trying to help me. Now tell me the truth before I have to go to Galveston myself."

"No, Sylvie. Sit. I'll tell you. I'll tell you everything." Her throat tightened as her heart pounded in her ears. Anything to keep her from that.

Sylvia eyed her a moment but finally sat next to her on the bed. "I'm waiting."

"It's not that easy." Especially when she might have the wrong information. Eileen inhaled deep and exhaled slowly, hoping to bring her heart rate a little lower. She knew this day would come but had no idea it would arrive like this. "I met Doug at Anderson College. I was a freshman, and he was a sophomore." She choked back the horror of

Luke's words. Alive? It couldn't be. Doug was dead. She knew. But could she explain what happened so that it made sense? "I'd never really dated in high school. Seth would come by, and we did homework together or sat on the porch and talked. Your grandmother made sure we were always chaperoned. But what she didn't realize was that we were falling in love. He was a year ahead of me in school and left for Anderson with the understanding we'd get married once I finished at KHS." She took in the wide-eyed shock in her daughter's stare.

"He stopped writing me. I was hurt and angry. He left me wondering why, what I had done. When he showed up with Luke, well, it brought back those feelings and increased my fear for you." She stole a glance at the drawer where she still kept his class ring that she never gave back. The loss for what might have been nearly yanked the breath from her, but then the realization settled over her, like a comforting blanket. She wouldn't have had Sylvia.

"I never knew what happened until Seth told me the other day. Your grandmother wrote him in my name saying I'd changed my mind and to not contact me again. When I got to Anderson, he was gone, transferred to another school. I was devastated. But then this guy in my English composition class began pursuing me. At first, I wasn't interested. I was still heartbroken. But he wouldn't give up, so I finally went out with him, and I found him charming and funny. And he was attentive. I needed that. Before either of us should have considered such a thing, he proposed. I agreed on condition we elope. I knew my mother would try to wreck things." She risked a peek at Sylvia, who seemed to be following, but her eyes reflected nothing of what might be going on in her head.

"Afterward, when I was sure she couldn't do us any harm, I called to tell her. She started making trips to see us, trying to get us to get an annulment. But we refused. Then one evening Doug didn't come home from work. I had some news to share and was so excited. But he didn't come home all night. Instead, the next day, my mother stopped by and tried to comfort me. I said I would wait until I had word from Doug, something had to be wrong. A day or so later, the mailman arrived with a letter from my husband. He didn't want to be married anymore and said I could divorce him for abandonment. He wouldn't contest it.

"I never wanted to divorce him. But I couldn't find him. So I kept going to my classes and hoping he'd change his mind and come home. Something else was happening too. The reason I'd been so excited for him to come home was that I'd learned I was pregnant. Now my mother was really after me to leave Anderson and come home, but I refused.

"Then came the day she said she'd tried to find Doug for me, that she hated to see me that way and that a baby needed its father. But she had bad news. Doug had been killed in a car accident out of state. She took me to her lawyer who said I needed to sign some pages, and everything would work out. I was so devastated I would've done anything I was told. That's when I went home with my mother and had you." Eileen chanced a small smile, but when it wasn't returned, she picked at a thread coming loose from the quilting on her bedspread.

"It didn't take long to see we would never survive living under her roof, so I finished up my teaching certificate at IUK and found us this apartment. It was hard to pay for things, but I refused to ask her for any help. She insisted we eat Sunday dinner with her and Father. I refused, but she told me she would tell you how stupid I had been to run off and get married. She said she wasn't even convinced I really was married, and that she'd tell you that you were illegitimate."

Eileen took a long breath and glanced at her daughter to see the impact of her story. She'd never shared it all with anyone. But now she'd had to with Sylvia.

Her daughter slowly rose like a looming giant. "You expect me to believe you never knew my father was still alive and living over in the next county?"

"Sylvia, I told you the truth. I can't imagine who this is that Luke says is your father."

"I've always trusted you, even when I didn't agree." Tears streamed down her cheeks. "I knew you wouldn't lie to me. But you did. You have my whole life. I can't even look at you. I am out of here."

The door's slam vibrated through to the depths of Eileen's heart.

Sylvia halted in front of her bedroom door. Should she pack before leaving? Returning here was not on her to-do list, but she needed to get to Luke fast. He'd just have to come with her when she gathered her things to move out.

Move to where?

Grandparents? She shuddered. There was no way she'd live under Grandmother's roof even if her grandpa was the sweetest man she knew.

Find Luke. That's what she needed to do. Together, they'd come up with a plan. In the meantime, he was her goal. The rest would work out.

She started down the street toward his house, a ten-minute walk at the most. Just as she turned the corner at the end of her block, she spotted his bright yellow Skylark headed her way.

He pulled to the curb next to her and jumped out. "Are you okay?"

"No. Get me out of here."

"Where to?" He held the passenger door for her.

"I don't care. Galveston?"

He didn't answer her until he'd slid back into the driver's seat. "Are you sure? I'll take you anywhere you want, but you might want to talk with Uncle Seth first."

"Why?"

Luke refused to meet her gaze, seeming to scrutinize the road ahead with scientific intensity.

"Luke, why do I need to speak with your uncle?"

"Because he's the one with the information. I just found it on his counter when I stopped by to see him."

His uncle knew? Why? How? "I don't understand."

"Sylvie, I did something I shouldn't have. I lost it with your mom. I was trying to maintain my cool, thinking I could fix it for you to talk with Uncle Seth, but I blurted everything out, and he doesn't even know I saw the note."

"Oh." Then maybe the guy wasn't her father. It could be just like her mom said. "Will you get in trouble?"

"Probably. But I think your need to talk with my uncle is more important than me getting yelled at for sticking my nose into something I shouldn't." He stopped at a red light and gave her his attention. "How about going to my house? You can meet my mom, and then I can track down Uncle Seth. He wasn't home when I went by earlier. I was looking for him when I found the message on his counter. Besides, you don't need to be there when he loses his cool over this."

She got why he didn't want her there when he confessed, and her heart melted for him at the prospect of what he intended to do. "Okay. I'd like to meet your mom. Maybe she can help me figure out where I'm going to live now."

Luke hit the brakes, and she stiff-armed the dashboard. "What do you mean?"

"I'm not going back. I heard your conversation with Mom and made her tell me what was going on. I can't tell if she's still lying to me. At the very least, she's been lying by keeping things from me. I can't be around her anymore." The words brought a sudden loss of identity. She'd no longer be Eileen's daughter, and that's all she'd ever been. What if the guy in Galveston wasn't her dad? She'd be without a parent. Or what if he was? What if he was her father but didn't want anything to do with her? She'd still be alone in the world. No matter how much she blinked, the tears wouldn't stop.

Luke pulled to the curb, shoved the gearstick into park, and switched off the radio, cutting short the Jimmy Castor Bunch in the middle of "Troglodyte." "Hey, babe, c'mere." He drew her to him, caressing her face between his hands, and wiping her tears with his thumbs. "It's gonna be okay. Let's get you to my mom. She's pretty smart."

Sylvia nodded between his fingers before he leaned in to kiss her wet lips. She pulled back. "I'm sorry. I'm a mess." She could just imagine her snotface, and she blindly searched for a tissue in her purse.

"Babe. It's fine. Really." He lifted her hand to his lips before putting the car back in drive and pulling onto the road.

She dabbed at her face and hoped her eyes didn't look too messed up. They were undoubtedly rimmed with red. "Do I look okay? I hate this. It's my first time to meet her, and I want to make a good impression."

"You're perfect. Did you know my mom knew your mom back when they were in high school?"

"Nope. Were they friends?" She couldn't imagine her mom with girl-friends.

"I doubt it. Mom was a freshman and was aware Uncle Seth had a thing for your mom. That's all."

"Oh." Was that good or bad? Did his mother hold a grudge against hers?

He pulled in a driveway, and she suddenly wanted to run back home despite everything that had occurred in the last hour.

"It's gonna work out, Sylvie." He hopped out and got her door, holding out his hand.

Sylvia needed it more for moral support than for getting out of the car, and she didn't let go even after he locked up.

He took her around to the back and up a short set of steps. Squeaky hinges announced their entrance into a kitchen. "Mom, hey Mom. You here?"

A pretty brunette came around the corner, carrying a laundry basket of clothing. "Luke, how many times do I have to tell you... Oh, you have a guest. Hi. Um. You must be Sylvia. I'm Tammy, Luke's mother." She slid the basket to balance on her hip and stuck out her hand.

It was so fast that Sylvia froze. But the manners Mom had instilled rose to the surface, and she shook hands with the woman who looked to be about the same age as her own mother. "Nice to meet you, Mrs. Rafferty. Luke has told me so much about you."

"He has, huh?" His mom cocked a brow at him.

"All good stuff, Mom. I swear. Anyway, have you talked with Uncle Seth today?"

"Nope. Was I supposed to?" She set the basket on the kitchen table.

"I'm just trying to locate him. In the meantime, Sylvia has a situation."

The room grew silent.

Mrs. Rafferty dropped to a chair. Luke's face turned red.

Sylvia's face heated as she caught what his mom was thinking.

"No, Mom. She and her mother got into it, and Sylvia needs a place to stay. Can she crash here?"

The look of relief that passed through his mom's eyes flickered into something else. "Um, I'm not so sure that's a great idea."

"Mom, we're engaged. We're getting married. Plus, I'm not asking for her to stay in my room."

His mom gasped and stared at the two of them. Then she shook her head. "We will discuss the first part of that news in a moment. But as for the rest, be assured that will not happen, mister." Mrs. Rafferty paused as if she figured out something. "You're looking for Seth?"

"Yeah, we need to talk with him."

"Well, while you're chatting, see if you can bunk at his place. If he agrees, then Sylvia is welcome to stay here." She caught Sylvia's gaze. "I won't have your mother worrying about your reputation. But if Seth says yes, then I do, too."

Luke pulled his mother into a hug. "You're outasight, Mom. Thanks."

It was funny to see how he could be so demonstrative with her, and she gave right back too. Why couldn't her mother be like that?

"Don't think you can butter me up and get away with your land-mine announcement. Just remember we have a discussion waiting here, buster."

"Gotcha. Okay, then, I'm going to go track down Uncle Seth. Babe, why don't you hang out here and get to know my mom?"

Sylvia glanced from Luke to Mrs. Rafferty before nodding. But the truth was, she was too nervous to make a sound.

Twilight fell as Seth finally turned down his street. It had been an intense conversation with Leenie's ex, Doug Avery. One that had the potential for a punch in the mouth thrown by either of them. But they'd kept their cool and had come to an agreement. Now he just needed to talk with Leenie.

Except when he pulled into his drive, someone was sitting on the porch. Luke. Petting Muncher. His poor dog. This move was supposed to give him more time with the mutt, but that hadn't happened since he got re-involved with Leenie. He turned off the ignition and blew out a breath. Better see what the kid wanted.

Luke stepped down from the porch to meet him. "Hey, can we talk?"

"Sure. Want to sit on the porch or inside?"

The boy fell in step with him. "Out here's good." He got silent while moving back to the white metal lawn chair he'd vacated and burying his fingers into Muncher's fur.

"Must be pretty big if you're having trouble getting started."

Luke nodded. "It is. I did something. And I need advice. You're gonna hit the ceiling, but can you wait until you get it all first?"

Whoa. "Okay." Seth leaned back in his chair, prepared to keep quiet until he'd heard everything.

"I stopped by here earlier. Something about the night of the dance has been bugging me, and I wanted to see if you thought I was losing my mind. Anyway, I walked in but couldn't find you—of course—but I noticed a paper on your counter."

Seth's tension rose and trepidation of where this was going formed a knot in his gut, but he kept his mouth shut as promised. Should've taken that paper with him.

"I figured you ought to talk with Sylvia, so I called her place, and her mother answered. Mrs. Avery wouldn't let me speak with her, and I lost my cool."

"You told her what you found? What did you say?"

Luke stared at the painted cement and nodded. "It wasn't good. And apparently Sylvia picked up on the extension and heard, too. They had it out, and now she's walked out on her mom. She's staying at my house if you'll let me bunk here. Mom's rule."

"What?"

Now the kid finally met his gaze. "Yeah. Is it okay? I'm sorry, I messed this all up. Is that Avery guy really Sylvia's dad?"

"If he is, don't you think it would be better for Sylvia and Eileen to find out about him first? You really stuck your nose where it didn't belong." How was he going to fix this one?

"Yeah, sorry. What were you going to do before I told you all this?"

Seth shook his head. Could his plan still work? "I was going to speak with Eileen. Now I'm not sure she will even be in the same room with me."

As if on cue, a car pulled up in front. Leenie.

"Kid, if you know what's good for you, beat it out of here. Go get your things, and let us have this conversation in private."

Luke didn't bother to answer but jumped over the side rail of the porch and took off to his car while Leenie climbed out of hers.

"Is that Luke? Where's he going? Where is my daughter?" She stormed the steps, shouting the whole way.

"Hi, Leenie. Have a seat." He motioned to the chair Luke had warmed.

She didn't sit. Instead, she crossed her arms and glared. After a beat, she swallowed and then dropped her voice. "First, where is Sylvia?"

"She's at my sister's house." He raised his hands at her gasp. "Luke is staying with me, so there will be no males in that house. My sister's stipulation."

Leenie's fury lessened a touch. "Where did Luke get the ridiculous idea that Doug is still alive?"

Did she really believe the guy was dead? She hadn't been faking? "You need to sit down. I promise to tell you everything."

She hesitated a moment but then plopped on the chair with a loud sigh. "Fine. But Doug's dead."

"How do you know?"

"My mother. She had a private detective look for him. Found he had died out of state. To take care of the creditors who'd come after me, she had me sign a bunch of paperwork with her lawyer. It was before Sylvia was born. I was so miserable and alone. I couldn't believe he'd just left me." Even in the darkening light, the tear slipping down her cheek glistened.

This would be harder than he'd thought. Up until now, he'd figured she'd used widowhood to hide her embarrassment of being divorced. But if she really hadn't known... "Leenie, I spoke with Doug today."

She gasped and stood. "I never took you for a liar, Seth."

"I'm not. Stop a moment. Between me and your mother, who is most likely to lie to you? Who is the one you'd trust to tell you the hard truth?"

The trembling started and she began to topple as realization crashed over her. Seth jumped to her side and guided her to the chair.

"She lied to me."

And he'd only begun to explain. "There's more. Doug can fill you in on the rest, but it was your mother. She arranged the divorce and got him out of the picture. He signed something promising never to contact you, so he had no idea about Sylvia. The guy is married with three kids of his own."

"We're divorced?" She shrunk deeper into the chair.

"Yes, I saw the decree."

"He'll take Sylvia from me!"

Seth dropped in front of her, winced, and grasped her hands. "No. That is not the plan." He paused until she calmed a little. "With your permission, and if Sylvia agrees to it, he'd like to meet her. When I left, he was about to tell his wife and kids. But he made a point of saying he had no intention of uprooting Sylvia—only to meet and maybe get to know his daughter. He was just as stunned to learn about her as you've been to discover he's alive."

Leenie wrapped her arms around her middle and rocked. "Why would she do this? What did she hope to accomplish?"

Seth pulled her to him as the dam burst. Her sobs broke his heart. She'd said they'd not had an easy marriage, but had she loved this Avery guy so much? Did she and Seth have a chance?

That thought pinged in his brain, fighting with the one that reminded him he'd decided they couldn't be together because of his condition. He would not do that to a woman.

"I hate her." Leenie pulled back. "I didn't think it was possible. I mean, I've always been afraid of her. But now I hate her."

Seth ran his fingers beneath her eyes. "You are in pain. Honestly, your mother is not my favorite person, either. But hating her is only going to poison you. Forgiving her—"

"Forgive her? Are you crazy? Look what she's done! She cut off our relationship with lies, she destroyed my marriage with more lies, and she's held me captive all these years with the threat of telling lies to my daughter. And, by the way, who do you think Sylvia will believe? Not me. It's not enough my so-called mother isn't happy to keep me from a loving relationship. She has to alienate me from the only one who has ever loved me."

"Leenie. Sylvia still loves you. She's upset and confused. Give her some time. You are not alone."

Her eyes narrowed. "You mean God? The same God who let my mother do all this to me and didn't stop it?"

"He brought us back together."

She froze at that, and he wished he'd used other words.

"I need to leave. Where does your sister live? I'll go get Sylvia."

He laid his hand atop hers, but she brushed him away. "Wait. You've both received a lot of truth today. Let her process it. I promise she'll be safe, and like I said, Luke is staying with me while Sylvia is there, so you don't need to worry."

"She's my daughter, my responsibility."

"She is eighteen years old. Unless you want to destroy your relationship, give her the space she needs. I promise she'll want to talk with you after she cools off."

If her glare were a weapon, he'd have been incinerated. But then it softened, and another tear slipped free. "What am I to do alone? I don't know how to live by myself. She was the reason I kept going."

"Then maybe it's time for you to think about you."

And maybe it was time for him to rethink about them.

Chapter 12

Sunday, April 30, 1972

E ileen could not get used to the quiet. That had been the hardest part of everything. She remembered feeling that way after Doug disappeared. Their little trailer had been silent but for her bouts of sobbing. Here it was happening all over again.

She'd tried to stick with her normal schedule. Work had been a balm, distracting her for short bits of time, only to realize she was glancing out her classroom windows for a glimpse of Sylvia. Of course, she could have had one of Sylvia's teachers send her to her classroom, but there was always the chance of someone else walking in and overhearing. Besides, what if Sylvie refused to come?

Saturday had been brutal. The hair appointment alone. No shopping or chatting. None of the things Eileen looked forward to because she did them with her daughter.

And now today. The thought of going to church by herself had been more than she could stand. There was no going, pasting on a smile, unobtrusively searching for Sylvia while pretending everything was fine. All the happy faces and she knew, *she knew* they'd all ask where Sylvia was because the two of them were inseparable. Who was she if she wasn't Sylvia's mother?

That was a question to ponder. A stabbed-through-the-heart, lonely cat lady? She didn't even own a cat. Did she need one or two? Her stomach clenched.

So she'd stayed home, already labeling herself as stupid, gullible, a dupe, naïve. The list could go on.

And more than once she'd picked up the phone to blast her mother, lay into her for real. But what if Mother made good on her threat? What if now that Sylvia hated her, she heard lies she was illegitimate and that her mother was some wanton woman simply trying to hide her past?

Seth told her that Sylvia had the truth of the story and just needed time to absorb it all. For her daughter's sake, she was giving her that space. Another reason she'd stayed home from church.

Had Sylvia gone without her?

Or had she started attending Luke's family's church? She and her mother attended different ones, so that wasn't beyond the realm of possibility.

Eileen was suddenly thirsty. Sipping water, she could handle. Eating was a whole other story. Her appetite left with Sylvia, and even though common sense said she needed to eat, she couldn't make herself.

As she filled a tumbler of water from the faucet, footsteps sounded on the stairs leading to her apartment. Before she could get to the door, there was a knock. Sylvie?

She raced across the room and yanked open the door. But it was a stranger. A woman who looked sort of familiar. Dark hair. Blue eyes. She'd seen those eyes before.

"Eileen Avery?" The visitor stuck out her hand. "I'm Tammy Rafferty, Seth's sister."

"Luke's mother." Now she knew why the woman seemed so familiar.

"That, too. May I come in?"

Eileen ran her fingers through her hair and stepped back, allowing entrance. What did Tammy think of the tiny space that had been her home, her sanctuary for all these years, and the fact she was still in her housecoat at two in the afternoon?

"Thank you for seeing me. I tried calling, but there was always a busy signal."

Manners kicked in. "Please have a seat. Can I get you something to drink?"

"Water is fine. Thanks."

Eileen had a feeling it was as much a moment of reprieve for her visitor as it was for her. A chance to gather thoughts. Why was she here, anyway? After filling another glass, she took it and hers out to where Tammy sat on the edge of her seat, her hands locked between her knees. Well, if she came all the way over here, she had something on her mind, so Seth's sister—Luke's mother—would have to start the conversation. Eileen handed her the tumbler.

"I'm sorry if I've barged in. I just felt we needed to talk, and Sylvia was worried when she didn't see you at church today."

"She was worried?" Really? Not that she'd wanted to cause alarm, but that was the first bit of hope Eileen had felt in days.

"Yeah, she said you never miss unless you are too sick to attend."

"I didn't know if she would be going there or with you. Besides, I didn't feel like seeing people."

Tammy's gaze grew soft. "I get that. Don't know if you were aware, but I lost my husband about a year ago. I've no idea what I would have done without my kids. They've kept me sane."

"I'm sorry." There was kindness in Tammy. Just like the kindness in her brother, even if he had a bad habit of digging into things that were none of his business. That thought made her sit straighter. "Does Sylvia want to come home?"

"Would she be welcomed?"

"Of course. Did she think otherwise?"

Tammy shook her head. "No, I just wanted to be sure. Let's just say I'm working on that for you. I think it's possible. But she's still feeling like you withheld information from her. Seth spoke with her, and now she gets that you really were unaware your husband was still alive and how manipulative her grandmother is." She glanced away. "I should have put that better."

"No. You said it correctly. My mother is the queen of manipulation. How does she live with herself?" As long as they were being upfront, Eileen decided maybe she could talk with this woman. "I wasn't answering the phone because I expected my mother would try to call because I didn't come over after church. I don't think she'll risk being seen in my neighborhood or attempt to climb my stairs, but she will keep calling, probably all night. So I took the phone off the hook."

"Can't say as I blame you. I'm sorry. You have to be hurting a great deal."

The kind words felt like someone debriding a wound. "I am. I don't know what to do."

Tammy reached for her hand. "May I pray with you?"

It was such a simple request. Before Eileen could remind herself just how angry she was with God, she was nodding. No words could make it past her vocal cords. With her hands encased in Tammy's, Eileen bowed her head.

"Father, thank You that You already have the answers. Thank You that You are in control and not Eileen's mother. And thank You that there is forgiveness and love beyond this pain. I ask that You wrap Your loving arms around my sister here. Infuse her with hope and fill her with Your wisdom to do and say only what You instruct. I also pray that You would speak to Sylvia and that she would hear You clearly. You've taught her to honor her mother, now show her how to do it in Your love. And for Eileen's mother, I pray You would open her eyes to the pain she has caused. Bring her to a full understanding and help her surrender to You before it is too late. Nothing is beyond You. And You can work this all to Eileen's good and Your glory. So in Jesus's powerful name, we leave these requests with You and trust You to do what is best. We love You, Father. Amen."

The sobs overwhelmed Eileen to where she couldn't breathe.

Tammy pulled her close and rocked her back and forth.

Eileen couldn't remember her mother ever doing that for her, even when Doug left or when she thought he was dead. It was something she'd tried to give Sylvia when she needed it, but to have someone hold her and show her this compassion, she didn't know how to respond. She only didn't want it to stop.

And then it did.

"Can I get you anything?"

Eileen pulled away, wiping her hands over her face.

Tammy held out a tissue from the box on the coffee table.

After blowing her nose and swiping a few more Puffs, she had her face cleaned though she knew her eyes were bright red, and her nose must resemble Rudolph's. "No. I... You're very kind. Thank you."

"You know that verse about showing comfort with the comfort you've been given? I've got wonderful people in my life who have done that for me—people in my church, my brother, my kids, my m..."

"Your mother?"

Tammy nodded.

"It's okay. Some people have loving parents. I'm glad you do. She taught you well."

"Thank you. Sometimes she makes me crazy, but I never doubt she loves me. I think that's how Sylvia looks at you. She does know you love her."

Something Tammy said brought up a thought. "You said you have kids. More than just Luke?"

"Um-hm. I have a daughter who is a freshman this year."

Eileen sighed before plunging into the question. "How did you decide on how strict to be and when to allow them to try things?"

"Like what?"

"I've just been terrified to let Sylvia out of my sight. She's a good girl, and she's highly intelligent. But I'm afraid she is naïve and could be tricked into situations."

Tammy patted her hand. "That's why we talk with our kids, look for those teachable moments. By the time they are in high school, I figure I've poured into my kids the important lessons and now I need to give them enough space to apply their understanding but still be close enough for them to ask questions. And I ask, too. It brings around great discussions. But ultimately I have to allow them to make their own mistakes. My husband and I were a team about this. We knew there was a time the kids would have to try things on their own before they went to college. High school was a thicker safety net, going away to school still provided a bit a safety. The prayer was that once they had their degree and were out in the workforce, they'd be capable of making the hard decisions on their own, though we'd—or I'd, still be there as a sounding board for them. Seth has sort of stepped in on that, too. But eventually, the decision is th eirs."

Eileen huffed. "My mom is still trying to make decisions for me and for Sylvia. She's never let go. How do I do that for Sylvia?"

"You're doing it right now. She's in a safe place. I insisted that Luke stay with Seth because I didn't want you to worry about her reputation.

In the meantime, she is choosing to finish up her school year. She wanted to go to church today. I think she hoped you'd see she was making good choices. Anyway, she's managing a bit of freedom. Does she have her driver's license?"

Eileen shook her head. "Sylvia thinks I haven't let her get it because I'm holding her back, but the truth is..." She looked away. This was too embarrassing. "The truth is I can't afford it. I keep the roof over her head and food in the kitchen and clothes on her back. But extras like adding her to my car insurance? That's beyond my budget."

"I see. I had to go back to work part time at my brother-in-law's insurance office, so I get it. But why didn't you want her to realize how tight money was?"

"I never wanted her to worry. She needed to feel safe and secure."

Tammy shook her head. "Because you never did. Right?"

Eileen stared at the woman. They'd only spoken for this short time. Yet Tammy just summed up her entire life.

Thursday, May 11, 1972
The bell rang, and Sylvia gathered her books.

It had been over two weeks since she'd left home. She still double checked each choice daily to make sure she was behaving and not creating waves in the Rafferty family. Guess it was a habit she'd never out-grow.

So much had happened, yet nothing seemed to change. At least not enough.

She'd made a point of wandering past her mother's classroom whenever possible but never stopped. Once, Mom spotted her. They locked gazes, and the pain of separation nearly crushed the fragile determination to build her freedom and maturity. Neither of them spoke a word, and Sylvia had hustled to her next hour class.

Luke took her to meet with the Weather Girls. The original appointment had been rescheduled due to everything that had happened that day. After taking a tour of Ferguson House, Sylvia knew that was where she wanted to get married. Not that they planned or could even afford a large wedding. It would have to be small. What did Stormy call it? Intimate. Yeah, that was a pretty way to put it. Seriously, who all were they going to invite? Luke had more relatives than she did, and of those she had, only her mother was worth inviting. Well, maybe Grampa, but not Grandmother, and he probably wouldn't come without her. Sylvia wasn't even sure Mom would agree to attend. And she had yet to speak with her father. Would he want to come? Meeting her half-siblings at her wedding seemed a little strange.

She hugged her books closer to her and headed for her locker. Somehow, continuing to finish up her final year and doing her best in her classes made her feel more adult-like. Hardworking, determined, focused. All attributes needed to make it in this crazy world, and even with her sheltered life, Sylvia knew crazy when she saw it.

Just like she recognized that something was weird when she approached the bank of lockers where hers was. Paper stuck out from the crack. A note.

She'd just talked to Luke before her last class, and this didn't seem to be Mom's speed.

Meet us on the Central Building playground before you go home.

Who?

Then her mind called up all sorts of possibilities but dismissed each aside from the persistent one. Lyla and Karen. The Stardust Ball was over. What more did they want?

Was it even safe to meet them? What if they tried something else?

No, the playground that had once belonged to the elementary school until the high school took over the Central Building was out in the open.

But it was far enough away from the Main Building that it could take time for help to get to her.

Should she ask Luke to come along? Then he'd have the answer to the $100,000 question, and she wasn't all that sure he'd remain silent. Not when he was in his protector mode.

She'd just have to brave it.

Her last two classes dragged, making Sylvia reconsider, but each time she did, she ended up with the same conclusion. She needed to meet with the girls alone and get it over with.

Finally, the last bell rang. After gathering her books and things at her locker, Sylvia squared her shoulders and marched down the main staircase, out the door, and across the street to the Central Building playground. The girls were already there. Lyla took one more puff on her cigarette before dropping it to the ground and grinding it with the toe of her penny loafer while she breathed out the white vapor.

Like a dragon set to crush and incinerate her prey.

Sylvia swallowed as her feet slowed. No, she would not show fear. But she did send up a quick prayer as she covered the rest of the distance. "I'm here. What do you want?"

The girls looked at each other, and Lyla shook her head. "You were right, K."

"I knew she'd come." Karen smirked and held out her hand while Lyla slapped a dollar bill in it.

"A bet? That's all it was? I don't have time for this." Sylvia turned to go.

"No. Wait a sec. We just... I mean, you didn't..."

Karen gave Lyla a withering stare before facing Sylvia. "What ditz here is trying to say is we don't get it."

"Get what?"

"Why you haven't told anyone who..."

"Who poured red punch all over me before I was to go on stage in front of the whole school?" Sylvia cocked an eyebrow. They had no trouble committing the act but couldn't even get the words out to say what they'd done?

Lyla nodded and shoved her hands into the pockets of her culottes. "Yeah. That. Why?"

"What was the point?"

"You don't want to get even with us?"

"Do you want me to?" Somehow, questions rolled out of her mouth, and she realized she wanted those answers.

"No. I mean..." Lyla glanced at Karen before continuing. "We're sorry. Even Roxie was ticked that anyone would do that, and she didn't know it was us."

Sorry? That's what this was about? Or were they just trying to make sure Sylvia didn't plan to say anything? "I accept your apology. Thank you." She turned to leave again.

"So, are you going tell Miss Winslow?"

"Is that why you apologized?"

They both stared at the crumbling blacktop and shook their heads.

Sylvia shrugged, but then an idea occurred. Lyla and Karen might not go for it, but if she sold it, they might put an end to this whole mess. "Look. I'm not out to blow this into a bigger deal. But the office wants to know what happened bad enough that they might end up blaming an innocent person." The thought hadn't even occurred to her until that moment. "The only way around this is if you tell Miss Winslow yourself."

"Are you out of your mind?"

"Thought you were supposed to be smart."

Sylvia held up her hands. "Listen. It's gonna sound crazy, but here's the deal. I don't think you want someone else punished, and really, if you are the ones to confess, it will show maturity. They'll probably go a lot easier on you. If they do find out—and I'm not telling anyone, not even my boyfriend—then it would probably mean suspension, and right before the end of your senior year? They might not let you walk at graduation."

The girls peered at each other as if the world around them had changed. Karen finally found her voice. "We never thought of that. But if we do go to the office, they'll call our folks, and that would be the worst scene ever."

"Yeah, mine will go ballistic."

"So, you tell them yourselves. Do it tonight, and then go see Miss Winslow first thing in the morning."

Lyla ground out the already smashed cigarette with her toe. "I've got a dentist appointment in the morning. I can't go tell until I get back."

"Fine. It's only a suggestion. I think it would be the right thing to do. But I really have to go now." She could see Luke watching the Main Building exits, probably keeping an eye out for her. "My ride is waiting." This time, when she moved to leave, they didn't stop her. Maybe she'd given them enough to think about. But the thought that by this time tomorrow the mess could be all over made her want to skip to the senior parking lot.

Luke leaned against the fender when she arrived. Arms crossed over his chest and a small smile spreading when he spotted her. It warmed her cheeks.

His sister sat in the backseat already starting her homework.

Luke straightened and got her door. "Everything cool?"

"Yeah. Just needed to meet with some people. A last-minute thing. But we're good." She climbed in, and he took her to her new address while Harry Chapin sang about his "Taxi."

Tammy was baking in the kitchen. "Hey guys, how was school?"

"Okay."

Grunt.

"Fine."

"Well, that says a lot. Oh, laundry is done, and you'll find your stacks on the dining room table. Please take them to your room. Luke, figure out what to take to Seth's and grab his stuff for him while you're at it, then get back to school for your track practice. Be sure to put it away for him before he figures out the laundry fairy is me."

That made Sylvia giggle.

"Will you be here for dinner?"

"Yeah. I'll just leave the clothes in the car so I won't forget them." He brushed a kiss on Sylvia's cheek, grabbed the stacks of men's apparel, and raced back to his Skylark. No need to make the coach and team wait for him again.

"By the way, Sylvia, I noticed that all your clothes are handmade. Didn't catch that at first because it is so professionally done. Who makes your clothes? Your mom?"

Sylvia swallowed. Hard. "Yeah, she's always made my stuff."

"Well, she does beautiful work."

The memory of her ball gown came back along with the realization that it must have taken hours and hours of patience to embroider all those tiny flowers besides the time to make the gorgeous dress. "You should have seen what I wore to the Stardust Ball. She made it by hand, too. It was the prettiest thing I've ever owned."

"I'm sure it was lovely. Such a shame it was ruined."

Sylvia couldn't agree more.

The rumble of tires on gravel made Seth glance at his watch. He'd been painting the floorboards on his screened-in back porch and lost track of time. No wonder it was getting dim.

Luke charged through from the front but didn't come on out. He knew it was Luke not only from the sound of the motor but the familiar tread—quick step with boot heel clicks on the porch flooring before the front door slammed and carpet muffled his walk. Only his nephew made that entrance. Seth had grown attached to the noises as well as the kid.

Moments later, Luke emerged from the hallway. "Hey Uncle Seth, Mom sent over dinner since you didn't show." He set a brown bag on the table and opened it to reveal filled Tupperware containers.

"Thanks. Guess I got lost in my project." Seth pulled a plate from the cabinet and started to dip up. "Did you eat yet?"

"Yeah. Stayed for dinner so I could spend more time with Sylvia." He paused. "Think we could talk, Uncle Seth?"

Seth dropped to a chair and motioned for his nephew to take the other one while he forked a bite of pork chop. Applesauce and au gratin potatoes rounded out the main course, but he'd noticed a foil-wrapped packet that he hoped contained dessert. "What's on your mind?"

"What isn't? I mean, who knew getting married could be so expensive? We were doing it this summer so we could save money at school but now I don't see how we'll ever pay for just a tiny ceremony. Sylvia is head-over-heels about the Weather Girls' place, and she's not even hoping for something big. Just the main family. But when she saw the balcony off the ballroom and heard that girl, Stormy, describe a sunset ceremony, she set her heart on it. And I want her to be happy. What do I do?"

Seth sighed. "You're not thinking I've got the answer, are you? I can't tell you what to do."

"Oh, no, I get that. It's just... I used to be able to bounce things off my dad. He wouldn't just hand me the answer, but he'd ask a few questions

I hadn't thought of or maybe I'd avoided. Got me thinking until I could figure out the best course."

"I miss your dad. He was a good man. I think he'd be proud of you."

Luke blinked a few times and cleared his throat. "Thanks, I needed to hear that."

Best get back to the subject at hand. "When you say small wedding, who all were you thinking of inviting?"

"You, Mom, Kimmie, Gramma, and dad's brother Uncle Kurt. Sylvie says maybe her mom and grandfather. Says he probably won't come without the old battle ax—"

"Respect." Seth locked gazes with this kid until his manners kicked in.

"Sorry. Just after hearing all the crap she's pulled on people she's supposed to love, I can't find any for her. But for Sylvia and maybe some for Mrs. Avery, I'll watch it."

Seth got it. Boy, did he. But family had strange dynamics, and it wasn't a good idea to fall into bad habits that could come back and hurt you. There was no need to mention how many times he'd wanted to go charging over to Mrs. Lawson and lay it all on her, but he knew deep down, Leenie would never be free until she faced her tyrant of a mother on her own. He was happy to lend support, but this was her battle to fight, win or lose.

"Anyway, that's about it. We're not even sure Mrs. Avery will show."

"She'll show." Seth knew that like he knew his name. "She might not be so happy, but she wouldn't destroy her daughter's big day even if she didn't agree. The one thing you can count on is that Eileen Avery loves her daughter."

"She has a funny way of showing it, keeping her all prisoned-up."

"That's where you're wrong. Leenie was doing the best she could with the only training she had. She was determined to keep Sylvia safe and unharmed. But sometimes adults need to step back and allow the mistakes. That's what's been so hard. She's this way only because she wants what's best for her daughter and because of what she went through."

Luke sighed. "Okay, I guess I can see her side, too."

"Did Sylvia say anything about inviting her dad or his family?"

The kid shook his head. "She never talks about them. But even with that small a group—no groomsmen or bridesmaids or any of that stuff—the price is still up there. I can either save what I have to help us get through our first year of college, or I can blow it on this wedding, and we'll not have anything but our scholarships to get started at Anderson. How do I tell Sylvie that?"

Seth sat quiet while an idea formed. Luke had refused handouts in the past, and he wasn't asking for one now. Just ideas. "I still have a lot of work I'm doing around this place, and frankly, some of it is harder on my back than I figured it would be. As long as you're staying here, why not take on some of it and I'll pay you?"

"Aww, Uncle Seth, I'm already getting a room for free."

"Yeah, but your mom feeds me and does my laundry."

Luke's dark eyebrows shot up in shock. "You knew?"

"Of course. There's no laundry fairy. Did she tell you there was?"

His nephew cracked up. "She said you weren't supposed to know she *was* the laundry fairy."

"Well then, I think we're even with your rent, so I'm happy to pay you to help here when you're not working at the radio station. What do you say?"

They shook on it, and Luke seemed to feel better. They cleared the kitchen and watched some TV. Luke swore that his uncle would dig the *Mod Squad*—it was a little too hip for his taste—and *Kung Fu*, which was better, but had some surreal moments that Luke had to explain. After that, Luke went to bed and left Seth with his thoughts.

The dean of boys, Frank Stucker, had called that afternoon with a proposition. After Luke had finally gotten around to sharing his suspicions that a couple of guys from his track team might have had a clue that something was up because of the way they called him over to get his attention before the incident at the dance, the administration had been looking for a way to put that clue and Seth's background skills to good use. They finally had him cleared to be a supervisor for the boys track and field team. He was to show up at practice tomorrow and see what he could uncover.

It was a long shot, but at this point, without Sylvia talking, that was all they had.

Come morning, Seth reminded Luke that he'd be at the practice. They'd decided it was best not to let the other boys know they were related, as least not right away.

But then that gave Seth time to get another coat of paint on the back porch floor before stopping for a quick bite and grabbing a shower to get ready for his new job.

He found a parking spot in the faculty lot and started the trek for the office. They wanted it all to look official, so he'd need a badge and a whistle.

As he stepped into the office, a young girl, no doubt helping during her free period, smiled. "How can I help you, sir?"

At once, Seth knew he'd seen her before. And he knew where. It was the young lady who'd come out of the restroom about the same time as Sylvia. "I need to speak with Mr. Stucker. And I think you should, too."

Despite her dark skin, she paled, and her eyes grew larger. "Me?"

Seth nodded as the dean of boys came to the reception desk, probably having heard his name.

"Mr. Matthews. Glad you're here. Want to come on back?"

"Yes, and I think this young lady should join us."

"Carma?" Mr. Stucker glanced from the frightened girl to Seth. "Let's go in here." He led them to his office.

Seth hated that the girl seemed so afraid. She'd been alone when she left, and Sylvia had said there were girls, so she was more likely to be a witness.

She sat on the chair where the dean indicated, her gaze roving back and forth between the men.

"Carma? Your name is Carma?" Seth started out gentle. No need to make her panic.

She nodded.

"Well, Carma, I'm Mr. Matthews. I hope I don't frighten you. I promise I'm not an ogre. But I need to get to some facts. And that's all I'm after. Facts. Think you could answer a few questions?"

Carma nodded again while twisting her fingers in her lap.

Mr. Stucker sat at his desk and remained silent, probably ready to jump in if Seth crossed a line.

"I believe I saw you at the Stardust Ball. You were there, right?"

This time she used her voice, though Seth had to strain to hear her. "Yes, sir."

"I believe I noticed you coming out of the girls' restroom about the same time as Sylvia Avery after someone poured punch all over her. Is this true?"

"Yes." She spoke in the softest of whispers now, and a tear rolled down her cheek.

"I have to say I don't think you are the one who did it. I'm right about that?"

"Oh, no sir, I didn't do it. I promise. I tried to help her get cleaned up." That came out clear.

"I had a feeling. But then, you know who did it, right?"

"Sylvia asked me not to say anything to anyone. She said they'd not stopped her, so they wouldn't try it again anyway."

"Did you actually see it happen?"

Carma shook her head. "I came in right after."

Seth rubbed his jaw and caught Mr. Stucker's glance. It would at least give them names.

There was a knock at the door.

Mr. Stucker excused himself to speak with a woman who looked to be a colleague. Then he closed the door. "Carma, thank you for coming in. You can go back."

Seth wanted to stop him. Carma was about to name names, he knew it. But he needed to proceed with caution.

"Have a seat, Matthews. You were doing a swell job, but that was our dean of girls, and the two culprits just turned themselves in. It's over."

It was over.

Seth wilted onto the nearest chair.

Chapter 13

Friday, May 12, 1972

The last bell rang, and Rachel Hess, one of the girls from Eileen's advanced baking class, lingered. "Mrs. Avery, I'm sorry we didn't get everything cleaned like we should. Time went so fast trying to get our mystery cookies finished. But if you want, I can go to the office and call my mom. I'm sure she'd let me stay after as long as she knows where I am."

Eileen started to refuse the offer, but after glancing at the mess her class had left for her, especially since it seemed all of them had done that today and she needed to get the cookies to Miss Winslow and couldn't count on Sylvia to help... "Thank you. I appreciate that. But call your mother so she won't worry."

"Okay, I'll be right back."

Oh, it had been a day. Eileen rubbed her temples. All five of the kitchen stations were a disaster with the students racing for the exit at the bell. Yes, it was her own fault, she knew that. She'd given them too large an assignment for one class period, even though they'd gone over everything yesterday in order to prepare. And she could have held them back until everything was cleaned. Most teachers would have. Something she really should have done. But it was Friday afternoon, and part of her wanted to get out of here as much as they did, if only to just slip off her pumps. Still, the quiet of her classroom gave her time to think.

It was a different quiet than that at home. Home only reminded her that Sylvia was gone. The ever-familiar gut clench at the memory returned, intensifying. Really, had she ever been without it over the last couple of weeks?

Here, her daughter was never in her class as a student, so it wasn't quite the same. Though in the past, Sylvia had helped a lot after school. Eileen missed that.

Great, she was going to make herself cry again.

No. She couldn't do that.

Eileen pressed her finger into the crumbs of the cookies at station two. Um, yummy.

The assignment was to come up with a traditional recipe and make a change with a mystery ingredient. She'd made a list of acceptable ones with a note to avoid peanuts and peanut butter. It never hurt to remind them. The students were to bring the secret ingredient from home and write out their adjusted recipe on an index card they sealed in an envelope. Only the name of the cookie would be presented at the mother and daughter tea. The attendees would complete a survey about what cookies they liked and why. Only then, afterward, would Eileen open the envelopes and give each station team their grade.

It was an assignment the advanced class looked forward to each year. The first year class simply made cookies from the standardized recipes.

But this was a time to shine, be creative. She pressed her finger for a little more before going to station three and doing the same.

So far, the students had come up with good ideas. However, just because the crumbs tasted great didn't mean everything was right. They would also be graded on coloring—underdone, overdone, just right. Size—did they get the right number of cookies from the batch, or were they too big or too small?

The questions made her feel like Goldilocks.

However, she couldn't help but think Miss Winslow would enjoy this year's efforts.

She stopped to box up the cookies from those two stations before continuing. The boxes from earlier stood completed and stacked on her desk. Once she had her last hour students' offerings ready, she'd pull out the rolling cart she kept in the back pantry closet and load it for the trip. Good thing the weather was nice today. She'd be dragging the cart to the gym, a block away on the other side of the Main Building and across the street. She'd bet that the officers of the Girls' League were already at work decorating with streamers and banners going on about mothers and daughters, probably working until late in the evening.

All at once, the pain of Sylvia's absence stabbed her. They'd never missed the tea in all of her daughter's high school career. But this year, when she was a senior and set to be valedictorian, they wouldn't be there. She grabbed for a tissue from her desk. When would she run out of tears?

There was nothing else to do. She had to get this together. So, after wiping her eyes and washing her hands again, she moved on to station four. Their cookies weren't really a mystery. They simply added choco-late chips to the oatmeal cookie recipe. Great taste, but way too easy for what she expected from the assignment. They needed to hope that they hit full credit on the other criteria.

"Mrs. Avery?"

Eileen turned to find Rachel and a younger boy in her doorway.

"My mom needs me to get my brother home right away. But she said I can come back. If it's okay with you, I can bring my little sister along. She's in junior high at Lafayette Park and is in Mrs. Jolly's home ec class there. We don't live far. I can hurry."

Eileen slumped. The help would be nice. The wait would be hard. But it would give her a chance to give the other stations of cookies her first evaluation. "Sure. Thank you, Rachel. I'm going to keep at it, but if you get back quick, I'm sure I'll have things you can do to help. I appreciate your offer."

The girl smiled and waved. The boy followed.

When would this day end? Eileen plopped at her desk. She needed to get so much accomplished, and her brain just didn't want to think. She started a list of everything she had to get done, then looked at the clock and realized she was running out of time.

Sort of like her life. She'd run out of time to tell Sylvia her story, and now her daughter didn't believe her, wanted nothing to do with her.

If she wanted this one place where things were still semi-normal to remain so, she'd better get moving.

Where had she left off? Oh, yes, stations five and one. She headed in that direction.

Sylvia packed up her things as the last bell of the day rang.

She still could not believe what she'd seen. Mrs. Chapel had sent her to the office to drop off a note, and she arrived in time to see Mr. Stucker and Luke's uncle call Carma into a room and close the door. The fear on the girl's face was hard to miss. And no one would let her tell the men they had the wrong girl. Miss Winslow was busy, and Mr. Stucker was not to be disturbed. The secretary told her she could come back later.

Sure. That would work. Right.

Who had pointed out Carma?

She knew this had to be regarding the ball incident. There was no other reason for Mr. Matthews to be involved. On the ride to school, Luke had mentioned that his uncle was going to be digging with the administration to get to the bottom of things. Which made Sylvia glad she'd spoken with Lyla and Karen and that they'd agreed to talk with Miss Winslow. If they kept their word, that is. She sent up a prayer that they did.

Sylvia took a moment to run past the office and glanced in to see if Carma might still be working, but she didn't spot her.

Luke would be waiting, but the anger building at the unfairness of it all demanded she go face the one person responsible for having something to do with Carma getting blamed. And she knew, *she knew,* that's what happened.

A little voice said to wait. Get all the facts.

But it was too late for that. The one person who helped her, who gave her the courage to not let mean girls stop her, was now facing disciplinary action. It was so totally unfair.

Would Carma keep her mouth shut? What if she got scared and named Lyla and Karen to keep from getting into trouble herself?

It wasn't as if Carma and Sylvia were best friends. They'd hardly spoken since that night. That realization slowed her steps.

However it went down, her mother had to be at the root. If the woman couldn't bug her on a daily basis, she'd find ways to delve into what was none of her business. Why couldn't Mom just trust her to handle this? It wasn't as if it had happened to someone else.

Better to get this over with. Show Mom the problem she caused.

She charged down the steps of Old Main and across the walkway to the Vocational Building, through the doors and down the hall. There was no hiding. She was on a mission, and it was best to stay out of her way.

Jim Hect rounded a corner. "Hey Sylvia, how did you do on—"

"No time, Jim. Later." She kept going, stopping only when she got to her mother's room. Grabbing the door handle, she huffed out a breath and yanked it open. "Where do you get off telling the office about Carma?"

Mom glanced up, her finger stopping in front of her face. She'd been crumb tasting again. "What do you mean? Who's Carma?"

"Don't play dumb, *Mother*." Maybe that would let Mom know who she was behaving like. "You have her sister in class. She was the one who helped me at the ball. She *helped* me. She didn't dump the punch on me. But you couldn't leave things alone and let me manage it. Didn't trust me, right? I'm not smart enough or capable enough? You have kept me wrapped up like some prize on a shelf and haven't let me live my life. But now this? Did you think for one second you might be wrong? What happens when the office calls her parents? Did you think of that?"

"Sylvie, I swear—"

"Don't want to hear it, Mother."

Mom bit her finger as tears welled in her eyes and her face reddened. Good, she felt bad.

No, Sylvia would not let emotions sway her from what was right. Making Mom understand what she did. That was right.

"I didn't talk to anyone, Sylvie. I didn't even kno..." She got a funny look on her face. "Sylvie." Mom's voice grew husky, and she tried clearing it. "Um, something's wrong."

"You bet it is. I had planned to come see you after school anyway. I thought maybe, just maybe, you'd want to make my wedding dress. Tammy and I talked about the beautiful work you did sewing my clothes, and I stupidly thought this might be something to help us heal. But no.

You had to stick your big, fat nose into it, and now you have the audacity to lie about it to my face."

Her mother sagged at the counter top.

"Don't go getting all dramatic on me, Mother. I'm done." Sylvia stormed out. She needed to get to Luke as fast as she could. Besides the fact he was probably waiting for her, he was the only one who could understand, talk her down.

Just as she hit the breaker bar on the door leading outside, she spotted Seth heading toward the building. She shoved hard and stomped his way. "And don't you try to weasel out as well. I don't want to talk to either of you."

Barely registering the look of shock on his face, she marched past and practically ran the rest of the way to the senior lot. Much like yesterday, Luke leaned against his bumper, waiting.

"I'm sorry I'm late again. Do you have practice or the radio station today?"

He shook his head. "Nope, practice was canceled, so I was hoping we could spend some time together."

That was the best news she'd heard all day.

Luke held her door for her.

Kimmie was stretched out on the backseat, her nose in *Eleanor* by Joseph P. Lash. It was a book Sylvia hoped to borrow once the girl was done. That is until her brain got filled with all this betrayal by her mom.

She climbed in and closed her eyes, slowing her breathing until she felt more calm.

God bless Luke. He didn't try to get her to talk. It was like he understood and respected her right to herself.

After they pulled in at his house, she stepped out long enough to flip the seat forward to let Kimmie exit. Then she returned to the car and faced Luke. "I cannot believe my mother."

"What'd she do, babe?"

"I'm not sure exactly, but I'd bet anything she's at the source. The one person who helped me at the Stardust Ball got pulled into the office. She's the only other person who knew the names of the girls. And your uncle was there. He was in on it. I'm so angry I could spit. This girl helps me, and she's getting blamed."

He cocked his head. "Are you sure about that?"

"I was at the office when they dragged her back there."

"That's weird. Uncle Seth said it was all over because the girls who did it confessed to Miss Winslow."

Sylvia stared. What did he say? "You mean...?"

He shrugged. "All I know is that he didn't need to go to my practice today, and the coach had already made plans. Uncle Seth was supposed to be in charge for the day. So they canceled our track practice. When I asked him about it, he said two girls went to Miss Winslow's office and told her they were the ones who poured punch on you."

"Then why did Carma get called into Mr. Stucker's office with your uncle?"

"No clue, babe."

Sylvia stared at him until her thoughts fell into a semblance of order. "Oh, I have a bad feeling."

"What?"

"I said some awful things to my mom. Maybe she wasn't lying to me. Oh, Luke, what did I do? Can you take me back? Maybe I can get there before she leaves."

"Sure, babe." He pushed the gearstick into reverse and backed out of the drive.

Sylvia's head swam. She'd been so cruel. What could she say now? Mom would never forgive her.

And she'd be right for not doing it.

Seth stared after Sylvia. What did she mean? Hadn't anyone told her yet that it was all over?

Probably not. There hadn't been all that much time. Besides, he was here to let Leenie know, so there was no way Sylvia could've gotten the information from her mother.

He huffed and shook his head. Teen-aged girls were a rare breed. Women were hard enough to fathom, but when they were in their pre-adult years, there was no understanding them.

Seth continued down the hall, following the room numbers to the one the secretary had given him. Leenie would be happy to learn at least this mystery was solved. Maybe it would help with healing the ruptured relationship between her and Sylvia. He could only hope. But based on what he witnessed as he approached the building, he had a few doubts. Something had thrown a monkey wrench into the mix.

He opened the door.

The room looked empty at first.

"Leenie? It's Seth. You here?" Then he noticed a black shoe sticking out on the floor between a pair of counters. Everything in his background kicked in, putting him on instant alert as he rushed forward.

She sat on the linoleum, her back propped against a set of low cabinets. And she was gasping. Her face was flushed and swollen around her mouth.

"Leenie." He grabbed her hand, and her eyes flew open.

"Pea. Nut. Can't. Breathe. Dizzy." She blinked between each word, her voice a hoarse whisper.

"I'll help you." Seth steadied himself before scooping her into his arms.

Just then, the classroom door pulled open, and two girls popped in. "What's wrong with Mrs. Avery?"

Seth had no time for questions. "Where's the nearest phone?"

The older one nodded. "The front of the building."

He pointed to her. "You, go there. Dial the operator and tell them to send help to this building for a peanut allergy reaction." Then he addressed the younger girl. "You stay with me. Open the doors. Let's go."

Both girls charged ahead, but only one took off at a run. The other held the door while he maneuvered Leenie through.

"Which way did your friend go?"

She nodded. "My sister went this way."

They headed down the hall that he'd just traveled. He couldn't remember seeing an office in this building, but as they rounded the corner, he noticed the school bookstore. Yeah, they'd have a phone. Good thinking, kid.

Just as they got inside, the older girl faced him, the receiver in her hand. "They're on their way."

Should he take her outside? Meet them to save steps? Seth leaned against the counter to adjust his hold. "Hang on, Leenie. We're getting you help. Keep fighting."

He wasn't sure, but he thought she nodded.

Seconds later, he heard the sirens. That made up his mind, and he headed for the exit.

Students and a few adults gathered, the group growing larger as the ambulance pulled onto the grass.

Mumbles of "what's going on" stirred around him as he headed toward the vehicle.

Two men hopped out from the front seat while a third climbed from the tail. He wore a white lab coat and raced Seth's way while the first two pulled a gurney from the ambulance's back end.

"I'm Dr. Marney. How sure are you it's a peanut allergy reaction? That's pretty rare."

"I've known her a long time, I know she is allergic, and she told me when I found her. Help her, she's having trouble breathing."

The guys with the gurney pulled up then.

Seth laid her on it, and the doctor kneeled next to her. Moments later, he took a syringe from his bag, added some medication, and gave Leenie a shot in her upper arm. "If you're right, she should quickly get some relief. Let's put her into the ambulance. I want to do a thorough exam just in case."

The gurney guys carried her to the back of the ambulance and slid her in.

"What hospital are you going to?" Seth knew he'd need to drive there himself. There wasn't room to ride with Leenie, and he shouldn't be in the way.

Dr. Marney turned back to answer. "St. Joe's. We'll meet you at the E R."

Then the men closed the doors and climbed in the front. Sirens blaring, they took off toward the hospital.

Seth turned to head for his car when someone grabbed his arm.

"What's going on, Matthews?" Mr. Stucker gave him the look that he knew had made boys quake when needed.

"Mrs. Avery somehow ingested something with peanuts. She has an allergy to them. I found her in time. Just hoping that was the real problem because the doctor wasn't sure."

"There was a doctor?"

"Yeah, I didn't question it, but now that you mention it, that's a little strange. I'm headed to the hospital now. If you'll excuse me, I'll keep you informed as I learn anything."

Mr. Stucker patted his shoulder. "Thanks. Go."

He needed no more incentive, just people to keep out of his way.

Seth raced to his car, probably moving a lot faster than his medical team would want. But he had to get to Leenie.

At the hospital, he grabbed the first parking spot he found and raced for the emergency room doors. His back and legs were growing stiff, but he kept going.

A nurse and a guy in scrubs stood behind a desk.

"I'm here for Eileen Avery. An ambulance just brought her in."

"Yes sir, we were informed you were coming. They're getting her hooked up right now. Let me see if they are ready for you to go back." The nurse placed a call while Seth paced. Four steps left, pivot, four steps right, repeat.

"Sir?"

"Yes?"

"Are you family?"

The question froze him. Did he lie? Did he flash his badge? "No, not yet." But maybe if she'd have him. "I'm the one who found her. Please."

The nurse spoke into the phone again, smiled, and hung up. "I'll take you back to her. Come with me."

Thank You, God. Seth hadn't realized he'd been holding his breath. But he followed the nurse to a cubical with a curtain.

She pulled it aside and let him go in.

Leenie lay on a bed, wan-looking but breathing. The swelling had decreased from her face.

He couldn't help himself and reached out to trace her still slightly puffy cheek.

Her eyes popped open at his touch, her hand moved his to her lips where she kissed his fingers. "Thank you, Seth. I thought I was going to die."

He leaned in. It wasn't the place for anything passionate, but he needed to taste those lips once more. He'd almost lost the opportunity, and he would not take any more chances.

She didn't pull away. Instead, she wove her fingers through his hair and returned his kiss, making him realize he had been a dead man walking until this moment. Leenie flipped a switch inside him, sending electrical current to parts of him he'd forgotten existed.

Someone cleared their throat. "Sorry to interrupt."

Seth pulled away, but Leenie captured his hand and held on.

Dr. Marney held a clipboard. "Mrs. Avery, your response to the antihistamine solution was exactly what I hoped for. You were having an allergic reaction to peanut. Good thing your friend was there to let us k now."

She looked up at Seth. "You're right. He's a godsend."

Seth's neck got warm. "I'm only glad I showed up when I did. So, doc, how long does she need to stay?"

"I'd like to keep her overnight for observation. They should have a room ready for her in a few minutes. But I think we're through the worst of things."

That's when Seth recalled the question. "Dr. Marney, how did you happen to be with the ambulance?"

The doc gave a half grin. "All interns are required to do ride-alongs once a month as part of their rotation in the ER. There isn't always a doctor on call, but today you got lucky."

"Today God was looking out for Leenie." Seth had no doubt about it.

Chapter 14

Breathing had never felt so good. Eileen drew in another lung-full of air, noting the scent of Seth's aftershave. Old Spice. Just like back in the day.

She should probably let him sit rather than holding tight to his hand. But ever since the doctor stepped away, she'd hoped for another kiss. The last one ended too quickly.

Instead, a nurse popped in with a guy in scrubs. "Time to move you to your room. Do you have everything?"

Eileen glanced at Seth. He was all she had here. But somehow that was more than enough. "We're good."

"Okay, then, sir, you can follow us. Roger here will wheel the bed to the room."

As if following instructions, the guy in scrubs kicked at the brakes on her bed while the nurse managed the IV pole.

Seth took her hand again once they were through the doorway until they reached room 241. He couldn't get through the door frame with her, so he let go and waited in the hall until they had her situated.

He paced, and every so often he stopped to shake his leg like it had gone to sleep. She must have been pretty heavy for him to carry all that way, but he never complained. Better to keep an eye on him.

"You can come in now, sir." The nurse put the buzzer to the floor station by Eileen's hand. "Please press this if you need anything. For now, you have the room to yourself since we aren't busy, but you might have a roommate before long." Looked like she addressed that piece of information to Seth. Was that her way of mentioning a lack of privacy? "I'll be back in a bit to make sure you're comfortable." Then she left.

Seth used the opportunity to come back to her. She never knew she could miss someone so quickly but having him close proved she didn't want to be without him ever again.

Transport guy Roger followed the nurse. What was her name?

Who cared? Didn't matter, everyone was gone. Finally, she and Seth were alone again.

"Pull that chair closer so you don't have to bend over me. I want you near, but no need to make you uncomfortable." She flashed him a smile that she hoped told him she wouldn't mind more of his kisses.

He got the message and leaned over to touch her lips and curl her toes in a happy way before breaking it off to draw the chair next to her bed rails. "We ought to talk, Leenie."

"I like doing what we've been doing. Talking is overrated." But something in his eyes told her there were important words to be discussed.

He flashed a lopsided grin. "Me too. But I was coming to tell you something good when I found you."

"Something good? I could use some good news." Images of Sylvia's face as she stormed out played through her brain. "I need to find out what happened in the office. Sylvia was so upset. She said the girl who helped her at the ball was pulled in for questions."

Seth nodded. "I know. That was my fault. I recognized her when I stopped by to see the dean. But while we were talking, the girls who poured the punch on Sylvia confessed. It's all over now. And it wasn't race related."

"You thought it was?" Where did he get that idea?

"I wasn't sure. The girl I saw, Carma, is black. I just didn't know and wondered if Sylvia was keeping quiet so there wouldn't be more riots." He leaned back in his chair, weariness radiating from his face. "I was wrong about that."

"Seth, the instigators last semester were primarily outsiders. Mr. Moore, our principal, and the committees he put together to investigate and come up with plans to keep things from happening again have done their job. We've had a much more peaceful end of the school year. That is except for my home life. Which is another story."

He enveloped her hand. "It's going to work out. I have a feeling once Sylvia has all the facts, it'll get better."

As if on cue, Sylvia and Luke stood in the doorway. "Mom?"

Eileen's eyes blurred with moisture. "Sylvia, come in."

Her baby girl rushed to her side. "Oh, Mom, I am so sorry I said all those things. And I didn't realize what was happening to you. You could've died, and it would've been all my fault." Sylvia clung to her, sobbing.

Relief and gratitude flooded Eileen as she ran her fingers along Sylvia's silky hair, moving it away from her daughter's face. "It's okay, Sylvie. It's okay. I'm fine. God was looking out for me." She glanced at Seth with a shaky smile while continuing to comfort her daughter.

It took a few minutes, but Sylvia finally raised up. "I'm so sorry, Mom."

"I know. I forgive you, sweetie. We're good. Maybe now we can work through the rest of the garbage I let build between us." Staring death in the face had given Eileen a chance to rethink some things. "If you and Luke want to get married this summer, I won't stop you. And I'd be honored to make your wedding dress."

Sylvia gasped and hugged her. "Thank you, Mom! Thank you!" She pulled away again and wiped her hands over her face before glancing at Seth and then Luke. "I must look a fright." After scanning the room, her gaze landed on the restroom door. "I'll be right back." Sylvia slipped out.

"Luke, I'm sure Sylvia could use a moment. Why don't you take her to the cafeteria and get her a Coke?" Seth held up a dollar bill, and his wink was hard to miss.

So was Luke's grin. "Will do."

When Sylvia reemerged, her face was less mottled, and her mascara-streaked eyes cleaned.

"C'mon, babe, we're going to get something to drink. Can we bring you back anything, Uncle Seth? Mrs. Avery?"

Eileen shook her head, as did Seth, and the two young ones left.

The silence was comfortable. For the first time in her life, Eileen enjoyed just listening to the quiet and holding on to Seth's hand. She closed her eyes, letting the peace blanket her.

"What is going on? Why are you in my daughter's room? Get out now!"

Mother. And shattered silence. All rolled into one explosion.

Eileen opened her eyes. "Stay put, Seth." She squeezed his hand. "What are you doing here, Mother, and how did you know where to find me?"

"The school office called. I am your emergency contact, you know."

She'd fix that as soon as she got out of here. Eileen glanced to see the furrowed brow of her father's worried expression over her mother's shoulder. "Hi, Father. I'm okay."

He gave her a small smile but remained out of the way.

"Never mind your father. Why is that man here? I gave you strict instructions to have no contact with him."

Blood rushed to Eileen's head in a hot flood, making her temples pound. The sheer audacity of the woman. Especially after Eileen had learned all the inexcusable manipulations she had pulled to destroy any happiness that might have been. "You have no right. Not after all you did. I know about Doug. I know how you paid him and sent him away. I know he's alive and remarried to someone else and that you tricked me into believing he was dead. I know about the letter you sent to Seth to separate us. Every chance I had at a loving future, you tried to covertly destroy. If anyone is leaving, Mother, it is you."

After the initial look of shock, her mother narrowed her eyes. "You leave me no choice, Eileen. I will have to make good on my promise."

"What promise is that, Mother? To try and convince Sylvia that she is illegitimate? She already knows about her father. She knows everything. You've lost us both. Now get out." Her voice shook as she pointed to the door, but the freedom of standing up to her mother while Seth pressed courage into her hand made her breathing even easier, as if her lungs had expanded to twice their size.

Mother's face reddened. "Let's go, Carson." She turned for the door.

"Ethel. How could you?" Her father's voice was edgier than she'd ever heard.

"I did what needed to be done. Now let's go."

"No."

"What do you mean?"

"It's a simple word, Ethel. I am refusing to do as you say. You told me you knew more about how to raise a child than I did, that since I'd missed such formative years while in the war that you needed a free hand. Well, I allowed it. I'm truly sorry about that, Eileen." His glance her way showed tears brimming in his eyes. Then he straightened. "But no more. You've been proven wrong here today. So if my daughter doesn't mind, I'd like to stay with her a while. Just to make sure she's okay."

"I'd like that, Dad."

He smiled while a tear slipped free, and he brushed it away. "You may take the car, Ethel. I'll get a cab when I'm ready to leave."

Mother's eyes grew enormous, and Eileen feared she might have a heart attack on the spot. Instead, she ramrodded her back and marched from the room with only a *humph* floating back over her shoulder.

Dad came close, squeezing her other hand before locating the guest chair for her nonexistent roommate and pulling it up across from Seth. "Thank you for letting me stay."

"I'm glad you want to, Dad."

Seth cleared his throat. "Actually, Mr. Lawson, I am too. I wonder if you could do me a favor?"

"Of course, if I can."

After releasing her hand, Seth patted it and grasped the arms of his chair. "I think I need a little help trying to stand. You see, I can't feel my legs."

Eileen gasped. He'd done too much to help her and it had cost him. "Dad, go get the nurse. Quick! Seth, why didn't you say something sooner?"

Her father raced from the room, returning with a nurse in tow.

"Sir, you can't move your legs?"

Seth shook his head. "I have a spine injury and was told this could be a possibility one day. Guess that one day arrived." His face went gray at his words.

The nurse pulled a cord, and a team raced into the room within seconds. Once they realized the patient wasn't Eileen, they transferred Seth to a wheelchair and sped down the hall.

"Dad, please follow them and let me know what is happening."

Her father leaned over and kissed her forehead. "I will." Then he was out the door.

Along with the joy of the good things this day had brought.

Sylvia drew the last of her Coke through her straw.

"You know something I like about you?"

She glanced at Luke, figuring he was trying to help her feel better about how awful she'd been to her mom. Even if her mother forgave her, she wasn't sure she could forgive herself. "No, what?"

"When you say you want a Coke, you don't mean just any cola or soft drink, you mean exactly what you say. A Coke."

"I never thought of that. I guess if I want a Sprite or a Pepsi, then I ask for that drink."

"That's what I mean. You are clear and know your own mind."

But did she? Ever since she learned what happened from Miss Winslow, she'd second-guessed every decision she made. How could she have been so stupid? The one thing she always knew, no matter what, was that her mother loved her.

Yet she'd treated her mother as if she were her grandmother. They were nothing alike. And on top of it, Grandmother had actually done the things she'd been accused of, but Mom didn't. Her mother had told the truth. Even though it had hurt her—and Sylvia knew it had when she recalled the look on Mom's face in the home ec room—Mom had done the best she could.

Too bad Sylvia couldn't say the same about herself.

No, she'd jumped to conclusions. What if she was doing the same thing when it came to marrying Luke? What if she was running headlong into something her mother was trying to protect her from?

Because, as Sylvia now realized, her mother actually knew something about getting married young.

"Luke, I want to go back and talk to Mom."

"I think Uncle Seth was hoping for some alone-time with her." He smiled. "Just think, when we hatched this plan to give her a love life to keep her busy and out of ours, there was no way we could guess something like this would happen. It's like Romeo and Juliet getting back together after a couple decades. That is, if they hadn't offed themselves first."

Sylvia giggled. "You're right. My mom and your uncle. Who would've figured? How long should we give them?"

He glanced at his watch. "Maybe another half hour?"

She nodded. But then she spotted someone coming into the cafeteria, glancing about. "There's my grandfather. Wonder what... Oh, no. Do you think Grandmother went up to Mom's room?"

Grampa saw her then and came to their table. "Sylvie, I'm sorry, I have some bad news."

"It's Mom. What happened?"

He shook his head and turned to Luke. "You're Seth's nephew?"

Luke nodded.

"Your uncle hurt his back. They've taken him to emergency and are running tests. Eileen thought you should know and could call your mother. I need to get back. I'm sort of the go between for Seth and Eileen. If you wait in your mom's room, Sylvie, I'll get word to you all there."

Grampa left.

Luke's face lost color. "I've gotta call Mom. Where's a phone?"

She spied a bank of pay phones on the wall across the way. "There. Oh, Luke, I'll start praying now."

He nodded and headed for them while digging change from his pocket.

Sylvia bowed her head. She was still praying when he came back to her.

"Told Mom to meet us in your mom's room. Let's go." He gathered their paper cups and dumped them in the trash before capturing her hand.

There was a difference in the way he held it. More like he needed her strength than giving her his. Could he feel how much she loved him and feel her prayers for his uncle?

Mom had her face turned away from the door as they entered. She ran her palms over her eyes before greeting them. "I'm glad Dad found you. Were you able to contact your mother, Luke?"

"Yeah, she's on her way. Told her to meet us here, so we'd all be together." He released Sylvia's hand and paced.

That's when she realized what was really bothering him. It had only been a year since they had rushed his father into emergency surgery. And he didn't live through it. This had to feel like déjà vu.

"He's going to be okay, Luke. Right, Mom?" Sylvia glanced at her mom for reinforcement.

"Yes." Mom wiped her face with her sheet and didn't meet Sylvia's gaze.

She didn't believe he'd be all right, either.

The thought burst in Sylvia's brain, causing doubt to run amok. What would this mean for Luke's family? For Mom? How could God let this happen when Mom and Seth had finally found each other and learned the truth?

He works all things together for those who love the Lord and are called according to His purpose.

All things. Not some things.

But what if Seth died? Or was bedfast? Or... The awful scenarios bombarded.

All things.

That still small voice remained firm. She just needed to focus on it.

"Mom, Luke, it will be all right. God has this."

Tammy stepped through the doorway. "Any news?"

Mom shook her head. "No. My father is with him and comes to tell me when he learns something. Right now, all they know is he can't wiggle his toes or move his legs. He has no feeling from his hips down."

"What happened? Did he fall?" Almost as an afterthought, Tammy stared at Mom. "Why are you in the hospital?"

Mom glanced at Sylvia, and she feared her horrible behavior would come out.

"I had an allergic reaction. Seth found me and got me help. But I think I'm the reason for his problem. You know how he isn't supposed to lift heavy things, but he hoisted me from the floor and carried me from my classroom to the ambulance. I felt him adjusting me while he held on and then saw him acting like his leg went to sleep when we got to this room." Mom took in a ragged breath. "If he can't walk anymore..."

"Don't go there. We don't know if this is permanent or temporary. Besides, what was he to do? Let you die? You know not one person could've made him not carry you. He has to be the big protector." The last statement sounded almost bitter.

Grampa entered, looking a little winded. "They are prepping Seth for spinal surgery."

Tammy's eyes grew wide. "He told me his injury was inoperable."

"The situation has forced them to try. They need to get the pressure off his spine. I was told it could be several hours before they know anything."

"I guess we should go to the surgical waiting room then, Mom." Luke held out his hand to Tammy.

Mom looked like she had an idea. "I just remembered something. If it's going to be several hours anyway. Luke, would you take Sylvia to my classroom and make sure all the cookies are boxed and delivered to the gym? My room should still be open. I'll call Miss Winslow from here to let her know. I have most of them ready. And Sylvie, you know how I work that survey. Think you can get that set up? It will give you something to do while you wait, and Tammy can stay here. We'll keep each other company. Dad, maybe someone at the nurse's station can let the surgical waiting room receptionist know where she is, and they can call up here if there's any word."

Sylvia kissed her Mom's forehead. "Good plan, Mom." She knew it would give Luke something to keep his mind off his fear. "We'll get it all done and be back in a while."

Mom was picking up her room phone and asking the operator to put her through to Miss Winslow's office as they walked out the door.

Luke groped for her hand, and she knew he needed her.

"It's going to be all right, Luke."

"You don't know that."

But somehow, she did.

237

Noises. Low voices. Curtains sliding on metal rods.

Slowly Seth became aware of his surroundings, at least auditorily. It was too much effort to open his eyes.

"He's coming around." A woman's whisper.

Drat. What did he do that caught their attention? All he wanted to do was sleep.

"Mr. Matthews. Seth. Can you open your eyes?" This voice was male and all business.

As Seth obeyed, light burned at his retinas, and he squinted, hoping that was enough.

"Bright." His voice sounded foreign, raspy, and he realize his mouth was a barren desert. "Water."

Someone touched his shoulder and put a straw to his lips. He sucked the liquid, pure heaven.

"Easy. Just enough to get you going. Thanks, nurse." Sounded like a doctor-in-charge voice. Too bad Seth couldn't place it.

The straw moved out of reach, and Seth could now open his eyes more fully, focusing in on the man in the white coat at the foot of his bed.

"Doctor?"

"I'm Dr. Stevens. I have to tell you, Someone up there must love you a lot."

Seth tried to move and winced. "Why's that?"

"I just came back from training on a new procedure for spinal injuries. Two months ago, I couldn't have done this surgery. I know you probably think that means you were my guinea pig, but I did extensive training at Johns Hopkins, where I assisted with over a dozen surgeries—all successful, I might add. I only returned last weekend. So, though you were my first of this type here in Kokomo, I was definitely familiar."

He might still walk?

"You have questions. I can see them in your face. Let me cover a few things, and if I don't answer something, ask. First, there is no way to know the full results of the surgery until the swelling goes down. From the look of things, it should be positive. I was able to get the fragments out. Nasty little things. So, if everything goes as we hope, you won't be in danger of them causing more problems."

Dr. Stevens glanced at his clipboard. "You want to know how long, too, right?"

Seth nodded.

"First, swelling takes time to leave. Then your nerves will need to start communicating. I'll be recommending physical therapy no matter the outcome. But I think we can kick you out of here in a week. A back brace while you learn to get around again. The exact time frame for your healing, though, has a lot of variants. It will depend on how your body

responds, how well you heed my advice, and how much you want to get w
ell."

"I will get well. That is a given, Doc."

The doctor sighed. "You say that, but I've seen patients who hold back
once they face the work required."

"You have nothing to fear with me."

"Good. Then I'm out of here. They'll be taking you to your room in
a few minutes. Meanwhile, I'll head upstairs to a certain person's room.
I understand she is hosting your family and they are all waiting to hear
about you."

Seth couldn't hold back the smile at the thought of Leenie with his
family. "Tell them... Tell her I love her."

Dr. Stevens chuckled. "I think she'd rather hear that from you." He
winked and pulled the curtain away as he left.

A nurse replaced him. "Your room is ready now, so we're going to
wheel you on up. Let me give you something just in case the moving
bothers your back." She pulled out a hypodermic needle and pushed
something into his IV.

The next thing he knew, he was floating.

"We're here, Mr. Matthews." They didn't try moving him to a new
bed in the room, just substituted the one he was on. Maybe he wasn't
supposed to move. That was fine because sleep sounded like a lovely idea.

When he opened his eyes again, his room had grown dark, but he could
tell someone was in there with him. Did he have a roommate?

He tried to get his bearings. The TV was off, no light came in the window, but the fluorescents spilled just enough illumination in from the hall to notice the form sitting in the chair next to him.

"Sissy."

She raised her head. "Oh, Seth. How are you feeling?"

"Groggy. Thirsty."

She jumped up and grabbed a cup with a straw. "Here." She got the straw to his lips. "By the way, they said you can eat if you are hungry, but you must lay flat, so it's only soft foods, and I get to feed you. They want you flat at least through tomorrow. Then they'll raise the head of your bed a little."

He grunted. If following doctor's orders meant getting better fast, he'd be the most obedient patient that man had ever seen. "How's Leenie?"

"She's good. Better since you got out of surgery and Dr. Stevens came to talk with us. She's been upset, believing she caused this." Tammy sat the cup back on his nightstand.

"No. What is she thinking? I couldn't let her just die. And she would've. By the time I got her outside, she was almost unconscious from it being hard to breathe. I would have done anything to save her. You tell her that."

"Tell her yourself." Sissy stood and pointed toward the doorway. Luke pushed Leenie in a wheelchair while Sylvia followed.

"Lucky for us, we're on the same floor, just a few rooms apart, so I could convince them to let me come here." Leenie motioned for Luke to stop and took over wheeling herself to his bedside. "We make a pair, don't we?"

He chuckled. "I guess we do."

Leenie brushed hair from his forehead, her touch waking him up completely. And causing thoughts that he should have considered before this to break through all the others. "Tammy, kids, could I speak with Leenie alone, please?"

"Sure." Tammy gave him a knowing grin. "We'll go take a walk."

"Right. I'll be back to wheel you to your room, Mrs. Avery." Luke smiled at them, but Leenie didn't turn toward the kids.

Instead, she zeroed her focus on him and traced his cheek with her fingertips. It probably felt like sandpaper. "Trying to imagine you with a beard."

"Why would you do that?"

She shrugged and kissed him.

Oh, those kisses.

No, he had to do this, say this. Before it went any farther. "Leenie." He captured her hands in his. "I need you to hear me." His heart raced as he prepared his words. "The doctor gave no guarantee. Even though he is optimistic, it's not a sure thing."

"You will be fine. I believe it, Seth. Don't worry."

He shook his head. How did he explain that he'd decided years ago about the worst-case scenarios? "I hope for that. But I have to be realistic. If it all works out, by God's grace, then I want us to begin planning our future. But if it doesn't, promise me you will go on. I can't have you hanging up your life because I can't walk—" he swallowed hard, "—or be a husband to you."

She pulled away. "Seth, what are you saying?"

"I'm saying I won't saddle you with a life where you have to take care of me, and I can't even give you a wedding night."

"What about for better or worse, in sickness and in health?"

"We're not married yet. You could still escape."

She stared at him. "Do you love me?"

"Leenie."

"I'm asking a simple question. Yes or no. Do you love me, Seth Matthews?"

"Yes. But it's not that simple. Because I love you, I can't do this to you."

He could see she wanted to stand over him, maybe even shake him. Instead, she white-knuckled the arms of the wheelchair and dropped her voice to just above a whisper. "Our life together was stolen from us once. I won't let anyone, not even you, take it from me again. I love you. I want to marry you. And I will do whatever it takes to make that happen. So you had better plan on getting better, bud. But if you don't, you still won't be able to get rid of me. So there. You think about that for a while."

Then she stood, placed her hands on either side of his face, and kissed him until he felt it in his toes before she plopped back into her chair and wheeled herself out of his room.

Oh, yeah. He'd definitely be thinking about that for a long while.

Chapter 15

Saturday, May 13, 1972

"Your chariot awaits."

Eileen glanced at the door to her hospital room to see Roger, the orderly, entering with a wheelchair. Nurse Sarah followed with her clipboard of paperwork.

"How are you getting home?" Sarah never raised her eyes but read off the question.

Luke and Sylvia grinned at each other, waiting for Eileen to make their idea of driving her home a reality.

She nodded at them. "They'll take me." It was the only way since Sylvia didn't know how and Seth wasn't in a position to do it. After what happened with her mother, she would never ask such a favor of that woman. Her father would have done it, but that would require calling her parents' house, and if her mother answered, well, it wouldn't be pretty.

"Okay, all you need to do is sign here, and Roger will wheel you out." Nurse Sarah turned to the kids. "You run ahead and bring the car to the front entrance. We'll meet you out there."

The kids rose from their chairs, Sylvie stopping to kiss Eileen's forehead before they took off out the door.

Since she'd only arrived with the clothes on her back, she'd expected to go home that way. But Sylvia had been thoughtful. She rescued Eileen's purse from her classroom and stopped by the apartment to get clean clothes and necessities. After her morning shower, Eileen felt more human. At least on the outside. Her daughter had brought a skirt and blouse more suitable for church than going back to the apartment. But she had to admit she'd rather not be wearing her normal Saturday clothes after this adventure and was grateful to Sylvia.

Inside, she was still worried about Seth. She hoped she'd gotten through to him, but who knew? And then there was the mental battle of whether she should come right back to sit in his room. That's what she wanted to do. But would it help him see her point or push him farther away?

Luke's yellow Skylark sat parked with its motor running. Both kids hopped out to help her into the front bucket seat.

She waved goodbye to Roger and Sarah and turned around to see Luke climbing into the backseat while Sylvia slid behind the wheel. "What's going on?"

"I have my learner's permit, Mom. Luke's been teaching me to drive. Since you're a licensed driver, we're going to drop him off at his house, and then you and I are going to attend the mother/daughter tea. Unless you aren't up for it." Sylvia peeked her way a second before signaling and pulling safely from the curb.

Eileen's nerves called for a vote to riot, but her heart knew this was special for her daughter and vetoed the rise of panic. Sort of. "Okay. So that's why you brought my good clothes. But what about my hair?"

"You look fine, and everyone will be glad to see you attending. I rescheduled your hair appointment for next week, anyway. I knew you wouldn't get out of that place in time to go."

Her daughter had taken charge and was doing a fine job. Pride and loss mixed to make the realization bittersweet. "Thank you. You've thought of everything."

"I tried. After the tea, I'll take you home. You can rest before you come over to Tammy's for dinner and then go see Seth during evening visiting hours. He should be wanting to spend some time with you after missing you all day. Tammy is going earlier to let him in on the plan so he won't panic." Sylvia turned into a driveway and braked, popping the gear into park like a pro and hopping out to allow Luke to exit. "You're sure you're okay with me taking your car, babe?"

"Yeah, no worries, baby. You can drive my car. Go, have a good time with your mom." He kissed her cheek. "I'll see you when you get back."

Sylvia flashed him a grin and returned to her ten and two position, expertly backing from the driveway and heading toward the school.

Why had she kept her daughter so sheltered? The young woman driving this vehicle was confident and capable. All things Eileen had desired for her but had failed to help her obtain. She'd come into adulthood on her own, breaking free of the silken threads Eileen wove around her for protection.

"Mom, I want to let you know about our wedding plans. Do you think we could talk about them without getting into an argument?"

Wedding plans? Eileen's guilt at trying to force Sylvia into doing things her way had kept her from being a part of those plans. That knife cut deep. "Sure. Is there anything I can do to help?"

Sylvia made a quick glance at her. "Of course, Mom. We're just getting started. You've agreed to make the dress. I wanted to give you time, so we've set the date for Saturday, July 29th. It's going to be small. You, Luke's mom and sister and Uncle Seth, if he's up to it. We'd like to invite Grampa but aren't sure how to do it without causing a problem with Grandmother."

"When she was at the hospital, I sort of exploded on her." Not that Eileen was sorry for what she said, just for how she said it. She wouldn't feel regret for the truth, but there should have been a way to keep the honor-your-mother commandment instead of what she did.

"Grampa told me. He was proud of you for standing up to her and terribly upset that he never realized the extent of her manipulations. I don't think I would have wanted to be Grandmother when he got home from the hospital last night."

"Oh?" That was something Eileen couldn't begin to imagine. Her mild-mannered, hen-pecked father standing up to her domineering and narcissistic mother. There were no words.

"So, I need to choose colors. And I thought I'd ask Carma to be my maid of honor." Sylvia pulled into the lot behind the gym and parked. "I have one other thought, but I need to discuss it with you. Don't say

anything about it now but know your answer will be what happens."
She took a breath. "Even though Doug has contacted me through Seth,
I haven't responded yet. He'd like to meet. I don't want to do anything
about it until you are okay with that happening. That includes inviting
him and his family to the wedding."

Doug at the wedding? That would mean she'd see him again. And his
wife and children. Those children were Sylvia's half siblings.

Suddenly it was hard to breathe, almost like when she'd tasted those
peanut crumbs. No, maybe not that bad, but even so, it was difficult to
think of Doug being there.

But Sylvia said for her to think about it, and she would. Her daughter
was offering obedience and honoring her. No going behind her back.
Like Eileen did with her own mother.

That took a foreign type of courage. Something Eileen had trouble
grasping.

"Let's go in, Mom. Remember, you don't have to decide on this now.
Think about it. You've got time. Besides, there's a celebration waiting
inside." Sylvia grinned.

Celebration?

Eileen climbed from the car and walked with her daughter to the
entrance.

A girl at the door with programs in her hand raced inside. "She's here."

They were expecting her?

The next thing she knew Sylvia slipped away, and Miss Winslow was
at her side. "Eileen, we are so glad to see you. I have to admit you had me

worried, but your sweet Sylvia kept me updated. Welcome. We've got a seat of honor for you."

They escorted Eileen to a table at the front near the microphone stand. Miss Winslow spoke with a few more women before taking charge and welcoming everyone from the mic. "There's been a last minute change to our program as we have an honored guest. Eileen Avery has attended this function since her daughter became a freshman WildKat at KHS. But she has also been supplying the cookies we enjoy that whole time, as well, as part of her home economics class. She's never said no to any request and has only delivered top quality in all that time. She's acted as a sponsor or chaperone again and again, and I've received countless stories of her selflessness in privately helping students. You might not know this, but we almost lost this valued educator yesterday to a mishap. The fact that she's out of the hospital and here with us is a miracle. So would you all stand with me and give Eileen Avery the round of applause due?"

Chairs scooted back while a standing ovation—for her—took place all around the room. Tears burned her eyes. Did they realize she'd done all that for selfish reasons? To keep her daughter cocooned and safe? To hang on to the only means of support she had? And the helping other students... The truth was, she cared for each girl who went through her class. It was no bother to offer something when she did. This was so unnecessary. She felt like a fake.

The applause died down. Sylvia went to the mic. "Mom, I..." She motioned around the room. "We all want you to know you are loved and appreciated. That your efforts are noticed even if sometimes they felt a little over-the-top." She winked as others chuckled. "So, as we enjoy this tea, a few WildKat girls have some things to tell you."

A line formed. One by one, each girl took her turn at the microphone and thanked Mrs. Avery for something she'd done. More often than not, Eileen couldn't even remember doing what they said, or to the extent of their praise.

Before they were finished, tears streamed her face. How had such a broken mess as she made any difference at all?

Miss Winslow returned to the front. "At this time, we're going to go back to our original plan for today. The choir will sing a song and then the daughters may serve their mothers cookies and refreshments."

As the girls' choir opened with an a cappella version of "Lean on Me," Eileen couldn't concentrate. Her brain still swirled. She knew she didn't deserve any of that.

Rachel Hess approached, pulling her from her scattered thoughts. "Mrs. Avery, I owe you an apology."

"What for, Rachel? You were the one who came back and from what I learned, you got the ambulance called for me. I think I owe you for all your help."

The girl's lip trembled. "But you see, it was my fault. I didn't understand how dangerous peanuts were to you. It was my job in the group to bring the mystery ingredient. We decided to add cookie crumbs to the flour. My mom always has packages of cookies in the house. But the night before, all I could find were Nutterbutters. I scraped the filling off—I was super careful to do that. But I never thought about there being peanuts in the cookie part. Or maybe I somehow missed some filling. But however it happened, I'm to blame. And I'm so sorry, Mrs. Avery." The girl broke down, and Eileen wrapped her arms around her.

"I'm okay. It all worked out, even some personal things that needed fixing got worked out because of what happened." The words came without her thinking them through.

Rachel drew away and flashed a smile, wiping her eyes before she moved to the microphone. "Just wanted to let you know if you have a peanut allergy, you don't want to try the Chocolate Crunch cookies. Trust me on this."

Eileen chuckled and tossed the girl a wink as she remembered her prayers.

God works all things for good for those who love Him and are called according to His purpose.

That had to be the answer. It was God.

Wednesday June 14, 1972

Sylvia straightened her skirt and leaned into Luke as Windy snapped another photo for their engagement pictures. They had to pick one to go into the *Kokomo Tribune,* and her mom said to choose a few more for an album.

Mom had been so supportive even though Sylvia realized there was a lot happening in her mother's life. First, she had to wrap up the school year. That meant tests and grades. Then Seth was never far from her mind. He'd been released from the hospital a week after his surgery, just as the doctor said, and moved into Tammy's house until he could get around on his own. As the swelling went down, he found he could move his legs and feet. With physical therapy, he'd finally begun walking, though slowly and with a walker.

Sylvia glanced to where Mom and Seth stood watching the photo shoot. He appeared to be studying her mother more than what was happening under the big sycamore.

"It's time for the kiss photo. Both of you stand right there. Sylvia, put your arms around his neck. Luke, embrace her so your hands clasp behind her waist. When I say go, start kissing." Windy made an adjustment to her camera. "Go."

It didn't take much inducement. Kissing Luke was pure pleasure, and getting to be his wife soon excited her.

But of late, she'd also had a few... They weren't exactly doubts. The desire to marry him was not the problem. But the question of timing still raised its head. Was it really the wisest idea to do this before leaving for college? Would they really be saving money? As the bills from the wedding trickled in, she knew he was concerned, though he never said anything.

They'd decided they were paying for it all themselves. It meant cutting corners and dipping into Luke's savings. It also meant she'd gotten an after-school job working at Fenn's soda shop. That was the edge Jim Hect needed. She'd maintained her A average in class but had missed a question on the chem final, solidifying her place as salutatorian. Not that she minded. Jim had worked hard, too, and he deserved to be valedictorian. Even with going to full time at Fenn's now that graduation had happened last Saturday, it wasn't much income for them to save.

Would a work-study program at Anderson be better as a single person? Could they plan a better wedding for next summer?

"Got it. Relax a minute while I switch cameras."

Luke stared at her. "You're thinking hard about something, and it's bothering you. What is it?"

"Are we are rushing too fast?" The whispered words were out before she could swallow them away.

"I don't know. Maybe." He shrugged. "I only know I love you and want to marry you."

"I feel the same. I love you and want to marry you, too. But should we wait for next summer? We'd have a better idea of what we're facing with school and more time to save."

"Is this you or your mom?"

She couldn't get angry for his asking that. He'd been patient to get them to this point. "No, I haven't said anything to her, and she's been great about supporting us." Sylvia glanced over again at her mom and Seth. They were out of the way of the pictures, but still beneath the old sycamore. Just as Seth leaned toward her mother and planted a sweet kiss on her cheek, a flutter of red settled on the branch over their heads.

"Mom, Seth, you've got a cardinal."

They both peered at her and then up above in the tree.

A bright red bird stared back at them, chirped, then with another fluff of his feathers, took off.

"You know what that means, right?"

Mom and Seth both shook their heads.

"You are meant to be."

Luke squeezed her hand. "Yeah, Uncle Seth. You need to propose because, well, the cardinal knows this stuff."

"Where are you getting this?" Mom stared as if Sylvia were talking baby talk again.

But then Windy looked up from her tripod. "They're right, you know. That's why we take the engagement and wedding photos out here. When I snap the shots of couples kissing, they are all hoping for that little guy's appearance. The legend of the cardinal is something we can't explain, but it goes back to the days of the native tribes in this area. And so far, we haven't seen him miss once."

That made Sylvia pause as the big question settled on her shoulders. "Did we get a cardinal?"

Windy smiled. "I usually like to surprise my clients, though sometimes I can't wait. But yes, you got a cardinal. You'll see him in your photos. I have a few more to take if you're ready?"

Luke turned her to face him. "It is up to you. I understand what you're feeling, and I'm not worried about your love. If you want to wait, we will wait. If you want to move forward now, then that's what we'll do."

"Can we get these photos and then go home and think about it? I mean, pray about it? That's what I haven't done yet, and I need to."

"Yeah, I agree. I should've been asking God for His idea about all this, too." He flashed her his grin, the one that kept doubt at bay, and turned to Windy. "We're ready."

They finished the poses, but Sylvia couldn't get past the cardinal. Both for her and Luke and for Mom and Seth.

Could God be using the legend to guide their decision?

What was He saying about all this?

Meant to be.

The words echoed in Seth's thoughts.

Leenie had stayed by his side throughout his recovery—one that was taking much longer than he wanted. Though he was up walking, thanks to physical therapy, it was still with pain and his walker and back brace.

What if the pain never went away? What if this was as good as he got?

Meant to be.

He knew Leenie wouldn't shy away from a life with him no matter his condition. But would she come to resent it? Resent him?

She wandered over to where the kids were regrouping after their photo session. He'd seen her loosen her death grip on Sylvia's life and turn it all over to God. The trust she'd built in their Heavenly Father shamed him at times because it was so pure, so complete. At least from his vantage point.

Did he need to save her from herself?

Trust in the Lord with all your heart and lean not on your own understanding. In all your ways acknowledge Him and He will make your paths straight.

The verse popped in his brain as if a direct answer to his question.

His heart said he loved Leenie. He always had and always would. It was his pride that put up the roadblocks, making his path crooked. Could he trust that deeply? Could he surrender before knowing for sure that he'd be able to be the husband Leenie deserved?

She and the kids were laughing, smiling. It wasn't that long ago that something like that would've been an impossibility. Yet there they were.

God was the God of impossibility. With Him, all things were possible.

"Hey kids, want to go get a bite to eat?" Maybe changing locations would get his mind out of this battle of wills.

Luke glanced at Leenie and Sylvia, who gave a tiny nod. "Sure. Where'd you wanna go?"

"How about the Casa Grande?" He watched as Eileen's cheeks brightened, most likely at the memory of their last trip there the night of the Stardust Ball.

But she was a trouper. "Sure. Good with you kids?"

They agreed, thanked Windy, and trekked to their cars. Leenie had driven him since he wasn't supposed to be doing that himself yet, and Luke brought Sylvia.

Once alone in the car, he let her get moving before the thoughts in his head forced their way out his mouth. "So, a cardinal."

"Do you believe in that stuff?"

"I believe God can speak to us through various means. They may not sell me on the superstition, but I think God was trying to get through to me."

To the untrained eye, there was no difference in her appearance. But Seth had been a student of Eileen Lawson Avery's nuances for an exceptionally long time. He noted the change in her breathing, the tighter grip on the steering wheel. She was hanging on to hope.

"What do you think He was saying to you?"

Seth chuckled. "Oh, I know what He was saying to me. I'm just not sure I can fully do it."

"What's that?"

"Trust Him completely. Just relax and let Him do what He wants. I've been the one to make decisions and protect the ones around me. That's my job. But slowly He's removed me from that ability. I can still use my brain and figure things out, but physically protecting anyone is out, at least for the time being."

"Maybe we don't need your protection as much as we need you. Could be God can protect us much better. Just you in our lives is what we want from you."

Seth noticed the touch of crimson creeping up her neck as she spoke. "We?"

"Okay. Me. I love you for saving me. I would be dead right now if you hadn't. But I have loved you for a much longer time because of who you are, and that's not just as a protector. You're a man of integrity and courage and compassion. You love with your whole being, even laying your life on the line if necessary. I see you, the real you, and you are so much more than a warrior. You are a man of faith and courage. I just wish..."

The silence dragged on until they hit a stoplight. "What Leenie? What do you wish?"

"I wish you had the courage to put faith in our love."

That nailed him. Right between the eyes.

Did he? Could he believe in the strength of their love to weather through his injury and rehab? That it would be strong enough to withstand anything else life threw at them? He toyed with his ring while choosing his words. "I do, Leenie. I believe in our love. I'd just like to be able to walk down the aisle as man and wife without the use of a walker or cane. To stand on my own feet and carry you over our threshold."

"Carrying me is what got us into this situation."

"No, no it's not. I was holding back before that, but now I do have hope."

She turned into the parking lot of the Casa Grande, pulled into a space, and shut off the car before facing him. "Hope enough to take a chance?"

"Leenie, I don't think I can get down on one knee to ask you."

"That's your pride talking, Seth. You need to keep listening to what God is saying." She opened her car door. "The kids are waiting for us. Let's go."

He reached for her hand, but she pulled back and climbed out. Now she was angry. He could feel the heat. But they needed to get inside.

She came around, bringing his walker from her trunk. "Here." Yep, angry for sure. The tone of her voice chilled the summer air.

And he couldn't blame her.

Seth followed her to the door where Luke held it open for them all.

The waitress took them to a table and got their drink orders before Sylvia and Leenie excused themselves for the ladies' room.

"You okay, Uncle Seth? Has this been too much for you today?"

If you only knew, kid. "I'm all right." Nervously, he played with his pinkie ring. "I just have a lot on my mind."

"I get that. Me, too."

Seth didn't probe. Something about his nervous tick finally clicked in his brain. And he decided. Pride had gotten in his way too many times. He didn't care anymore.

The women came back.

He waited until they were seated, then stood. "Leenie, you are right about a lot of things. But you are wrong if you think I don't love you more than my pride. This isn't the way I'd always planned things, nor the way you deserve, but it is from my heart because I love you and want to spend the rest of my life with you. If you are crazy enough to take a chance on me, to have that faith in our love, then I am asking you, Eileen Marie Lawson Avery, would you please marry me?" He carefully lowered himself to one knee using his walker and slipped the pinkie ring from his finger.

She teared up again, but the smile she gave him touched him deeper than anything ever had. "Yes, Seth, oh yes."

Epilogue

Saturday, July 29, 1972

E ileen stared at the mirror reflecting Sylvia standing behind her. "Mom, you look amazing."

She patted her daughter's hand that rested on her shoulder. "So do you, Sylvie. You are so lovely I could cry."

"Well, don't. We don't want our makeup messed up. Who'd want to see us with raccoon eyes?" Sylvie kissed Eileen's cheek and reached for the veil which hung from a hanger. It wasn't long, just simple, like their dresses. Simple elegance is what Tammy had called them.

Eileen glanced about the room for a clock. "How much time do we have?"

Tammy spoke up then. "You're doing fine. I asked Stormy the last time she popped in about why there were no clocks in here. She said it was to help the bride trust those in charge to get her where she needed to be on time. I think she has a point. So just relax. Everything is falling into pl ace."

She was right. Eileen knew it. Everything she'd trusted God for had come about better than she could've planned. Seth not only asked her to marry him, he was healing faster than his doctor could believe.

Her father had continued his contact, building a relationship with her she could never have imagined.

And she'd agreed to go with Sylvia when she met Doug for the first time. It was a little strange. Doug brought his wife, Sylvia had Luke, and she held onto Seth's hand through the whole meeting. Afterward she couldn't shake the notion that all three couples were with the right people. Doug and his family had welcomed Sylvia but without pressure. They were building relationships as well. With God, all things were possible.

There was a knock at the door, and Stormy entered. "Just making sure everyone was decent before I brought in the father of the bride."

Eileen glanced over Stormy's shoulder to see her dad, his eyes filled with moisture. He would walk her down the aisle to Seth.

Sylvia was her maid of honor. Who else could she have chosen? The kids had mutually decided to wait until next summer to get that one year of classes and routines under their belts. And they finally agreed to letting her and Seth help pay for things. They were going to have enough surprise expenses that adult life would bring. No need to make things harder.

"Are you ready, Eileen?" Dad tucked her fingers in the crook of his arm while Sylvia placed the petite veil on her head.

"Ready. Have you seen Seth? Is he okay?"

Dad chuckled. "He's pacing around like a caged tiger. Getting plenty of exercise today."

She tried to imagine.

But then five months ago she wouldn't have been able to picture any of this in her future. Only God knew how He could work this all out.

Stepping out in faith was far better than anything she could imagine.

"Let's go."

Acknowledgements:

Abba Father, thank you for the stories. Thank You for the drive and encouragement. And thank You for touching lives through all this. To You be the glory.

To my wonderful P.I.T. crew who prays me through each story keeping me accountable—Annie, Deb, Lori D., Julie, Alyssa, and Dorothy—you've had a lot to pray about for me over the last couple years. Thank you! I love you all!

Thank you to my cover artist, Stephanie with *Alt 19 Creative*. You took my imaginings and gave them substance. You get me—don't know if you should be scared about that or not, but it certainly makes for great covers.

My Beta Readers and Street Team, you are such a huge support. Thank you! And extra thanks to Kathrine Karrol, Diana Brandmeyer, and Brenda Poulos who went over and above for me.

To my editor and friend, Liz Tolsma, you have no idea how much you encourage me with your expert help. I cannot thank you enough. Hugs!

My extraordinary family is so encouraging—Phil, Jaime, Jonathan, Alyssa, Juan, Natalia, Meg, Mat, Owen, Kami, Amy, Rick, Rusty, Sandy, and all my extended loved ones. I couldn't do this without you all.

And, as always, E.B. I still miss you—say hi to your gramma for me.

Author Note

Moving from Kokomo to Phoenix in 1972 was traumatic for my six-teen-year-old self.

I know it was the right thing for my family, and God has been faithful. Yet there's a part of my heart that is pure Hoosier and always will be I guess. Maybe that's why 1972 stands out so much, calls me to write in that setting. I've been back home many times, and as Thomas Wolfe's title reminds me, I really can't go home again.

Except, in these books and memories.

I remember sitting in my first hour Biology class on the bottom floor of the Main Building at KHS in early November 1971 and seeing feet run past the windows that were high on the wall—our classroom was technically in the basement. Not long after, someone from the adminis-tration office opened the door and told us we were to go straight home. That they were dismissing us class by class, and that we'd be told when to come back. If memory serves, it was about three days before we returned to school.

One of the most brilliant things Mr. Moore, our principal, did was to include students in the process of learning what happened, how it happened, and why it happened. Seriously, when your school is one of ten in the nation to be written up in *Life* magazine for its race riots, you want answers. There was a parent committee, a staff committee, and a student committee. I'm not sure how they all worked, but I do remember the convocation where the students gave their report of what they'd learned. The biggest point I took away was that it wasn't any of the students who instigated things, but rather outsiders who caused trouble with a divide and conquer mentality. It's been more that half a century, but I remember.

I couldn't stay true to that time and write about Kokomo High School without acknowledging what went down, but I tried to be sensitive. I hope I was successful.

A special thank you goes to Steve Barlow, class of '73, who not only read an early (unedited) version of *Sylvia's Mother*, but he shared stories—my favorite being the fact that he was the one who made the track and field team late getting back for the Stardust Ball because he was a pole vaulter. I added that bit with his permission, putting the blame on Luke.

I also had help from former classmates—yay, class of '74—who helped me get the lay of the land, so to speak, for the Vocational Building. I never had a class in there, but needed to know where there might be a phone line. Tom Tull and Alan Bourff came to my rescue with not only information but photos. My thanks to them both.

I also had help with the ambulance scene from my cousin Jason Burger who not only has worked for the fire department for a lot of years, he is second generation and knows a lot of the retired guys who remember what it was like back in the day. I explained Eileen's situation and asked what would have transpired. Also need to thank my cousin Darlene Burger, Jason's mom, who was the go-between to gather all the data. That's how I knew they would have used an antihistamine injection in the arm rather than epinephrine. A lot of what ifs were asked and considered. So thank you to Jason, Dar, and all their connections for getting me the info I needed.

The best piece of research came by accident. And I wasn't even researching for this book at the time. Chuck Buell was a DJ in Chicago at WLS back in the day and I found he had an interview that had been recorded and saved where he told about crazy things that happened when he met some of the groups. He got to talking about Dr Hook and the Medicine Show—something about being in Monterrey, California and hanging with Dennis Locorriere (the lead singer) on a houseboat and asking about where he got his songs.

Dennis said to follow him and they went to a different houseboat a few docks over where Chuck Buell was introduced to the lyricist who wrote "Cover of the Rolling Stone" and "Sylvia's Mother"—Shel Silverstein. Yup, that Shel Silverstein. Before *The Giving Tree* and *Light in the Attic*, there was some rock and roll going on. Shel Silverstein also wrote the words to "A Boy Named Sue." I never saw that coming. Thought my first encounter with the poet was with his children's books that I loved. I even taught from them. But now I can't hear those songs without hearing his rhythms and style.

The next book in the *Weather Girls Wedding Shoppe and Venue* series will be *Runaround Sue*. I'm enjoying getting to know Sue and Mac. Hope you will too. If you want a sneak peek, keep reading.

It should release sometime around May 2023. So, until we meet in those pages,

Abundant blessings!

Sneak Peek of Runround Sue: Book Three of the Weather Girls Wedding Shoppe and Venue series

Chapter 1

Tuesday, June 20, 1972

   Wabash Community Church, Kokomo, Indiana

"I'M NOT BEING DIFFICULT, Tracy, nor am I a misanthrope." Sue Mitchell ran her hand over her forehead, swiping her bangs from where they were slipping out of the bobby pins she'd used to pin them back. There wasn't time for this discussion while she was supposed to be working.

That is, if there was anything that still needed doing. It hadn't taken long to plow through the to-do list Pastor Mussing had left for her.

She glanced around the church office reception area. Even the plastic philodendrons had been wiped clean. But Tracy didn't need to know she'd knocked out her work already.

The voice on the line suddenly acquired a lofty air. "Let me put this in a way you will understand. Your arcane attitude is bumming me out. I want to have some fun with my best friend. I've let you have space to pull yourself together, but now it's time to get off your callipygian and party hardy."

Sue snorted. "A pretty pukka effort. Do you have your thesaurus open next to you?"

"Nope, you aren't the only one who attended college. Besides having roomed with you for so long, I sort of absorbed your vocabulary." Tracy followed up with a sigh. "Please? The only thing we ever do together is work with the girls on Wednesday night. I have tomorrow off, and I promise we'll be home tonight by ten-thirty, eleven at the latest. C'mon, whaddya say?"

It was Sue's turn to sigh. Her friend was right. They hadn't gone out for fun in forever. Which was fine with Sue. If she didn't see another soul, it would be pukka with her. Ha!

But Tracy had been there when she needed a friend and offered her sanctuary. Even helped her find this job. She owed her friend. "Okay, but we stick close to town. Or head toward Galveston. Nothing south or west. Got it?"

Tracy squealed and Sue pulled the phone away from her ear as the chatter continued. "Yay! I can't wait. I'll see you when you get home. Oh, we're gonna have some fun. Bye!"

The line clicked before Sue returned her bye. Stuff like that happened when Tracy got excited. That girl never had a down moment, never met a stranger, and never doubted anyone's story. Gullible and dewy-eyed, that was her roomie.

Sue picked up the stack of finished folders on her desk and tapped them straight before setting them right back where they were. What else could she be doing? Everything from her in-box was completed, her out-box emptied. Sometimes it was a pain to be so competent.

And then she realized that if she didn't keep busy, her brain would be creating what-if scenarios about this evening. Like what if she ran into someone she knew from Russiaville? Oops, she'd mused herself into exactly what she wanted to avoid.

But what if she did? What would she do? She needed a plan.

Hmm, she could head for the restroom and lock herself in until Tracy found her. Or she could play dumb, like the person was mistaken—she'd changed her appearance enough that it was possible. Sue shoved the black cat-eye glasses with nonprescriptive lens up to the bridge of her nose. Maybe she just shouldn't go.

But she'd promised Tracy. And she owed her roommate more than she could repay.

Okay, what if she dressed frumpy? Would Tracy let her out of the apartment raggle-taggle?

Absolutely no. She'd take it as a personal affront to be seen in Sue's company when not coiffed and styled appropriately.

Great, now what did she do?

"Sue, could you do me a favor?"

She pulled herself away from her concerns to find the pastor's wife, Gloria Mussing, standing at her desk. When had she entered the room? Mercy, this day was growing obdurate about giving her a hard time.

"Of course, Mrs. Mussing. I'm happy to. What can I do for you?"

The woman had a basket of cards and envelopes with a list. "I just got a call and need to run an emergency errand. These cards are for the hospital, nursing home, and shut-in visits this Saturday. Would you please get them signed and in the envelopes with the person's name on the front for me? I'll get them grouped by who is taking them out. Thought I'd get this done today because the rest of the week is stuffed full, but now this."

"I'll do it for you. In fact, I was trying to think of something else I could work on."

Surprise raised Mrs. Mussing's brows. "I saw the list Jim left. You finished it already?"

Sue nodded, then added a smile to keep it friendly.

"I can honestly say we get our money's worth out of you. My goodness, you not only work hard, but fast. I told him it would take you three days to get that all done."

"It wasn't so much." She shrugged, hoping it didn't sound boastful. The truth was, the training she received in college prepared her for much more than the simple filing and typing required at this job. In fact, the hardest part was keeping the smile on her face when people arrived. It would be so much better if she didn't have to deal with the public, or even the congregation. Maybe she was a misanthrope, a little bit.

"Well, I'm glad you're here with us and that you'll take this off my hands. Good to know we've got someone we can trust to get things done." The pastor's wife set the basket on Sue's desk, waved, and headed out.

This time, the smile was genuine. Sue didn't hear a lot of praise as a rule and Mrs. Mussing's words felt like Noxzema on a sunburn—only without the sting. Just the cooling sensation that made her want to say "ah."

She pulled out the list of names and began by addressing the envelopes. It'd be nice if her old church did something like this. Then maybe someone would be filling out a card for her brother while he sat at home. But she didn't recognize anyone on the paper. She hadn't been attending all that long—only since she started her job. There was no way she'd be going back to her home congregation and since she hadn't found another place to attend, it only made sense to come here on Sundays. Plus, turns out Pastor Mussing was not only a great boss, he knew a thing or two about preaching sermons.

Once she had the envelopes readied, she found the name on the list, noted if the person was in the hospital or a nursing facility or was just homebound and chose an appropriate card, signing it with her best penmanship—Blessings from Wabash Community Church.

Mrs. Mussing hadn't said how to sign the cards, so she'd spent a moment thinking up the best message to write. After a couple, she picked up a rhythm and soon had the stack completed and filed back into the basket in three stacks and in alphabetical order. All done.

Sue stood and stretched and began pacing the room. If she couldn't do her exercises, she could at least move. Despite the ease of the job, it had a peaceful setting, kind colleagues, and a safety that made it all worthwhile.

No one around her recognized her. She could stay cloistered in this office until... Until she didn't have to.

Ten minutes later, she settled back at her desk and decided to start of list of jobs she could get done if Pastor wanted her to. Keeping busy helped, and it was no trouble. She'd gotten to number seven when the notion about the safe and serene nature of this job shattered. The church office door opened, and he walked in, causing her to retreat behind a persona loup of efficiency.

She wasn't sure if she was repelled or attracted, just that he turned her stomach to flying confetti and her pulse rate to jackhammer. Either way, he scared her and that wasn't good. With effort, she kept that professional mask in place.

There was a slight shuffle to his gait, and he pulled off his motorcycle helmet to reveal a matted, beach blond mane and full beard. A guitar case hung from a strap over his shoulder as he approached her desk.

No, this wouldn't do. He made her too uneasy.

"Is Professor Day in?"

Sue swallowed hard and found her voice. "Um, who shall I say is calling?"

"Just tell him Mac is here for the appointment." The guy glanced around the room, spotted the couch next to the potted fern, and headed that way.

The space between them increased, granting her more breathing room. Not that he smelled bad. She hadn't noticed anything like that. Just that his mere presence made her nerves take up conga lessons. She called into the music director's office. "Mr. Day, Mac is here for an appointment."

"I'll be right out." Click.

"He's on his way."

She should ask if she could get him something to drink. But starting a conversation meant acknowledging his presence again, and she wasn't sure if that was such a wise idea. Still, part of her job was to be the office hostess. A part she had hoped she would not have to deal with regularly. Pastor Mussing had made it clear that she was the first impression visitors got, so it was important that she be hospitable. And it was getting summery outside. Logic told her his head had gotten warm riding with that helmet on. Fine. She'd play Jackie Kennedy. It might not be the White House with thousands of live TV viewers, but she would be as gracious.

"May I get you something to drink? We have water or coffee." Should she suggest that the church stock powdered Nestea for the summer?

He glanced her way and flashed a touch of a smile. "No, thank you."

Well, that was that. She'd tried. Had she really? "What about a magazine?"

He shook his head, and the matted, probably sweaty, clumped strands swung a little. "No. But thanks."

At least he was polite. Even if he just sat there, not trying to talk with her.

That hadn't happened in a long while. Recent history had proved that, given the chance, a man would try to start a conversation with her whether she wanted to talk to him or not. Well, not super recent. Not since she'd changed her appearance.

Maybe it was working. The thought tickled at the corners of her mouth, and she caught a genuine smile trying to sneak out. But it was followed up with a little sadness. Did that mean she'd never again get attention from a man? Part of her wanted to cheer that notion across the finish line. But another part wondered if she'd always feel this way and if she'd sliced off her proverbial nose to spite the face that had brought her such heartache.

Mac ran his hands over his jeans, wiping the sweat away again. Despite the air conditioning in the office, his nerves were outdoing his deodorant three to one. He couldn't imagine why Professor Day had asked him to stop.

He moved his guitar from leaning against the couch to lay across his lap. Music had always interpreted Mac's life.

He'd spent adolescent summer days under the boardwalk and nights up on the roof with Ben E. King. Then he moved to the dock of the bay to hang with Otis Redding.

But at graduation, his Uncle Sam sent him on an exotic all-expense paid trip that cost him more than he could articulate. Eric Burdon spoke truth to him—he had to get out of that place.

It was bad. So bad.

Especially those first few weeks in the hospital.

Then came the years of trying to resurrect his life, of learning who he was.

These days, though, more often than not, he found himself with Doby Gray, grateful for the music that helped him drift away.

Music. The balm that poured out a measure of peace amid a chaotic world. Where was the music in this silent office?

"Sorry about the wait, Peter. Or do you prefer Mac?" Professor Day stood in front of him, hand outstretched.

Mac stood before meeting the handshake. Didn't do to let anyone think he couldn't stand on his own. "No problem, sir. And it's Mac. Thanks for asking."

Professor Day held a box under his left arm. "Give me one more second and we'll go back to my office." He turned to the secretary. "Sue, would you please run these over to my daughters at Ferguson House? They need it before four, but have a client until after three, so don't try to leave before then—they made sure I knew not to interrupt their important meeting, but that the next client needed these reel-to-reels." He chuckled as he handed over the box.

"Happy to take care of that, sir." Though she sat there ready to do his bidding, Mac had the impression the woman was a lot smarter than she was given credit for. He took a better look.

"Just Aaron is fine. Do you know how to get there?"

"Yes. Aaron. I'll make sure they are there on time." She flashed a smile that seemed rehearsed. Still, it lit her face a little, making two dimples pop like tiny parenthesis on either side of her mouth. Maybe they were spotlighting where the smile should go. She was better looking that she wanted to let on.

"Good, got that out of the way. Come on back, Mac, and I'll explain why I dragged you here." He laughed briefly, but it was the real deal—not like Secretary Sue's smile. One of the reasons he accepted the professor's request to come to the church to meet. He like the guy. Besides, how many advanced music students have a teacher who has sessions with Burt Bacharach, Herb Alpert, Brian Wilson, and Frank Sinatra on their resumes—just to name a few? If you want to be a professional musician, you need to learn from someone who knows the score.

Professor Aaron Day knows.

The hallway to his office wasn't all that long, only a couple of doors on either side. The professor stopped at the last one on the left and turned the knob, holding it open.

Mac stepped past him. The room was cluttered with books and instruments and sheet music in piles.

"Excuse the mess. I'm trying to get organized around here. Splitting my time between the church and the university means I never get around to combing through and deciding what to pitch and what to keep." He lifted a stack from the visitor chair and motioned for Mac to have a seat.

He did, still mesmerized by the sheer musical vastness represented in this small room. "How many instruments do you play?"

"A few. I prefer my guitars, especially my twelve string, and the piano. But I've played clarinet and sax for a few recordings."

Mac would bet there were more than those named. He glanced at his own ax—it was never far from him, like an extra appendage. But he was self-taught on the piano. Reading music was doable, but playing by ear, that was where he was freest. He'd picked up the harmonica because it would carry in his pocket in the Nam. That he hadn't played since he got home.

Professor Day cleared his own chair and dropped into it as if finishing a race. "So, I'm sure you are wondering why I asked you here."

Mac nodded and kept a tight button on his lip—too often he'd let the wrong word slip at an equally wrong time.

"If you noticed the class syllabus, you know you must put together a recital of your own compositions to be played by other musicians. You can choose what instruments, but there needs to be a mix of at least three. Most of your classmates will be scheduling use at the IUK auditorium, but I got thinking, this congregation might like to have a music night, so I am offering you a chance to do your final project here. You'd need to present before Labor Day. I happen to know there are a few musicians who attend, and I'll be happy to help you with contacts. The thing is you would want to have a theme that fits a house of worship."

Mac mulled the man's words a moment. "What does that mean? Only classical or hymn-like pieces?"

Professor Day shook his head. "No, it just needs to be God-honoring. I've even heard rock music that does that. Think of the songs from Godspell. There's several that fit that category."

"Are you requiring words for all the music? I'd have to find a singer."

If he knew a good singer. And no, he was not going to sing them himself. This final project was a giant step for him without that added feature.

"Only one piece needs lyrics. But you can add them to the whole recital if you choose. But as I looked over the roster for this class, I really felt moved to make you this offer. You don't have to do it." He paused, like he was waiting for Mac to give him direction on what to say next.

"Professor Day—"

"Aaron—as long as we are outside of class, I'm fine with that. Go on."

Mac cleared his throat and tried again. "Aaron, I'm not a super religious guy. I do believe in God, and I've got reason to be grateful. I don't know if I'm the right person."

"I think you are. I also think that as you work on this, if you pray and ask for guidance, you might find this is more for you than for your audience."

"I don't know any singers. Do you have a name or two to go along with the other musicians?"

Aaron grinned. "Do I have a name? Mac, you've come to the right place. The best pianist in town just happens to be my youngest daughter.

All three of my girls, as well as my wife, have beautiful voices. Sounds like nepotism, I know. But facts can't be denied."

"Oh. Okay. Think they'd be willing?"

"I got a feeling at least one could be persuaded." Aaron scribbled on a notepad. "Just want to make sure I remember. Okay, now, before you go, I'd really like to hear you play."

"Um, so it's decided?" Mac suddenly felt like he'd been steamrolled.

"You still want to think about it?"

Mac let his gaze skirt around the room before meeting Aaron's. "I'm in. This thing is going to stretch me."

"That's the point. Now get out your guitar and show me what you can do." Aaron moved to the piano and set the stack of books covering the seat on the floor before sitting down and playing a quick scale. "Do you know 'Classical Gas'?"

With his guitar out of the case, he slipped the strap over his head and played the opening chords.

Aaron joined in and soon the tiny room was filled with the jam session.

The door opened and Mac glanced up to see a middle-aged guy in the doorway as his fingers slowed to a stop on the frets.

"Keep going, sounds great."

Aaron stopped and spun around on the stool. "Oh, Pastor Mussing, come in. This is one of my students, Mac MacKenzie. Mac, this is our pastor, Jim Mussing."

Middle-aged dude walked on in with an outstretched hand. "Nice to meet you, Mac. You are really good."

Mac shook the guy's hand and struggled to get his voice to work. "Um, thanks, Nice to meet you too." He'd been having so much fun that his words felt like lies. He hadn't wanted to meet the guy right then. He wanted to keep playing and getting lost in the music. That was where he was truly free.

But his folks had drilled manners into him, and he use them. Besides, he was in church. Which was worse, to lie to say something polite or tell the truth and be selfish?

"Sorry to interrupt, I was just enjoying it too much I guess. Hope to see you around, Mac. I'll let you two get back to what you were doing." And with that Middle-Aged guy closed the door.

"Guess we got too loud?"

Aaron shook his head. "No, these walls are thin. It'd be hard for him not to hear. You're pretty good on guitar. How's your piano skills?"

"Eh?" Mac shrugged.

"Try this." Aaron pulled out a couple pages of sheet music.

Mac started to balk. It wasn't that he couldn't read the thing, he could. But getting his fingers to comply as fast as his brain recognized the notes was another deal. Well, maybe he should let his professor know the extent of his skill. Would he rescind the invitation?

He laid aside his guitar and inspected the music. It was for a hymn, "O Fount of Many Blessings." At least he'd heard it before. That should help. Mac sat on the seat, got his foot on the pedal and his fingers over the keys, and leaned in to follow the notes, humming them under his breath as he did. He could do this. Okay. Big breath.

The song started and as music tended to do, it flowed up his hands and arms and straight to his heart where he took hold of the nuances and textures, making it come alive. He played the verse a second time and repeated the chorus before drawing to a finish.

As the last note echoed away, he knew something had happened.

There was clapping behind him, but only one person. Aaron. Professor Day. His teacher. He'd pleased the man. Mac's heart pounded.

Maybe, just maybe, he could do this. Only he'd have to use his own compositions—not that he'd never composed anything. He had. Several pieces, some that would actually work for this situation.

No, the big thing was, he'd need to allow others to hear his work. An audience. And that might be the hardest part of this whole process.

About Author

Historical Christian Romance author, Jennifer Lynn Cary, likes to say you can take the girl out of Indiana, but you can't take the Hoosier out of the girl. Now transplanted to the Arizona desert, this direct descendant of Davy Crockett and her husband of forty plus years enjoy time with family where she shares tales of her small-town heritage and family legacies with their grandchildren. You can contact Jennifer via her website www.jenniferlynncary.com

Or use this QR code.

JENNIFER LYNN CARY

Also By Jennifer Lynn Cary

The Crockett Chronicles Series:

The Patriarch: : Book 1

The Sojourners: Book 2

The Prodigal: Book 3

Tales of the Hob Nob Annex Café

The Relentless Series:

Relentless Heart: Book 1

Wedding Bell Blues: Book 2

Relentless Joy: Book 3

Silver Bell Christmas: Book 4

The Traveling Prayer Shawl

The Weather Girls Trilogy:

Sunny

Stormy

Windy

The Forgotten Gratitude Journal

Cheryl's Going Home (A Weather Girls Novel)

The Weather Girls Wedding Shoppe and Venue Series:

Judy in Disguise (Book One)

Nonfiction:

<u>When God Holds Your Hand</u>

Or use this:

QR code for Amazon Author page

Made in the USA
Columbia, SC
28 January 2023

10614004R00186